DIABLO LAKE

A town founded by
witches and brimming
full of secrets...

Moon
Struck

NEW YORK TIMES BESTSELLING AUTHOR

LAUREN DANE

Also available from Lauren Dane and Harlequin

Diablo Lake

Protected
Awakened

Goddess with a Blade

Goddess with a Blade
Blade To the Keep
Blade on the Hunt
At Blade's Edge
Wrath of the Goddess
Blood and Blade

Cascadia Wolves

Reluctant Mate (prequel)
Pack Enforcer
Wolves' Triad
Wolf Unbound
Alpha's Challenge
Bonded Pair
Twice Bitten

de La Vega Cats

Trinity
Revelation
Beneath the Skin

Chase Brothers

Giving Chase
Taking Chase
Chased
Making Chase

Petal, GA

Once and Again
Lost in You
Count on Me

Cherchez Wolves

Wolf's Ascension
Sworn to the Wolf

The Hurley Boys

The Best Kind of Trouble
Broken Open
Back to You

Whiskey Sharp

Unraveled
Jagged
Torn
Cake (novella)
Sugar (novella)

Second Chances
Believe

DIABLO LAKE: MOON STRUCK

LAUREN DANE

carina
press

carina
press®

Recycling programs
for this product may
not exist in your area.

ISBN-13: 978-1-335-50809-6

Diablo Lake: Moon Struck

First published in 2016. This edition published in 2023.

Copyright © 2016 by Lauren Dane

For questions and comments about the quality of this book,
please contact us at CustomerService@Harlequin.com.

Carina Press
22 Adelaide St. West, 41st Floor
Toronto, Ontario M5H 4E3, Canada
www.CarinaPress.com

Printed in U.S.A.

This one is for Bernice
who wore White Shoulders.

DIABLO LAKE: MOON STRUCK

Chapter One

The rising sun and a huge to-do list drove Kit from the bed in the guest room of her best friend Aimee's house. Much better than the last two weeks on the couch at her parents' place. Or the hotel near the hospital, several hours' drive away, where her father was recovering from a stroke.

Diablo Lake, the place she'd run from a few years before. And still, no matter what, she'd always be from the funky little town full of witches and shifters in the middle of the mountains that had always remained her home.

Her absence from town was officially over. Starting today, she would take over running the Counter, the family-run soda fountain. That way her dad could do his job, which was getting better and her mother didn't have to shoulder the stress of trying to help him and run a business at the same time.

And while she was at it, Kit needed to get the shop back on track so her parents had an economic future and, she supposed, she needed to accept that *her* future would look vastly different than she'd imagined it just two weeks before when she got the call that her father had been taken to Vanderbilt by helicopter.

Kit's groan as her feet hit the floor made her roll her eyes at herself as she stood, swaying slightly, trying to wake up.

Coffee. Yes, that was a good first step.

She shuffled into the kitchen and spied the huge pan of cobbler she'd totally forgotten about. Well, surely it would be far easier to get moving that first morning back than it would have been without cobbler. It was science after all. Probably. She really didn't have time to look it up, but it sounded just right.

She rustled through some drawers and cabinets and failed to find coffee to go in the coffeemaker or a bowl so after a shrug, she simply spooned some ice cream directly onto the cobbler. Her people were pioneers after all; she could manage this fine breakfast without all the fancy stuff.

Aimee's place had been remodeled, she thought as she looked around more closely. Nothing staggering, just a new coat of paint and the stuff had been moved. Aimee had a cute house. It fit her personality and lifestyle with the open floorplan. Once every three years she redid a room to keep things fresh, but overall, the style was warm and sexy with deep earth tones and overstuffed furniture.

Katie Faith wandered through the kitchen and dining room, spooning her cobbler and ice cream into her mouth as she hugged the pan to her body.

And that's how Aimee found her, with a wooden spoon and an entire pan of berry cobbler. *Half* a pan of berry cobbler.

One of Aimee's eyebrows rose as she took the scene in. "Step away from the cobbler, Katie Faith."

Kit hugged the pan to her body a little tighter. "Shut

up. I'm a growing girl and I need a good breakfast before I go to work. I also need coffee. You've remodeled in here and I can't find it. How can I eat cobbler and ice cream without coffee? I know who raised you to be a good Southern woman. Your momma would be so disappointed in you. Just sayin'."

Aimee snorted as she breezed into the kitchen, Kit in her wake. "Just because you know I peed my pants in kindergarten doesn't mean you get to be grumpy and eat all my cobbler without sharing." Aimee went to the cabinet to the left of the sink and opened it up, pulling out a red canister. "I have coffee. And I told you I was going to redo the kitchen last month."

"I won't tell anyone about the peed pants if you make me some. Coffee not peed pants. I'll be your best friend," Kit said in a singsong voice and tried to look thirsty and pitiful all at once.

"You're full of it, Katie Faith. Just you know that I know it." Aimee did that thing with her finger pointing from her eyes to Kit.

"As long as you know it while you're making me some coffee." Kit winked and held the spoon, full of cobbler, her friend's way. "This is Sandy's cobbler, isn't it? I'm going to gain five pounds just being in the same room with it. I can't believe I missed the bake sale yesterday."

"There's always another bake sale. It's Diablo Lake." Aimee turned on the coffeemaker, pointed out a clean spoon to Kit and dug in, settling in next to her on the small kitchen bench. "You'll be moving back here permanently anyway."

Kit froze. "We don't know that for sure. Could just be six months or so."

"Doesn't change what's true anyway. Your crazy vacation in Chattanooga is over and done and you can come on home. Accept reality, Katie Faith. Your parents are getting older. You need to come back here for them if for no other reason. What's past is past. No one gives a fart in a high wind about Darrell Pembry."

It did seem rather silly now, three years later, leaving her home because of a stupid-assed man like Darrell. The humiliation was nearly gone. Nearly.

"You're such a delicate flower," Kit managed around her cobbler.

Aimee handed her a cup of coffee with milk and lots of sugar. "Thank goodness you're back because no one else is as cracked as you. Can't make the same kind of jokes with anyone. Sit at the table so I can get at that cobbler too. In a bit we can get dressed and you'll tell me what I can do to help today."

"You're going to make me cry." Kit moved herself to the breakfast nook.

Aimee's snort sounded a lot like her mother's. "Go on then. If a body being nice to you makes you want to cry, Katie Faith, you've been gone from home too long."

"We don't know for sure I'll have to move back." She brooded over her coffee in between huge spoonfuls of cobbler.

"Don't sulk. Imagine if your face froze like that." Aimee rolled her eyes. "Pull up your big girl panties! You don't belong in Chattanooga anyway. Every time I visited you there you were like a tourist. You're from Diablo Lake. You belong here. Look at you calling yourself Kit. Spending hundreds of dollars to ride exercise bikes and get yelled at by the instructor." Aimee paused her rant long enough to give Kit a sigh heavy with exasperation. "Your *people* are here. We want you back home, Katie Faith."

"You're one to talk about full names."

Aimee's eyes narrowed. "Hush your mouth. Don't even try it. Katie Faith is *not* a bad name. You're not named after someone everyone in your family hates because your grandmother hijacked the forms and changed your name from Aimee to something else. *You* are totally Katie Faith. You're not Kit. Kit is a car who talks to David Hasselhoff. God, I miss that show. Anyway, don't avoid the subject."

"You miss that show? You're dumb."

Aimee snickered as Kit giggled. It was an old joke, Aimee's given name and how her mother had cried for days when she found out what old Mrs. Benton had done. Later, Aimee's parents had gone and legally changed Larnamae Alvonia Benton to Aimee Marie as they'd planned to name her to begin with. But everyone knew Aimee started as Larnamae Alvonia.

"If I came back here, everyone would know my business again."

Aimee waved her spoon around after taking a bite of the cobbler. "Girl, everyone knows your business anyway."

True enough. Aimee's mother, Trula Faye—everyone called her TeeFay—was best friends with Nadine, Katie Faith's mom. They were the queens of gossip in Diablo Lake. If anything was worth knowing, they knew it and doled it out as they felt necessary and appropriate.

It had been a fine testament to friendship when, after the whole mess at the church three years ago, no one had said a single thing about it in public. She wasn't quite sure what all her mom and TeeFay had done, but they'd protected her the best they could under the circumstances and that had meant everything to Katie Faith.

Too bad everyone had looked at her like she was dying for the next six months until she finally just moved away to lick her wounds without all the pity. And—she could admit to herself—to see who she was apart from Diablo Lake. She needed to understand if she could survive without all that. And the truth was, she had a three-quarter life in Chattanooga. The heart of her life was right there in Diablo Lake.

Home meant the way the earth seemed to welcome her and fill her with magic every time she drove into town. It meant the roses bloomed in winter and fruit still hung on trees. Home meant safety and people you loved.

"I hate moving. And I'll have you know, *Larnamae*, spinning class is really hard! Keeps my ass from falling to my ankles."

Aimee grinned after tossing a balled-up paper napkin at Kit's head. "We need to find you a house lickety-split. If not, you'll be living over the garage back at home and you'll never get laid. You could live here, you know."

Diablo Lake didn't have a lot of extra housing, but she was pretty sure she could find something relatively soon. Location was important though. No way was she living on the Pembry side of town.

"I love you but we'd kill one another if we lived together too long. As for sex? Getting laid is at the bottom of my to-do list just now." She was going to complain about how it was dumb for women to tell each other they needed sex. But Katie Faith loved sex and it did make her less cranky overall. And, she thought it made Aimee's life better too.

"That's your problem. Orgasms on the regular keep you mentally well-adjusted."

Katie Faith sipped her coffee. "Listen, I don't need anyone else to have one of those. Anyway, when's the last time *you* got any action?"

"I've been broken up with Bob for eight months now. I don't miss him. But I can't deny he knew his way around my lady bits. Diablo Lake's stock is limited. What can I say?"

"You're a floozy and have weak character." Katie Faith shook her head sadly and then cracked up.

After a quick flip of her middle finger, Aimee went back to her breakfast. "That's me all over. Hey, so are you heading to the hospital today? We got sidetracked discussing sex and other dirty things."

Kit, *oh hell*, Katie Faith, stood, draining her coffee. "I'm going to stop over at the Counter first. Then I'll call my mom and see what's going on. I've got Curtis helping out while I'm back and forth to the hospital. And Miz Rose is going to help. She knows the place backward and forward anyway." Curtis was Aimee's cousin and Rose Collins had worked odd shifts at the Counter for nearly thirty years. She was eighty now, but spry and smart and she could run the place with her eyes closed. And the leader of the Consort of Witches in Diablo Lake.

"I need to shower. I'll go in to work for a bit. Call me when you're ready and I'll ride with you. I haven't seen your mom in a few days anyway. I'll also make sure all the pieces coordinating with his physical therapy and the rest are in place once he's home." Aimee's expertise with all the medical-related stuff was a huge help.

Katie Faith hugged Aimee tight. "Thank you. Really."

"That's what friends do." Aimee jogged from the room as Katie Faith began to tidy up the kitchen and wash out the coffee stuff.

She'd have to handle a lot of things. She'd need a place to live and not just to get laid, as Aimee so delicately put it. If—when—she came back, it would be for good and she wanted her own space to put her roots back down.

Roots were important. She had them here in Diablo Lake. Gradys had been there for generations. She fit there in a way she knew she'd never be comfortable anywhere else. At the same time, it was really important that she come back and make a place for herself on her own terms. She didn't want to be that woman who got herself left at the altar, or Avery and Nadine's girl. Not only anyway.

She may have not fit into Chattanooga as well as she had in Diablo Lake, but she was her own person there. She'd also learned a lot about herself. She would return, partly because her family needed her and partly because it was time. But she'd do it with some dignity. As much as she could anyway.

Looking through Aimee's kitchen window, she caught sight of a man jogging down the street in the early morning stillness. She leaned closer to see who it was, not that the long, powerful legs and shirtless torso weren't enough to enjoy in and of themselves.

As if she'd shouted a name, he turned and she stilled, her hands gripping the dish towel tight. How on Earth could she still be so totally gobsmacked every time she caught sight of the man? And how on Earth did he still look so good? And forbidden, which, well come on, what girl with a lick of sense wouldn't want that?

She did manage to lift her hand and wave. He must not have recognized her, either that or he hated her, because his wave in return was joined by a puzzled look and he kept on running.

Shrinking back from the window with a wistful sigh, she hung the towel up and headed to get dressed.

"I just saw Jace Dooley jogging," she called out to Aimee as she finished with her makeup and came back out into the living room.

"Shirtless, right? Tell me it was one of those days." Aimee waggled her eyebrows.

"Wait, this is a thing?" Katie Faith asked.

"Yes. He goes for a run every morning. You can see him twice if you're up early enough. Unless it's snowing he usually has his shirt off and tucked into his shorts. He's one of the Lord's finest creations." Aimee hummed.

"I can't believe you didn't even tell me. What kind of friend knows Jace runs shirtless past a body's kitchen window every single day and never bothers to say? It's like I don't even know you." Katie Faith shook her head.

"You're right. I sincerely apologize for my oversight. So." Aimee looked her up and down. "Is this a thing then? I just need to know how to be supportive. Like should I be cheerleading you taking up jogging so you can get yourself and your jiggly boobs in his path? Or is this just an idle trip down memory lane when you had the hot and tinglies for him?"

She thought about it for a while. "I don't know if it's a thing yet. It could be a thing. If he's single and I still like him. I've changed since then. I imagine he has too. But it's not something I came back to town to do. In the meantime, I'll be sure to set my alarm tomorrow so

I won't miss out. Just because I don't have time to do anything doesn't mean I can't look."

Aimee said, "It would be a crime against nature not to look at him."

"Thanks for enabling me. I love you." Katie Faith gave her a hug.

"Love you too. Now let's get out the door and kick today's butt."

Chapter Two

Katie Faith locked the front doors of the Counter. Three weeks had passed since she'd arrived back in Diablo Lake to take over. The weight of it was frightening, even as it comforted and anchored her. She'd expected to feel trapped. Instead she carried a tote bag full of ledgers to study in the evenings after she closed up and spent a good part of her days thinking on things she could do to improve business.

All that planning and work had kept her busy enough to not obsess over her father every moment of the day though it was impossible to get the memory of him normally so hearty, now pale and fragile, tubes running all over his body out of her head.

She'd grown up thinking her father was invincible. Now she knew otherwise and it terrified her.

Still, it was impossible not to smile as she turned and caught sight of Miz Rose patting her hair and straightening her sweater. "Good day today, Miz Rose. Thank you so much for all your help. I don't know what we'd have done without you these last weeks."

Miz Rose sent Katie Faith a raised brow. "Where else would I be? You think I got lots of social engagements I'm running out on?"

The woman was about four foot nothing and Katie Faith knew the hair tightly confined in her braided bun fell in deep auburn waves to her knees. She'd been a notoriously beautiful young woman in her day. Males from Diablo Lake, no matter their background, courted her and in the end, she'd chosen the quietly dignified Jefferson Collins. They'd made a passel of gifted kids who also had kids of their own. Miz Rose was an incredibly powerful woman and though Katie Faith loved her very much, she never forgot that.

"Miz Rose, if anyone in this town had social engagements it'd be you."

Miz Rose chuckled low and sort of naughty. She was family. Had been the first person, after her father, who held Katie Faith when she'd been born. She'd been a wonderful role model, a woman Katie Faith admired deeply. The feeling had been returned by Miz Rose. When Katie Faith had walked back into the church after being told Darrell had run off with Sharon Woolery, Miz Rose had clucked her tongue.

Shaking her head she'd said, pouring on her disdain for extra effect, *"Well, Katie Faith, you saved yourself some heartache, girl. He's about as useless as a back pocket on a shirt. Your children would have been as dumb as stumps. Let Sharon have him."*

It still made her laugh every time she thought of it.

Katie Faith bent to kiss Miz Rose's cheek, the soft scent of White Shoulders wafting from her, filling her with a childhood's worth of memories.

"You *will* call me if you need me in here tomorrow afternoon." An order given by someone accustomed to obedience with just a smidge of magic to underline her words.

"Thank you. I will." She waved to Miz Rose's grandson who waited for her at his passenger side door.

"Hey there, Katie Faith. Good to have you back in town. I guess I'll be seeing you next week at the meeting?"

Oh yeah, all that stuff. She nodded. If she was back she had responsibilities far beyond running the Counter. Her family made up one of the Consort—what they called the group of witches who'd banded together and then been part of Diablo Lake governance from the very start.

"Hey, Brandon. I'll be there." She walked alongside Miz Rose, not helping but being there in case she needed it. Pride was important. Dignity was important. Katie Faith had been raised right, so she saw Miz Rose safely into the car and stood back to watch them drive away.

She turned back to check the doors one last time before heading across the street to her next meeting. At the last all-town gathering where they held a census, four thousand people called the city limits home. Of course *city limits* meant a pretty large area sprawling through the already isolated Smokies. Not a lot of people really, but enough to keep a few restaurants, a dive bar and a brew pub open on Diablo Lake Avenue, the main thoroughfare bisecting the town and the only way back to the series of roads leading to US Highway 441.

The Counter, which was purely a daytime joint with limited food and drink options shared the left side of the street along with the Red Door Inn, the aforementioned pub. At the farthest end of the street lay Pete's, a creepy, windowless building where the old guys in town hung out to drink all day while bitching about the government and avoiding their spouses. It wasn't dangerous in there or anything, but your shoes stuck to the floor and she'd rather pee outside than even go into a bathroom stall there.

Luckily, Katie Faith was headed to Salt and Pepper to catch up with Damon Dooley, who sidelined as a realtor in addition to running the general store with his twin, Major.

Diablo Lake was isolated. On purpose and by design. They were far, far off the already remote US Highway 441. It kept humans away during most of the year and gave the citizens of Diablo Lake the anonymity—and safety—they desired.

But such isolation meant in order to pay bills, the denizens of Diablo Lake had to be creative and perform a variety of jobs. During the summer and fall, many locals hired out as guides through the surrounding Great Smoky Mountains National Park to save up money to get them through the generally hard winters that closed roads and isolated them even further.

But they were witches, who had a solid and very important connection to the earth. Being so far out in the wilderness was good for them. And shifters. Werewolves like the Dooleys and Pembrys and big cats like the Cuthbert and Ruiz families all loved the freedom to shift and run wherever they liked. Guide work was a natural thing for them, they were good at it and made a hearty living. Some of them even did backcountry and snow tours during the winters.

Pale green eyes met hers as she walked through the doors of Salt and Pepper. Damon sat at a nearby table, drinking a Coke, working his way through one of the diner's signature mega burgers and a huge pile of french fries.

The man was easily six and a half feet tall. Broad like

the rest of his kind. The kind of gaze that never missed a thing, even as he'd been flirting with his server. His deep-black hair was short just then, but Katie Faith knew when it got longer it grew into curls any girl would want to run her fingers through. Not that she ever had. Damon Dooley was so far out of her league she had to tiptoe just to see the edge of it. Didn't mean she couldn't look now and again.

Summers in Diablo Lake were her favorite time. The boys went shirtless and the shifter boys let their hair grow. All work-hard muscles, long hair and perfect teeth. Katie Faith smiled at the memory and suddenly moving back didn't seem so very bad at all.

Katie Faith slid into the booth across from Damon. "Hey."

"Hey, Katie Faith. How's your daddy?" Damon's eyes softened from flirting to concerned.

"He's doing good. He starts his physical therapy on Monday. Thank goodness for Aimee. She found a physical therapist who agreed to come out here three days a week to work with Daddy at the clinic."

He nodded. "Major told me to let you know he'd come out this weekend to see about adding some railings to the front and back steps. Should make it easier for your dad to get in and out of the house without help."

She *had* been gone too long because as she heard that, tears welled up. The outpouring of love and support for her dad had touched her deeply.

Damon gave her a moment to get herself back together before he spoke again, filling her in on the rentals and places for sale available in her price range and desired area, including an apartment above the mercantile, which the Dooley wolves owned and operated.

Given the very possessive nature of werewolves, she needed to avoid any part of town controlled or dominated by Pembry wolves. Otherwise, they'd lay claim to her, like a chair or the last piece of pizza.

"I don't want *anything* in the Pembry part of town." She said it quietly even though no one around was Pembry. It was still a small town after all; smart to keep your business quiet unless you wanted everyone to know it.

"I'm going to suggest you want to be in town or at least very close, in the middle of winter."

True. At least if she lived in town she could walk to the Counter if the roads got bad or the power went out. The market and mercantile would be close enough to get her through if they got snowed in for a few days. The main part of town was also the first to get plowed and sanded in icy or snowy conditions.

Yes, in town was the best option and, she thought, where most of the people she liked best were anyway.

"Can I take a look tonight? I do want to buy, but maybe I can rent while I keep saving. I'd like some other options. I've been here nearly a month so once I make a choice I'd like to get things moving quickly. I'm staying with Aimee, but I need to move my furniture from Chattanooga and get that all sewn up."

He nodded. "Don't know why not. I have the keys for both places. You want to look at the apartment above the mercantile? Major and I are good landlords."

She shrugged. Of course he and his brother would manage the place. "Sure. Why not look at all my options?"

"Always a plus, in my book." Damon grinned and her hormones did the cha cha. He was nearly as hot as his big brother. Nearly.

* * *

Jace Dooley looked up from the engine of a Chevy truck whose carb needed changing out to catch sight of Katie Faith Grady stretching those damnable legs out the passenger side of Damon's car.

She turned, pushing her sunglasses up to the top of her head and he felt it to his toes. Damn she was pretty. Always had been, even when she was small. But now she'd grown into herself. Her once unruly hair now tousled around her face, still curly but she'd tamed it somehow. Made the curls behave. The color was rich, not the shade she was born with, but what did he care? He liked the way it looked in the late day sun, like dark red wine and chocolate all bound together. It worked with her skin and eyes. Big hazel eyes. Eyes she'd gotten from her daddy's people. Eyes that branded her. And that scared him as much as it excited him.

She moved with purpose, as always. But grace had replaced the clumsiness she'd had as her legs kept growing all through high school until he wanted her so badly he'd nearly punched that idiot Darrell in the face for having her. But for a few hours on one night he'd never forgotten.

Of course, sadly, people run to type and Darrell had pissed it all away to sneak off with Sharon. Well, they deserved each other and he hoped Katie Faith knew what she'd so narrowly escaped.

Jace continued to watch like some pervert as she followed Damon up the stairs to the apartment above the mercantile.

That's when he realized what was happening. *Oh hell no.* Standing up straight, he banged his head against the hood and didn't stop the curse from escaping. Guiltily, he looked around, relieved his grandma had gone back inside and hadn't heard that one.

Crap. He wiped his hands off on a nearby rag and headed toward where they'd disappeared. If Katie Faith lived across the hall from him, he was pretty sure he'd die of want. Or he'd go to hell for all the self love.

At the top of the stairs, he caught her scent lingering in the air. Like catnip, electric and spicy. Her magic danced through it, calling to him.

Like it had years before.

Like it had and he'd pretended it away.

The door to the vacant apartment was open and he followed the sound of voices, hers a soft, sweet song, brushing against the low rumble his brother possessed.

They turned as he entered. Damon didn't bother to hide his smug smile as he sent a look of challenge to Jace. Jace picked it right up. "You were right, Damon." He grinned and looked to Katie Faith. "It *was* you who waved at me through Aimee's window a few weeks ago, right? Damon said you'd been staying in town. Glad to hear your daddy is back home."

She blinked up at him a few times and he noted the increase in her heartbeat. Not in fear. *Not at all.* When she licked her lips before speaking he nearly growled. Her skin warmed as she blushed, bringing her scent to him where it grew claws and dug in.

"Yeah, that was me. Good to see you, Jace. Or should I say Officer Dooley? Thank you. He's doing much better." Her voice had gone breathless in a few parts, which only got his attention more.

"Jace is just fine. Unless I'm arresting you. You plan

to disturb the peace?" He stepped closer, unable to stop himself.

She continued to look up at him, those big eyes of hers blinking slowly. Every time she licked her lips he had to root himself to the spot to keep from bending to take a taste of that mouth.

Damon rocked back on his heels, clearly pleased with himself. "I'm showing her the apartment. Mind if I show her yours? Just so she can see what it looks like with stuff in it?"

He did *not* need her scent in his house. He did not need her to live next door. It was too much. He'd never be able to avoid her.

Like he hadn't just thought all those very rational things, he found himself smiling down at her as he spoke to Damon. "Sure. Lemme go make sure it's picked up." He backed from the room and went to his door, cursing himself the whole time.

His place was relatively clean. He suspected his grandmother came in a few times a week when he was out to tidy up. Good reason to keep the *special* magazines and movies tucked away.

It wasn't too many minutes later when Damon walked right in with Katie Faith. She reached out to knock on the door as they passed through the entry, ever a girl with manners. He stifled a smile.

He made the mistake of taking a deep breath and he was done.

Chapter Three

Katie Faith took the place in while pretending she was totally cool. Meanwhile, in her head, she giggled while doing a dance at sharing a small space with two of the most intensely male specimens she'd ever seen.

Being around Jace transported her back to high school. The first time she'd seen him, she'd been out on the track, pretending to run laps when Jace, then a senior to her freshman, shirtless and sweaty, lapped her and her friends.

Katie Faith wasn't totally sure but she might have seen the Promised Land. All sorts of things happened to her body that she wouldn't really understand for another few years.

But she did now. Boy howdy, did she! The adult Katie Faith knew the pleasure—and the danger—of the major tinglies when a man like Jace doled them out.

Moving in across the hall would be flirting with trouble. She knew she had an affinity with the Dooley wolves, just as she had with the Pembrys. That was one of the ways Diablo Lake and its protective magic continued to be strong and vibrant.

Wolves and witches clicked. Their magic was complementary. Some wolves and some witches *really* clicked in the romantic and biological sense. Sure she could date and fall in love with anyone. It happened from time to time. But that *affinity* between witches and shifters meant she had a connection to them in ways she'd never have with other males.

After that little exchange back at Salt and Pepper, when she and Damon nearly broke light bulbs just by touching, being in this apartment would be like waving a red flag at a bull. Or worse, she'd be the juicy steak and all the Dooleys who came around would salivate.

Coming back to Diablo Lake meant facing the political and social realities of town. A witch living in the territory a wolf considered his would be a shiny lure. They'd want to collect her. Claim her for their family.

She'd been considered part of the Pembry pack when she was with Darrell so it hadn't really been an issue before. If she moved into this apartment she'd have to carefully guard her boundaries or she'd have Dooley wolves in her living room all the day long.

The studio for rent was way smaller, but technically not in anyone's territory. If she chose that one, she'd be avoiding the potential for future annoyance and dick measuring.

Katie Faith stomped her foot. In her head, because that's where a lady kept her tantrums. Which was a dumb saying her granny used and she scared people day in and out with her lively ways.

Lively was what her pops called his wife. Everyone else just said crotchety. Granny would move into this apartment and flip the bird to anyone who tried to stop her. Which, when she thought about it, was the way to do it. No one owned her or where she chose to be.

Katie Faith had done her time in Chattanooga, feeling totally unattractive and invisible. She'd healed from being dumped so unceremoniously. She was a woman in the prime of her life, could it be so wrong to want to look at gorgeous men every day? Would it be such a crime to be admired and to feel beautiful? Also, if something broke they all knew how to fix things. And they could reach high shelves.

She knew she had nothing to fear from the Dooleys, but also, if she moved into that apartment, that they'd consider her one of them above and beyond the whole connection between their magic. You lived on the same property, in the same space with wolves and they'd kill you, drive you out, or place you under their protection. Since Damon had brought her over there and they wanted to rent the place to her, she guessed they chose the latter. And protection sounded sort of nice. Especially when you compared the options of being killed or run off.

She also couldn't deny dread that eventually the Pembrys would seek her out. If she was surrounded by Dooleys, it would underline that Katie Faith was done with Pembry wolves.

The rent was doable, and it was central enough to the Counter and to her parents' house. It would be silly *not* to rent it.

She drew her attention back to Damon and Jace. There was something going on between the brothers, a whole conversation of looks and exhalations. *Boys.* Like she wouldn't know it was about her? She cocked her head and watched the interplay until Jace turned his gaze back to her and she got a major case of the tingly bits.

He waved vaguely around the room. "Go ahead on

and look around. This is a mirror of the place across the hall." Jace's voice was so low the bass of it vibrated through her belly and other places south.

She looked at them on her way toward the bedrooms. Damon was so handsome he was nearly pretty with it. But Jace was something else entirely. The kind of man who took up every bit of space when he walked into a room, even if he never said a thing. A good cop quality, she was sure. He was quietly intense. Intelligent, she knew. His nose was just a bit more crooked than would merit movie star handsome, and yet, with the wary eyes and the full lips, the combination made it impossible not to look and admire whatever it was he possessed.

She'd crushed on him in high school, where he'd been nearly four years older. Who hadn't? Jace had been mysterious. His energy had been all bad boy. Intense. His physicality had been different than Darrell's. They'd both played football in high school, but Jace had run the defensive line. Big and scary, but not really. Not in his eyes.

Darrell had been much nearer to her age. They'd been in the same classes and he'd been handsome and at times he had a great sense of humor. He'd liked her. Pursued her. Where Jace had been broody and intense, Darrell had been open and vivacious. The kind of guy who had an opinion about everything. And, because of that, she really should have known he'd have turned out to be a dick.

The ugly truth was he'd charmed her in his way. And he'd sort of led their relationship and she'd let him. She hadn't known better until after. But it was high school in a small town and so after two years of dating everyone assumed it would be forever.

Except for one night after the homecoming parade.
She'd gotten into an argument with Darrell. He broke up
with her then and she'd stormed off while he'd stayed.
Most likely to track Sharon down, she knew now. Katie
Faith had gone to the batting cages, hitting one after
another to work out the mad. No one knew she did it.
The batting cages were her secret. Her place to run
when she'd had enough because they all thought she
was still a clumsy teen.

And then Jace had been there. Leaning against the
cab of his truck. Long legs covered in pale denim,
booted feet crossed at the ankle.

He'd *seen* her and it had been a pretty big shock. Jace
had changed everything because he'd asked her what
was wrong and he'd meant it.

And in the telling she'd been so close to him and had
been crying in frustration. He'd hugged her. But it was
that he'd understood her tears were more from anger
than sadness—again he'd seen her—that had made her
hug him the first time.

And then when she pulled back he'd bent to kiss her.

For nearly four hours, they'd kissed and talked. Held
hands and touched. She could still remember the waves
of sensation that had rolled through her as he slid his
fingers through hers, palm to palm. He'd branded himself into her in a way she still carried even then. It
couldn't have been more intimate if they'd actually had
sex. But they hadn't and it was still the most explosively
sexual experience she'd ever had.

Then he left town for a month and she gave up, chalk-
ing it up to one lovely secret that would never be spoken about again.

And here she stood in the doorway to his bedroom,

looking at his bed and wondering what he'd feel like against her skin. She sighed heavily. This was dumb. Beyond dumb and back again. She should just see if her parents would let her borrow money from them to make her down payment larger. The two-bedroom house for sale had been everything she wanted in a house but out of her budget. Her monthly payments would be too close to the line for her comfort. She needed to rent while she saved up money and settled back into Diablo Lake.

They'd give her the money, but right then things were extra tight with her father's hospitalization. More stress on them would be a terrible thing. No. Waiting and saving was the financially sane thing to do. Even if she would be living across the hall from a man who rang her bell like it was dinnertime.

They'd both totally been checking out her butt and looked away quickly when she caught them.

"I'll take it. When can I move in?"

Damon moved to take her arm and draw her outside the apartment. In hindsight, a normal thing. But Jace's wolf had other ideas and he found himself grabbing for his brother's retreating body, a snarl on his lips.

Damon froze. "Just a sec, Katie Faith. Excuse us." Damon closed the door, leaving her in the hallway before he turned to face Jace.

Damon spoke slowly and carefully. Jace was higher ranked and, he knew, in a state of agitation after Katie Faith had just been in his space, her scent still in the air. "What the hell are you doing? Your eyes are changing like a fucking pup. Get yourself under control, Jace."

Jace unclenched his fists and took a slow, hard exhale and then back in. "I'm sorry. It just happened."

Damon shook his head. "Who do you think you're

talking to? You and I both know what this is about and she's right outside. We can work around that. Once people know it's that way, they'll back off."

What his brother meant was that a witch with her background living in the midst of a knot of Dooleys would bring the males around like bees to a flower. But if Jace showed he was the one Katie Faith belonged to, they'd leave it be.

Jace shook his head, denying what his brother had said. Lying and they both knew it. But he spoke anyway. "It's *not* about her. I'm just not used to her, that's all. It'll be fine. Go on or she'll think we're talking about her."

They'd been carrying on a hushed conversation, which was a big enough clue even if she couldn't hear the exact words.

"You *are* talking about me," Katie Faith called from the other side of the door.

That's when he started to realize the Katie Faith in the hallway was not the same shy, sweet girl she'd been before she left Diablo Lake.

Stupidly, he sort of dug it.

He gave Damon a severe look. His brother had the balls to roll his eyes.

"Oh you think just because we've got company I won't punch your face?" Jace asked in a very quiet voice.

"Go on ahead then," Damon taunted, wearing what their grandfather called a *shit-eating grin*.

Snorting, Jace reached out, whacked his brother's pretty head into the doorjamb and was checking his watch before Damon even figured out what was happening. "Thanks. I feel better now."

"Asshole." Damon punched his shoulder hard enough to make Jace grunt a little.

"Do you guys need more time to have whispered discussions about me and scuffle around?" Katie Faith called out from the hall. "If so, I'll just head back to Aimee's."

Before he could punch his brother once more, Jace opened the door to find her leaning against the wall across the hall. At ease. Her heart rate was slightly elevated, but she made the effort to stay calm.

"You know how to live around us already," he told her. If she'd been too close or had appeared anxious, he'd have responded. His own anxiety would have ramped up and it could have been weird.

Instead, she showed her control and she stood her ground in a way that was not aggressive.

"Werewolves are just men turned up to fourteen. You're not that complicated. So can I move in here or what?"

Damon eased out, staying in Jace's line of sight the whole time. His brother was right, he was acting like a fucking pup instead of the next in line to run this family. Jace locked his control into place and stood taller.

"Give us forty-eight hours to get the place cleaned and ready for a tenant," Damon told her with a smile.

Chapter Four

John Joseph Dooley looked at his grandsons as he drank his morning cup of coffee. "Patty tells me there'll be a new tenant above the mercantile."

Jace looked toward Damon, keeping his glance nonchalant. JJ Dooley never brought anything up lightly. He wasn't the Patron—the leader—of the Dooley wolves for nothing. And clearly his brother had gone to tattle because he was a shit stirrer.

"Katie Faith Grady's moving in this week. She'll be a good tenant. Quiet enough, no chore to look at. She's got a job. Big plusses in a renter." Damon winked at his grandfather, keeping it casual.

"She's a wildcard." Patty Dooley, JJ's wife and their grandmother put another heaping platter of hotcakes on the table before joining them at the opposite end from JJ.

Like pillars in a foundation, his grandparents had held this family together in the lean times as well as those of plenty. They'd stepped in to raise Jace and his brothers after their mother had died giving birth to Damon and Major. Their father, the Dooleys' youngest son, had been an outlaw wolf. Whatever he'd done got him killed.

As an outlaw, his name wasn't spoken. Their father

was a shadow shaped like a man. A weight of shame they bore without having really known him at all.

The reality for Jace and his brothers had been a life of proving to everyone that they were nothing like their father. It had forged a deep bond between the three. A unified front. His relationship with his little brothers was part of his armor. Even when he wanted to punch one of them he always knew they'd have one another's backs.

They figured out soon enough that whatever their father had done had most likely been selfish and stupid. JJ had to fight several challengers to keep his position as Patron in the two years following their father's death. That's when he began to train his grandsons.

Jace had been four years old the first time he'd had to fight to prove he was worthy.

It'd become something they all had to do. Battle not just to prove their strength but to build respect. Not just with fists, but with heart and brain. Lots of people wanted to knock the outlaw's sons down a few pegs. As a kid it had been a regular occurrence that he went to bed with bruises or some sort of injury from fighting or training.

One of his earliest memories was being jumped by three adult wolves. Knowing there was no way he—a seven-year-old—could beat them all at once, he'd led them on a chase until he'd been able to become the pursuer. Taking each one of them out at a time. He'd used his wits and though he'd been sore for a few days afterward, his grandfather had been proud.

JJ had sat on the chair near his bed. His grandmother had tended to him, cleaned him up and got him into bed to let time do the rest to heal him. She'd gone to check on the twins, leaving him alone with his grandfather.

Being raised by JJ hadn't always been easy. His grandfather knew Jace had to build up a thick armor. And he understood all the scar tissue from having to fight off challenges would be part of that.

Even through all that, Jace had always known his grandfather loved him and absolutely believed in his ability.

"Mercy is an important quality," JJ had told him. "I like that you didn't kill any of the wolves who attacked you today. You made a point to them and the rest of the pack. I also like that you beat each one of them badly enough that they'll feel it a while."

Jace had nodded, pride easing the pain of his broken rib.

"I want you to remember something. When you're in charge, you might have to be merciful to your wolves by being unmerciful in their protection."

Jace's eyelids grew heavy as the spell Miz Rose had provided to help him sleep began to pull him under.

"Well done," JJ murmured. "I'm proud of you."

All those years of having to fight for respect and their rightful place in the pack had his uncles willingly stepping aside, acknowledging Jace as Prime when he'd turned twenty-two.

Shoving that from his mind, he attempted to fish for info while keeping his tone light. "She's a wildcard, huh? What do you mean, Grandma?" Jace forked several more hotcakes onto his plate and smothered them with the warm berry preserves.

"I mean the girl's got lots of energy around her. Lots of magic. Could make her something strong, special.

Haven't seen her use it though." Patty shrugged and drank her tea. But Jace wasn't fooled by the pretend casual tone. He knew she was busily working out just how they could work this to their advantage. There was a reason she and his grandfather had such a tight bond. She was as politically savvy as he was.

"Pembrys aren't gonna like her in the bosom of all these Dooleys." Major, Damon's twin, wiped his mouth with a napkin and sat back with a satisfied sigh.

"That's just icing then, isn't it?" JJ smiled and Jace's protective feelings about Katie Faith intensified.

"I think she's had enough of a time with the Pembrys. Leave her be." Jace hadn't expected the level of vehemence he'd used. The entire table turned to give him a look. "What?" he asked, hoping to change the subject soon.

"Just interesting, how you seem so interested in her welfare and all," JJ said with a smirk. "I'm getting old. Your grandmother deserves a day off at some point. I think it's time for you to start thinking about taking over as Patron. You need to start a family of your own."

Jace groaned. Katie Faith had been back in town for less than a month and his grandpa was already planning for how many kids she was going to have with Jace.

"She's a nice girl. The Pembrys did her wrong. Let it go. The last thing she needs is to be fought over like a bone." Jace attempted to be stern, but JJ Dooley didn't care about that.

"Mmm. You sweet on her?" his grandmother asked.

He avoided her gaze. "I care about her because she's a *friend*. I'm gonna head out." He stood, picking up his dishes and putting them into the dishwasher. "Sheriff's got a burr up his butt about people showing up late."

Dooley wolves had built Diablo Lake. From the roads to the buildings. While the Pembrys liked to run things, holding office and filling up a lot of city type jobs, the police station tended to be full of Dooleys. His cousin Sam was a deputy like Jace. But it was Aimee's dad, Carl Benton, who was the sheriff. A guardian witch. Carl's magic helped to buffer the energy between Dooley and Pembry wolves.

Another thing that made Jace crave Katie Faith was the way their magical energies had an apparent affinity. A good balance between complementary magics was one of the reasons Diablo Lake's biggest secret remained safe from the outside world.

Here he'd been assuming he'd end up with another wolf and suddenly this delicious little witch dropped into his lap and he didn't plan to let that go.

"Hey there, Jace," Connie, the dispatcher—and his cousin—called out as he entered the station house. The squat concrete building was also the town disaster shelter and out back was the basketball court most everyone in town used all summer long.

There were two cells. Rarely used and even then it was bush league stuff. A scuffle at a party so someone might need to cool off overnight. Once or twice he'd arrested someone for domestic violence.

If they were Dooleys, his grandfather would handle the real discipline once they got out of jail. They didn't cotton to any harm of women and children. Once a Dooley violated that rule, the sentence would be brutal and nearly immediate. And permanent.

Thankfully it was mostly small stuff. Drunks and

dumbasses, but they generally avoided the crime plagu-ing human cities.

Jace booted his computer up before heading to get himself another cup of coffee because his PC was a hundred years old and slow as molasses.

"Getting a cup of coffee," he called out to Connie. "You want any?"

"Too hot for coffee just now. I'll stick to soda. Thanks though. I hear you have a new tenant over the mercantile now."

He goggled at her. That was fast, even for small town gossip.

She laughed. "You think everyone isn't buzzing around about Katie Faith being back and how pretty she is? And you go and move her in across the hall? Granddaddy must be giggling all day long."

That made Jace laugh. "She needed a place to live. We rented her one. But you're right that JJ is in heaven. I'm sure he'll find a dozen ways to rub it in some Pembry face before the week is out." Hell, part of Jace wanted to do that too.

Connie said, "He does like to stir the pot. Not that Dwayne Pembry and his litter don't deserve a good les-son in how not to alienate a gal as powerful and pretty as Katie Faith Grady. We're smart enough to see her value to Dooley."

This again? He gave his cousin a serious look. "*Leave her be.* Let her come back and make her way here. All this politicking is going to spook her."

As he spoke he knew how futile the effort was. Di-ablo Lake was what it was. Chances were, Katie Faith knew the same and was already steeling herself for the inevitable when she moved in.

"You're getting old. She's pretty. Good family. She'd be a good addition to the pack. Why not you instead of any other idiot in town?" Connie shrugged before turning her attention to the ringing phone.

"Any *other* idiot? So I'm an idiot too?" he asked but she continued to deal with the call.

Sure he was going to settle down. Someday. And sure he'd had a thing for Katie Faith for a long time. But this would be on his damned terms if it happened at all. And he wanted it to. At least to take it a little further to see how they were together. Still, the way his family tried to marry him off like he was sixty instead of twenty-seven annoyed him.

"There's been some vandalism down over at the Baptist church. I told Snuffy you'd be right round," Connie said once she'd hung up.

Lucky him. Snuffy Carson was a pain in Jace's ass. If he wasn't such a sour old jerkoff, his trees wouldn't get toilet papered by the youth of Diablo Lake all the time. But he took being offensive as his duty.

"Don't tell him I'm rushing over there for TP'd oak trees, Connie. The man has to understand where his problems lie in the big scheme of things."

"Like behind that big murder case you're trying to crack? Or the bank robbery that never happened because this is Diablo Lake and more toilet-papered trees down at First Baptist is pretty much the most egregious thing you'll be dealing with today? He's lonely and old and his wife died ten years ago. He probably hasn't had any since way before that. I'd be grumpy too," Connie told Jace. "You know how to handle him."

The old guy would rant and rail. Jace would take pictures and a report and he'd most likely have some time to stop over at the Counter to check up on Avery Grady's health and have a chocolate malted.

It was the neighborly thing to do.

Katie Faith put a glass of iced tea in front of her father. He wanted to come into work for a little while that day and both she and her mother thought it would do him some good.

He wasn't able to handle much. He was still healing. He had to use a wheelchair if he was going to be out for any real amount of time because he got tired very easily. His genetics would continue to aid in speeding his healing, but it would still take time.

He could flirt with all the customers, get fussed over here and there, he exchanged gossip with his friends when they popped in. It was good for him to remember how much he was loved and appreciated and welcomed back to the community.

He was alive. He was mending. Everything was going to be all right.

"I gotta say, Katie Faith, it does my heart good to see you here, making this place your own," her dad told her with a smile. "I sure did miss you, baby."

"I missed you too." And she had. The longer she'd been back in Diablo Lake, the more obvious it had become to her that she was back where she belonged. She finished cleaning up and turned back to him once more. "I have some ideas, opening up a bit earlier, staying open a bit later. And I'd like to add some simple food items to the lunch menu. Easily made ahead. Like a sandwich of the day. Chips instead of fries. I don't think we need to muscle in on what Salt and Pepper does. We can complement each other instead of stealing business."

In any small town that was important, but in Diablo Lake even more given their isolation.

"Good to think about how it impacts the neighbors. I raised you right." He winked and she was glad to see a little color in his face again. He wasn't full strength, but he'd started physical therapy and the paralysis on the left side of his body had gone. Being back in Diablo Lake where the land did so much to help speed his healing had vaulted him forward by at least a month.

She grinned at him. "I'm thinking of buying an espresso machine for the mornings. There's not a single coffee place for miles around. I wouldn't be stepping on toes. Mom still wants to keep her afternoon shift. I think we should keep Curtis on too."

The bell over the door jingled and they both looked up. Mayor Dwayne Pembry took up the doorway and inwardly she made the same sound her father made out loud.

"Like a bad penny," her father muttered and she had to fight back a hysterical bubble of laughter.

If he upset her father one bit she was going to chase him out with the broom. She hoped that showed in her eyes when her gaze met his, holding it steady. This was *her* territory.

"Mayor Pembry, what brings you down to this end of town?"

"Just stopping in to say welcome home and to check on your daddy's health." He turned his fake politician smile on Avery. "You're looking good. Scared everyone. Try not to do that again."

Once, what now seemed like a million years ago,

this man was going to be her father-in-law. He'd eaten dinner at her house dozens of times. He and Avery had been good friends even before Darrell and Katie Faith started dating. Their children's relationship had only strengthened it. And when Darrell had done her wrong, Dwayne had badmouthed Katie Faith. Most likely he'd been embarrassed, but the damage had been done. Even though he'd finally realized just what Darrell had done and took the time to publicly admonish him and apologize to Katie Faith on behalf of the Pembrys, it had been too late. He went on to lose the mayor's office, only recently taking it back when the prior mayor was killed in a hunting accident.

"Can I get you something?" Katie Faith asked, keeping it professional and pleasant but not an inch more. "I can still make a mean vanilla Coke."

He hesitated and then the smile he sent was more like the old Dwayne. "I shouldn't. If Scarlett heard about me having a soda, she'd get a switch off the back tree."

She risked a quick look at her father. Scarlett Pembry was a crazy woman. Hard, uneven, not incredibly stable and she took to making up fanciful stories when she got bored or took it into her head someone had done her wrong. It was entirely possible she would take a switch to her husband's behind if he broke some dietary stricture.

Dwayne slid himself onto the stool next to Avery's wheelchair. "What the heck? I haven't had a vanilla Coke in ages. Probably since the last time you were here." He paused as she began to make his soda.

Her father made small talk until she finished, placing the soda before Dwayne.

He took a sip and sighed happily. "This is just the

thing. Thank you, Katie Faith." His smile faded. "Is everything gonna be all right? Between you and Darrell?"

She cocked her head and looked at him long and hard. "Seems to me, Mayor, that's what they call a dead horse. There's nothing between me and Darrell to be one way or the other."

"This is my town, Katie Faith. I just want to be sure things run smooth-like. I know he did you wrong. But he's got himself two younguns and a wife. I need to know right up front if you have any plans to interfere with that." Oh that folksy thing made her want to punch him.

Anger burned through her and the lights hummed just a bit before she reined it in. "You come in here and ask if *I'm* going to mess in someone's relationship? *Me?* If I recall correctly, and excuse me here because I'm getting angry, but I was the one who had someone else interfere in *my* relationship." She shook her head and held a hand up to keep him silent. "No. You said your piece and now I'll say mine. I came back here because my family needed me and because this is *my* home. I don't want your son. I'm grateful every single minute of my day that he cheated on me and dumped me before I joined myself to him. He's someone else's problem. She's welcome to him and his babies. If you're lucky, they'll turn out like her sister, leastwise they'll be smarter than stumps."

Dwayne sighed deeply. "I know he did you wrong, Katie Faith. I've said so before and I'll say it now, I'm sorry for the things I did right after the wedding. He was wrong. But he's trying now. I'm asking you to respect that."

"Dwayne Pembry, I've never done a damned thing

to your son or his wife. I don't care about either one of them enough to spare their marriage a passing thought. I'm finding it hard to locate my sense of humor. I told you I don't want a part of any Pembry, especially Darrell. I don't care if you don't trust my word. The God's honest truth is that I'm the only one with credibility here. You need to go on now. I'm done with this conversation forever." She took his glass and began to wash it.

"I didn't mean to hurt your feelings, Katie Faith. I really am glad you came home." He stood and she looked up at him.

"You delivered your little message, now go. Rest assured I want no part of you all. Don't you come back here to upset my father again or there'll be the trouble you're so eager to prevent." His dumbass son was one thing, messing with her daddy when he was still weak? That made her furious.

With a heavy sigh, Dwayne turned and trudged out.

"And don't you call 'round election day asking for money, neither," her father called out. "Imagine! The nerve of him to come in here and treat you that way."

She shook her head and took his hand in hers. "*Please* don't get upset, Daddy, it doesn't signify. Let it go. I have. It's been over three years now. You can't afford the anger right now. Your revenge is to live a long time."

The bell jingled again, but this time the doorway held far more interesting fare than before. She grinned.

"Hey, Jace."

He removed his ball cap, what the cops in town wore, and ran his hand through his hair. He'd probably put that hat on while his hair was still wet from the shower. *Oh my.* She paused a moment, going to a very happy place.

She probably shouldn't be thinking about him in the shower. But she wasn't talking on a cell phone and driving, that was an improvement. Right? Her internal argument faded as she watched him move like the predator he was toward the counter. His uniform pants strained at the thighs as he walked, nearly silently. His button-down shirt fit him perfectly and she wanted to lick him. A lot.

He looked *good*. Taut and muscled and sun-kissed and hot damn, delicious.

"Good afternoon, Katie Faith." He smiled, a quick flash of white teeth. "Mr. Grady, how are you?"

"Sit down, son." Her dad indicated the stool right next to his. "I'm working on getting better. It's hard with two women hovering over a body all day and night." Her father sent her a look and she rolled her eyes.

"Must help that they're both so pretty, though." Jace grinned and winked at Katie Faith, who snorted.

"What can I get for you?" Katie Faith leaned over the counter. "It's on the house if you'll answer some marketing questions."

He laughed and settled in, resting his arms on the counter. His gaze locked on hers and she couldn't have looked away even if she had wanted to. Not that she wanted to.

"Shoot. I'm all yours."

Good Lord above, he made her all flustered. "What'll it be?"

"Is it too early for a milkshake? Chocolate?" He looked hopeful.

Werewolves and chocolate. Almost as bad as witches and their obsession with peaches. She smiled. "Never too early for a chocolate milkshake."

He made small talk with her father as she scooped the ice cream, followed by milk and chocolate syrup. It was like breathing, she'd done it so many times. She'd worked behind this counter since the age of ten or so.

Deftly, she poured the shake into a frosty glass. "I'm assuming you want the whole shebang? Whipped cream, nuts and a cherry?"

He just looked at her like she was crazy to even ask so she poked a straw through the pretty mountain of whipped cream and slid it to him with a spoon.

"Would you come in here for coffee if we served lattes and such in the mornings?" she asked him.

"Oh, is this the marketing portion of the program? I need to serious up." The smile hovering at the corner of his mouth made her a little dizzy.

"You're awfully saucy for this early in the day." She sent him a mock frown.

"My grandmother tells me I was born this way." He took a draw on the milkshake and moaned. "This is heaven in a glass. And I think it could work. There's no fancy coffee for miles and miles."

"You think people would spend four dollars for a cup of coffee here in Diablo Lake?" her father asked.

Jace thought and shrugged. "Four bucks?" He winced. "Maybe two fifty. We're backwater, not backwards."

Katie Faith waved it away. "I wouldn't charge four dollars anyway. That's city pricing. I just thought I'd have some coffee and a few baked goods in the mornings, a sandwich at lunch, just one, and then close up at five instead of three. Nothing major, just hopefully some extra business."

"Six to five is a lot to do on your own. Still, I like

that you're digging in. Putting roots back down." Jace's comment seemed flip but his eyes were serious. She just had to figure out if it was as a friend or if he was serious about her on a romantic level. Not that she should be sniffing around a werewolf of any make much less a Dooley. The generations-old beef between the upper-class Pembry wolves and the blue-collar Dooley wolves made any notion of dating either a stupid idea.

She shrugged, trying not to blush. Her father raised his eyebrows, looking back and forth between them, a ghost of a smile on his lips.

"My mom still wants her afternoon shift. Curtis will still be a part-timer so I think it's definitely doable."

More customers came in, half wanting to get a look at Katie Faith being back, but even those she lured in with sweet treats. Maybe she'd be better at this than she thought.

Not one failed to notice who and what was sitting at her counter, though. By nightfall she could only imagine how tongues would be wagging.

"I need to get back to the station to fill out some paperwork." Jace grumbled something about toilet paper. "Thank you for the company and the milkshake."

"Oh I see, come in, be seen, get the gossips all worked up that you're here and dash out again?" she teased.

"It's my greatest joy," he said, deadpan. "Especially if it comes with milkshakes."

"Any time." Like at two in the morning and he was in his boxers and came knocking on her door. She could whip up a milkshake whenever he needed.

He shook her dad's hand before turning back to give her a long up and down look. "I suppose I'll be seeing you soon enough, neighbor."

He looked *damned* good walking away in those uniform pants.

"That boy sure is sweet on you." Her father smiled into his tea.

"He's just being friendly."

"Pull the other one," he mumbled.

"Momma's gonna be here soon to pick you up. I'll be by later on for dinner." She wanted him to drop the subject.

"You be careful 'round them Pembrys. You hear? I don't like it that they came over here. It's as if they're preparing for Darrell doing something stupid."

She sighed and wiped the counter down. "I can handle them if a problem comes up. Which it won't because I have no interest in a single one of those lunkheads."

"Darrell Pembry is an idiot. Makes him more dangerous, not less. This isn't about your interest in them. You're a powerful girl, anyone can see. Power's a lure. Especially in Diablo Lake."

Katie Faith frowned a moment. "He's a fool. Even if I didn't already think he was worthless, I sure as heck wouldn't get involved with a married man. I'm better than that!"

"'Course you are. That's not what I meant and you know it. You're strong. Stronger than you were when you left. You need to work with Miz Rose on some stuff. I'll help when I'm all healed."

Before she could follow up, her mother came in and collected her father to take him home. It was easy enough to manage the fountain by herself for most of the time but right after the middle and high schools let out, things got very busy. Those hungry kids with some

disposable income would give her afternoons a profit-
able boost if she handled it right.

   She picked up the phone and dialed Aimee. She had
planning to do and the movers would be arriving the
following day with all her stuff so it would be her last
night in Aimee's spare room. They'd get together with
their other friend Lara to celebrate when everyone got
off work for the day.

Chapter Five

At a little past noon the following day, Katie Faith tipped the movers and said her goodbyes to them. She'd see them all again soon enough as the moving crew had been a bunch of local Dooleys with strong backs and a big truck.

"No damned chore to watch shirtless, sweaty dudes hauling stuff around on our orders, you know?" Aimee said.

"I'm in agreement with that." Wolves ran hot, so even through the winter, when they worked outside they frequently did it in shirtsleeves or even better, wearing no shirts at all. "I really like that beard Major is growing."

"I'm the president of the Oh-yes-I-like-that-beard fan club. Jace grew one last winter. Looked like lumberjack porn all night and day." Aimee hummed at the memory and Katie Faith tried not to throw the book in her hands at her friend's head.

"Lower cost of living isn't the only reason to be glad I'm back in Diablo Lake," she said, because she couldn't fault anyone for finding Jace Dooley gorgeous.

They both laughed as Katie Faith began to unpack the boxes with her kitchen supplies. "I already stocked the fridge up with beer if you want one. It's after noon on a weekend and we're moving so we get to day drink."

"Your never-ending resourcefulness is a balm to my heart, Katie Faith." Aimee cracked open two beers before joining in on the unpacking.

"If we had been Scouts of some sort I'd totally have earned a lot of flair. Badges. Patches. Whatever. You know what I mean. Maybe with a sash. On a sash, yeah, that would be so cute. Right?" Katie Faith made what she figured was the internationally understood movement for sash-type thingamabob.

Aimee shook her head and snickered. "Bless your heart, Katie Faith."

Katie Faith gave her friend another internationally well-known hand signal and went back to work.

Finally, after several hours of unpacking, hanging pictures and getting the place just right, Aimee paused to give their work a satisfied look. "You got yourself some nice furniture."

Katie Faith turned a circle to take it all in. Her view was of mountains and trees and nothing but. Her belongings fit there. *She* fit there.

"I was an accountant for a department store. I'd never have been able to afford it all without the discount," she told Aimee. Her boss had even told her if she ever changed her mind they'd have a job waiting for her.

She wouldn't be going back to Chattanooga because she'd accepted what had never been more true. Diablo Lake was her home. Her roots went deep, like the magic there did.

"I texted Lara to let her know to get her butt on over here with some food. You're goofy enough as it is. When you get hungry, you're destructively goofy,"

Aimee informed her of their friend whose family owned Salt and Pepper.

"You're going to spoil me with all your love talk."

"I notice you don't deny my claims of your goofiness."

"I'm too classy to dignify your remarks." Katie Faith sniffed and then shoved a caramel into her pie hole because she had no pie and she *was* known to get a bit unruly when she got really hungry.

On cue, Lara appeared holding several bags. "Burgers, fries, deep-fried cherry pies."

"We have beer! Perfect." Katie Faith snuck a french fry and sighed happily. They sat at the small table and looked out the windows, over the fog-shrouded sunset against the mountains and trees in the distance.

"When's the coven meeting?" Aimee grinned and Katie Faith groaned.

"Don't let Miz Rose hear you call us a coven. She's a mite testy about that." They were witches in the sense that they were all born imbued with magical powers of one kind or another. They drew their energy from the earth and met as a group every other Thursday night. But long ago, the Collins family, the strongest of their kind in Diablo Lake, one of the founding families who'd been in charge the longest, decided that *Consort* was a better word to use for what they were and it stuck.

"She *is* kinda scary." Lara leaned toward the windows. "Holy cow, is Damon Dooley a spoonful of yum."

"He sure did seem to think the same of you when we were at Salt and Pepper earlier this week," Katie Faith teased as she took the pickles off her burger.

"Can't say I'd mind living here so close to 'em all. Dangerous. Well, not really, which is probably why they're so hot, but they're big and manly and they all have those work-with-your hands manly jobs. The Pembrys are sort of soft by comparison." Aimee stole some fries and sipped her beer.

"Darrell wasn't all bad. He just wasn't good enough either." He hadn't been a total loser until the end. There were good times between them. It had taken a year or so before Katie Faith could remember that, but time did heal those wounds.

"Face it, he was with you for the power and position. Sharon came along, swished her tail at him and he strayed because she offered less power, but more sex." Lara's blunt delivery would have depressed Katie Faith had an epiphany not shoved everything else from her head.

She sat up from where she'd been slumping. "Power and position? What?"

"Don't tell me it never occurred to you? You're a beautiful woman, Katie Faith, but Darrell and his fellow Pembrys aren't in charge for nothing. They marry for *power and position*. Or, if they knock a female up. But really, it's all good for you because you're free and you're more powerful than they imagined you'd be. That must be killing them." Aimee snorted a laugh.

"You mean to tell me, you think Darrell Pembry only wanted to marry me because I had the potential to be a powerful witch?" Katie Faith was suddenly so angry she wanted to hit someone. Because she knew it was the damned truth.

"Yes, that's what I mean to tell you. I'm sorry it never occurred to you until now. It's not about you, he's the dick." Aimee made a rude noise.

"Dwayne came into the fountain to be sure I wasn't gonna try and wreck Darrell's precious marriage. As if I'd do that. As if I want him. I don't want him and I am more than however much talent I have."

"Of course you are. Who said otherwise here in this room?" Lara waved through the glass down at Jace, who grinned up at them, waving from where he stood talking with his grandmother.

"I didn't have much power back then."

Aimee turned to face Katie Faith fully. In the background, she heard the clomp of footsteps up the stairs. *Jace*.

Aimee stared at her, clearly weighing her words. "You're the daughter of an incredibly gifted witch and your momma is a very powerful guardian. What did you think you'd be?"

"I don't think about it! I'm just regular, every day Katie Faith Grady. No frills, no superpowers. Is that how everyone sees me? What I might be in the future? What if I'm a dud? Am I slated to marry some dude who lives in the root cellar? I only get a good one if I meet the magic standards test?"

Lara clucked her tongue. "Don't be such a drama queen. This is Diablo Lake. Always has been. Yes, these things are important and I can't believe you never thought about it before. It's who we all are, how things work here. Already in the south it's about who your people are, only here it's worse because we are all alone. Do you think Darrell is really smart enough to run an entire city department? He got the job because he's the son of the big cheese."

Aimee reached out and squeezed Katie Faith's hand. "My daddy runs the police department because he was born a guardian. I'm a social worker, because like many guardians, I'm drawn to the kind of work that takes care of people. Keeps order. Every single place to eat in this town is run by witches. Witches are the doctors, the teachers and the cooks. Dooleys fix and build, Pembrys manage. Everyone has a place. Is that so bad?"

Katie Faith knew all that was so, but still. "It is if everyone's potential is hindered by what they're born as."

"Oh yeah, cause that never happens anywhere else, Pollyanna," Lara said.

Katie Faith glared at her.

"And you're *not* hindered. Look at you! You've made something of yourself, haven't you? You were meant to do all you've done. You were born to be exactly where you are right now. Big baby."

"I was meant to be dumped at the altar?"

Lara nodded. "Good lord yes! Katie Faith, marrying Darrell Pembry would have been the worst mistake of your life. Unlike in the books, werewolves don't automatically mate for life or anything. They imprint. Or whatever it is they call it. Anyway, he didn't imprint on you. He liked you well enough, but if he'd have married you, he'd have cheated and it would have killed you and then you'd have killed him since his kind look so unkindly on divorce and such."

Aimee went further. "You can see the difference. JJ and Patty are married, yes, but they're something else, *something more*. You can see their connection the minute they enter a room. Same with Dwayne and Scarlett. She's mean as a snake and crazy to boot, but they're totally into each other. You'd have been some heifer Darrell married to bolster his position. That's dumb. Just like he is. You're way too cute and smart to be tied to a dimwit like Darrell."

"Do you know what was nice about being in Chattanooga? I was an accountant. Named Kit. Nice men asked me out on dates. No one cared who my people were. If I had a lot of magic, or none at all, it didn't matter. My boobs mattered, but you know, that's just reality. Plus they're pretty nice."

"You're special, Katie Faith. You can't get mad about it. You can't change it and you wouldn't even if you could, so hush up. This conversation is getting on my nerves." Aimee stood and threw her trash away and went back to putting books on shelves.

The good thing about having friends who've known you forever is that they know your triggers. Sometimes they pull them for fun, but usually they just called you on your crap and didn't hold it against you.

After they'd left, she stood at the top of the back steps, breathing in the night air, trying to let go of her anger and resentment. Her surprise and annoyance at herself for never thinking about something so obvious.

It'd been a while since she'd felt like such a fool and she didn't like it any more just then than she had before.

That's where Jace found her. He'd wanted to go to sleep but knowing she was just across the hall drove him nuts. Finally, he got up and followed his nose to where she stood, her body silhouetted by moonlight and starshine. Her hair was down from the messy ponytail she'd captured it in earlier and his mouth watered at the totality of her.

"Hey you," he said softly, sidling next to her. He put two bottles of beer on the railing. "Thought you might need one of these. Get everything moved in okay?"

"Just the thing." She grabbed the beer and took a swig before leaning into his body. His heart skipped a beat at the way she fit so perfectly against him. She smelled like cinnamon and anise. Witches usually smelled like cinnamon but the anise was all Katie Faith.

Without even planning to, he put his arm around her shoulder and she didn't stop him. It felt as good right then as it had all those years before on that one night they were together.

"All moved in thanks to Dooley wolves who did all that heavy lifting. Thank you." Her voice was soft, but he didn't have to strain to hear her.

"That's what neighbors do. So any more trouble from the mayor?" It infuriated him to know Dwayne'd had the audacity to come in to the Counter trying to intimidate her.

Pembrys were like that though. They made the mess and tried to make it everyone else's fault.

"As my daddy would say, Dwayne is as full of wind as a corn-eating horse," she grumbled and he laughed.

"You can take the girl from Diablo Lake, but you can't take Diablo Lake from the girl, I see."

She chuckled, turning toward him, his arm holding her close. Suddenly, her mouth was right there. He *knew* how sweet the taste of her lips was. He remembered that night so long ago when they'd kissed for hours. It had been so powerful for him, he'd been so moved, he had to leave town for a while. Despite Katie Faith and Darrell's on-again-off-again nature, the Pembrys had considered Katie Faith *theirs*.

His decision to go and stay away from her hadn't been about Jace and Katie Faith, though he'd wanted it to be. It had been bigger than that. Wolf business. Recklessness on his part could have started a war.

But the want between them hadn't ever really left. The memory of how she'd tasted was still fresh. So much so that there was no way he could stop himself from bending his knees and kissing her right then and there.

Her arms wrapped around his neck as she opened to him and the sweetness of her slipped through him on tiptoes, only to quietly turn his world upside down.

There would never be enough of Katie Faith for him.

Lips, so whisper soft, parted against his and his tongue slid inside. Their breath married as he deepened the kiss, holding her tightly, trying to ignore the pounding of blood through his veins and the rather noticeable sign of approval he pressed into her belly.

He needn't have worried about her being shocked, not his Katie Faith. She writhed against him, setting off little zings of pleasure through his body. By the time he was able to think clearly enough to stand back a step he knew two things.

First, Katie Faith Grady was *his*. She may not know it, but there was no denying it to the wolf inside or the man on the outside.

And second, when they finally got into bed, they'd probably bring the entire town's ceilings down. He couldn't wait.

Swallowing hard, he watched and groaned as she pressed her fingers to her lips.

"I've wanted to do that again for so many years it's sort of embarrassing," he managed to say around a tongue that felt too big.

She smiled, cocking her head to the side. "I've *wanted* you to do that for, well since the last time we did. I'm ridiculously giddy. What took you so damned long, Jace!"

He couldn't help it, he laughed and hugged her. "One

thing's for sure, Katie Faith, things between you and me ain't gonna be boring. We have time now. You don't belong to anyone else." But him. "Let me dazzle you."

"You dazzled me a long time ago. But I'm open to more dazzling. Any time."

He wanted to waltz her back to his place and give her some jazz hands, but he decided to let it go slow. To build that want until he nearly exploded with it.

"I have tomorrow afternoon off. How about a hike?" he asked her. He'd tuck a bottle of wine in his pack along with a blanket. Yeah. He liked the idea of kissing her silly under a wide blue sky.

"Uh. Like up hills so I'll get sweaty and stuff?" She had all the enthusiasm of a person who'd just been asked if she wanted to go to the dentist.

He should have been horrified that she was so averse to something he loved doing. But he was delighted instead. Charmed and bewitched.

"Why are you making that face?" Katie Faith asked him.

"I was just thinking you had me bewitched. Fitting I suppose." He tucked a tendril of her hair back behind her ear.

She frowned and he narrowed his eyes at the change in her demeanor.

"What did I say?" He wanted to fix it. His wolf didn't much like seeing her upset in any way.

She shook her head. "Nothing. It's not you. You're all good. At least for now." Katie Faith blew out a breath, visibly letting go of her tension. "I'll let you know when you aren't."

"Does that mean you're telling me you're mercurial?" He nuzzled her temple, breathing her in. He didn't even remember pulling her that last little bit of space separating them.

Her low hum was nearly a purr and it had him clamping down on his wolf. His wolf wanted more of her right that moment. Wanted to tease and seduce and play.

"I used to be malleable but that didn't really work out for me."

He tipped himself back enough to look at her better. "I prefer who you are right here and now."

"You say that now," she warned and he snickered.

"I'm next in line to be Patron of the Dooley wolves. You think mercurial is going to slow me down?" He knew not to mock her size or constitution. He liked his balls too much to do that.

"I guess we'll see," she said, grinning now.

"Right? I'm kind of excited to see what happens next."

"Kind of? I must not be doing this whole thing right if all I get is *kind of* excited."

Jace said, "I think we need to work up to me being *really* excited. But I think it's safe to say, you'll be there when that happens."

"That might make me more amenable to hiking. But not a whole lot more."

"If you get tired I'll carry you. I'm pretty strong, or so I've been told," he said, liking this energy between them.

"If you do it while wet I might be convinced."

"I do believe you're a far dirtier girl than I ever imagined."

Her laughter rang through the night and he let himself be eased by it.

Chapter Six

"It's probably because your butt is so fantastic."

Katie Faith sighed. She hadn't meant to say it out loud, as she huffed along behind Jace on the hike she'd agreed to go on while high on sex chemicals.

He didn't even look back as he kept going like some sort of camel. Or donkey. Or whatever.

He laughed though and he really had a good one. Sexy and masculine. It went with the ass. "I take that to mean you agreed to this date because you were somehow hypnotized by my posterior end?"

How was he not even winded?

"At the risk of getting all murdery on you, Jace, I really must inquire if we're close to the end of this hike? Or at the very least a place to stop so I can eat and rest. I'm not a mountain goat."

He did turn then, but kept walking without breaking a stride, only doing it backward.

"Now you're just showing off." She gave in and giggled because he was ridiculous and she never even stood a chance. Mercy.

He flashed her a grin. "Is it working?"

"I'm here on a Saturday morning. The sun has only been up like two hours. So I'd say yes."

Jace slowed until she reached him. "Despite all your complaining, we're nearly there. See that bend ahead?" He spun and turned to walk side by side with her on the trail.

If there was another mountain around that bend she was going to kick him in the balls.

"You're not even sweating. I hate you."

He picked her up and began to jog up the trail until he'd rounded the bend and the trail opened up with the lake down below, glittering in the sun.

"Wow."

"You're barely even winded. I can hear your heart rate, you know," he said as he set her on her feet. "You're in good shape for a city girl."

"You clearly ignored all that wheezing this last half a mile or so." Straight up a mountain like a Sherpa. Only she was not anywhere near that level of athleticism.

"Next time I'll give you a piggyback ride."

"You're totally serious." Katie Faith grinned as she shook her head.

"What?" He shrugged his pack free and pulled her closer. "Why be with a werewolf if you can't enjoy all the perks?"

It shouldn't make her all tingly. This was sort of caveman. Ish. Caveman adjacent. But it was just so… sexy when he did it.

"You make me want to take risks, Jace Dooley," she told him.

His grin again, this time it was all utter male certainty. "Yeah?"

She nodded. Katie Faith wanted to throw her head back, laughing at the beauty of this exact moment. Exhilarated that this male in the absolute prime of his life wanted her so much.

Showed off and preened for her.

It turned her head. Big time. And did marvelous things for the other parts of her. Jace was different. Different from anyone else she'd known. Different even from the boy he'd been years ago.

"You're the equivalent of eating dessert first."

His smile, before he claimed her lips with his own, was delighted.

A few minutes later they sat on the blanket he'd brought, drinking coffee and eating honey buns. Those he'd brought too.

"You're spoiling me," she said, licking her fingertip. "*Not* the hiking part. Just to be clear. That's me spoiling *you*."

"Goddamn, Katie Faith." He laughed. "I really do like you." He flicked the pad of his thumb over her bottom lip. "I *am* spoiling you. Glad you noticed."

She went still as she thought about that. Looked out over the lake as wispy clouds passed overhead here and there.

He didn't say anything else. Giving her space to process. This was serious for him. This date, the view and the treats, they were the werewolf equivalent of candy and diamonds. He gave her some flash, some romance, a piece of something he loved. Showing her his belly in one way.

Much like the ass, his belly was spectacular.

She wanted him right back. Wanted him more than anything else she'd ever wanted. So she slid her fingers with his, palm to palm, holding on as they sat shoulder to shoulder.

She answered the question he hadn't spoken. *Are you ready for what this relationship is going to be? What I am?* "Okay then."

He snorted, squeezing her hand slightly.

Okay then.

He was next in line to be Patron. A very eligible bachelor. He'd pretty much declared his intentions to her and she'd said, *okay then.*

Somehow though, it seemed fitting. He liked it. Liked that she accepted what he was. Liked the speed of her pulse when he'd touched her bottom lip. She wasn't a fawning innocent. Nope, not one bit.

She knew what she wanted. And he loved that.

What she wanted was him, which he also liked quite a bit.

"That smile you're giving me is pretty intoxicating." She rolled over to pick a nearby flower and in one easy movement was back at his side.

He nearly choked on his tongue at how lithe the movement was. Oh and the lovely jiggle of her boobs.

"I hear you let your beard get bushier over the winter. I didn't see that and I'm bummed. You'll need to do it again this year so I can get a firsthand look," she told him.

Somehow they'd gone from relationships to his beard with no real discernable transition.

"You were discussing my beard with people?"

Katie Faith kissed his neck, at the hollow behind his jaw.

"Not just your beard. You in general. Your brothers. Hotness of shifter boys with all that hair of yours. You'd never allow me to take a picture after I tucked wildflowers in your beard, right?"

"You're amusingly random just now, Katie Faith. But as it comes with kisses, I'm going along with it."

"No, would you? I mean, I saw someone who posted a photo of her boyfriend and he'd had all these wildflowers tucked in it. His beard, I mean. I remember thinking it was so sweet that he'd allowed it and then I laughed and thought it was probably just so he could keep on seeing her boobs."

"Boobs are a great motivator, in my personal experience. I'm pretty simple that way. And I suppose if it got me a sight of your boobs, I might just let you tuck flowers in my beard." If she was straddling him, shirtless as she did it. Yeah, that would be okay.

"And let me post a picture up on social media?"

He rolled her to her back, pinning her with his lower body. "Now you're being greedy."

"I totally am. Will you discipline me?"

He rolled his hips, grinding his cock into her so they both sighed softly. Longing.

"You're a dirty one, huh?" God he hoped so.

She looked up at him, coy but artfully, purposefully so. "I never really thought so, but now I guess yeah. When it comes to you, I'm filthy."

"I love that answer." He dipped down to kiss her, a brush of lips, hers so soft and warm. Inviting. Her taste, sweet lord, the way her magic seemed to burst through his system when he slid his tongue along hers. Her sigh was as delicious as her taste.

Katie Faith slid her fingers through his hair and then did it again, this time lightly scoring her nails over his scalp until he moaned. She tugged when he tried to move away, holding him close enough to nip at his bottom lip.

A shock of sensation moved through him, driving his senses. *More.*

He settled in, resting in the cradle of her hips, letting himself drown in the taste and feel of her.

Magic surged between them as her eyes flew open. She arched on a gasp. "Wow."

"Yeah."

"More," she said, tugging his hair to underline her point.

"Katie Faith." He paused to suck in a breath, which didn't help at all because all he breathed in was her and the magic they'd just made.

The pout on her mouth battered his control.

"I'm glad you know my name. Now, get back to it," she snarled.

"Christ. You're killing me," he said, torn between laughing and giving in to her demand. "To be blunt, I'm not in high school anymore. If this goes on much longer it's going to be a lot more than second base."

She nodded. "Yes." Again with the hair pulling.

"Out here. Outside. On a blanket," he added.

This time her nod was more annoyed. "I'm fully aware of my surroundings. You picked a nice soft spot. The ground under the blanket is dry and if it wasn't, I'd be on top because this hiking thing was your idea anyway so if there's a wet spot you get it."

Her delivery was so matter-of-fact there was nothing else he could do but laugh. "I just thought the first time between us should be in a bed and maybe a lot more romantic." Jace didn't want her thinking he was going to shirk on the romance, after all.

"I'm on the pill. Shifters are blessedly STD free. You're here with a *remarkable* package behind your zipper. I'm here saying use it on me, Jace. This is my ground. The magic here is good."

To underline that, she spread her arms out wide as she smiled, breathing in deep. The magic seemed to mist around her and his wolf wanted to roll around in it.

Generations of witches had lived and worked their gifts in Diablo Lake. The land had absorbed it, been fed by it and in turn gave it back to them. Jace had understood this in his head, as he'd been raised and learned about his history and that of the town.

But he hadn't understood the symmetry of it, the perfect symbiosis between witch and earth until right then as he looked at his gorgeous woman.

"I've never in all my life seen anything as beautiful as you," he told her because the truth was easily given as a gift.

Her smile deepened. "Thank you."

Possession seemed to fill him. Triumph that such a creature would be his.

"You can fuck me in a bed when we get back home later today," she said and then gave him a look that had him whipping his shirt off. "That's what I'm talking about."

Whistling sounded a ways down the path, followed by laughter.

"Are you kidding me?" he snarled, snatching the shirt back up and getting it on before anyone came upon them. "It's Damon and Major." Those shitheads were the worst cockblock ever.

Katie Faith laughed. "At least they didn't come upon us ten minutes from now."

They stumbled around that last bend, waving and calling out greetings as they did. Jace frowned hard but they ignored him, plopping down on the blanket like pups begging for scraps.

"Why are you here?" he demanded. "I'm sure you two have a job somewhere." It was a late summer day, with plenty of tourists still willing to pay for an experienced guide.

"We had a sunrise paddle with a tour and we just dropped them at the Mercury Falls. We figured you'd be around here somewhere." Damon's grin told Jace he knew exactly what he was doing.

Jace sent him a look right back that he hoped made clear just how even he was going to get with his brothers for this.

In the meantime they were eating Katie Faith's pastries and guzzling the coffee he'd brought for her. And he was not currently having sex with her, which he would have been if those two knuckleheads hadn't shown up.

Jace leaned down to snatch the bakery box away as his hard-on died a thousand deaths. "Those are Katie Faith's. You don't need to eat anything else."

"I don't mind sharing," Katie Faith said.

"If you're nice to them they'll only stay."

Katie Faith rolled her eyes and then smiled prettily at his brother, who'd been flattering her.

Just to poke at Jace.

Ugh.

"I think I know a few things about werewolves," she told him as he helped her to her feet. "It's not so bad to have them around."

Damn.

She made him tender in ways he hadn't known were possible.

"We were getting ready to head back anyway," Jace told his brothers. He had a bed and a door that locked and plans to use one on her and the other on Damon and Major.

Damon showed her a patch of wild strawberries, presenting them to her with a flourish. The same ones Jace had planned to point out to her on their way back.

He mouthed, *I'm going to fuck you up*, to his brothers as they headed back down the trail.

Chapter Seven

Over a week later, Katie Faith still hadn't consummated her relationship with Jace, which was frustrating, but also sort of fun.

He got delightfully annoyed when work had called, or one of the jillions of Dooleys popped over just to say hey and interrupt him when he was hurriedly trying to get her lying down or backed up against stuff.

And when he wasn't being interrupted, she was. Katie Faith had had to make a run, two hours away, to pick up a new fridge for her parents because their old one up and died.

Aimee had helped get all their food into the cold case at the Counter while Katie Faith had gone to get the refrigerator. All in all, it had taken up most of the day, and that night she had a girlfriends' night out so if she planned to ever end up in Jace's bed, she might have to steal him away to Knoxville or something just to have him to herself long enough to gain some carnal knowledge.

Unlike that hopeful anticipation, the dread over the looming confrontation with Darrell, rat-eating-pigdog-cheater, Pembry sank in her belly like a stone.

She'd heard he was looking for her, but since she

worked in the same place every day, she wasn't hard to find and frankly, she wasn't really looking forward to seeing his face when he finally found his balls and decided to man up and face her.

It would happen, one way or another, so she wasn't that surprised to look up to see him just a few feet away, looking like the egg-sucking dog he was. Even so, she groaned as she slowed her pace.

"I thought I smelled dog poop. I thought you'd stepped in some." Aimee first looked to Katie Faith and then over to Darrell where he stood blocking the sidewalk in front of Salt and Pepper. There was a crowd inside who'd all, *of course*, turned to watch the much anticipated confrontation.

"Turns out it's just the dog crap you nearly married." Aimee sneered up at Darrell and his handsome boy face darkened. "You so dodged a bullet, Katie Faith. Hell, he'd probably have loved it if you changed your name to Kit."

"Are you ever going to let that go?" Katie Faith asked Aimee with a snicker. "I swear you hold on to stuff for years. Like a hoarder."

Aimee flailed her hand, gesturing toward Darrell. "I kept my mouth shut about this lumbering moron and look what happened. I can't in good conscience allow you to continue believing you're suited to be called Kit. I need to crush all your pretensions in that direction or you'll try it again later. Like a goldfish."

That made Katie Faith guffaw. "You're a real friend. Please do feel free to tell me if I'm about to marry a hairball on legs, though, okay?" Katie Faith, now that she and Aimee got warmed up, really would have been just fine if they'd kept on walking and left this scene behind.

She linked arms with Aimee and continued on their way.

Naturally, Darrell needed to ruin that by blocking their path. "You're not needed here, Benton." The thin veneer of his charm slipped away as he spoke to Aimee, who curled her lip, crossing her arms and standing her ground next to Katie Faith.

Katie Faith wanted to punch him in the tin cans right then for being such a jerk all the time. Other big men didn't find it necessary to push folks around with their size. But he was barking up the wrong tree if he thought he could scare Aimee.

Laughter came from her then. *Barking up the wrong tree.* Aimee turned to her, smiling and waiting for Katie Faith to share the joke.

"I was just thinking how he was b-barking up the wrong tree if he thought he could scare you."

Aimee looked at her blankly for a moment and then got the joke, laughing along with her.

"Did he do that? Bark while you were, you know…" Aimee made the universal make-out sign, wrapping her arms around herself and making smoochy faces.

It was so terribly inappropriate Katie Faith got the church giggles and couldn't stop.

Finally, Darrell, grumpy he wasn't the center of attention, cleared his throat. "Grow up, Katie Faith."

Which was sort of like gasoline on a campfire. Her amusement melted away into anger. *She* needed to grow up? Her head snapped as she narrowed her eyes at him.

"Why are you blocking our way like a big, empty-headed sack of rocks?" Katie Faith demanded.

"I heard you'd moved back home."

She looked at him, waiting for more until she sighed. "Yes. As you and everyone in town knows, I've moved back."

He crowded her just a little more, getting in her space. Katie Faith didn't allow herself to move back. Darrell was playing some sort of dominance game and if she didn't stand up to him, he'd never let her be.

He growled a little but eased back.

"We don't need to have anything to do with each other. I live here but that's really the only thing we have in common these days. And I'm cool with that." Katie Faith added a hand at her hip because what she wanted to do was punch him.

"I'd been hoping you could finally let go of your grudge. Come on, let's not fight. We were close once." He sent his patented *guaranteed get to second base on the first date* smile her way. "There's no need to go turn your nose up at any other Pembry wolves because of old history. You don't need to go lowering yourself to Dooley level."

Katie Faith curled her lip. That was what this was about? "You get an A-plus at insulting and patronizing." *Gah*, she couldn't believe she'd actually let him get to second base once upon a time. Probably more than once. And way more than second base. But whatever.

"Yes, I'm back. No, I don't wanna be best friends and hold your hair back when you're sick. Yes, I'm sorry to see you're still a pimple on legs. Yes, I hope your wife can handle the skid marks you leave on your underpants. Lastly, have a nice day, Darrell Wayne." She fake-smiled at him and started to move around his body when he shifted, pressing her against a nearby wall.

His face was a mask of anger, his wolf very close to the skin. It scared her almost as much as it made her spitting mad. Darrell's nose nearly touched hers as he spoke. "Got anything to say now? Huh? All talk and then nothing? You used to use your mouth for something a lot better." Sneering, he used his chest to press her back harder, the bricks digging through her shirt.

Aimee ordered him to stop from where she stood to his right. He ignored her, keeping his attention on Katie Faith. Using his wolf to attempt to control her. Using his size to scare her into compliance.

That wasn't going to happen because strength didn't necessarily have to come from size.

That's what pushed past the fear. No one was going to treat her that way, least of all him.

"Get off! I'm warning you, Darrell Pembry, back your dumb ass right on up. Now!" Katie Faith kept her tone sharp, not letting any of her fear show through.

"Or what?" He sneered, his face just inches from hers. Aimee was now pulling on his belt loop to get him away from Katie Faith but he was six and a half feet of solid muscle; he wasn't moving anywhere. Not like that.

He knew it.

Before she could think about it, Katie Faith pulled her power up through the soil at her feet. Soil her people had nurtured and fed for generations now. Magic unraveled within her with sweet and seductive strength. It welcomed her back and offered itself up to her.

She hadn't even taken a breath after her last warning to get off her. Time snapped back into place as Katie Faith grabbed all that power with sure hands. With a whip of intention, she knocked him back and off the curb, stumbling a few feet and onto his ass.

The noise from the sidewalk and from inside the café all died away as people gaped at Darrell Pembry picking his sorry butt up off the pavement.

Wow, well wasn't that a surprise? Where had that come from?

Darrell's face darkened as he stalked back toward her. Fear filtered past her amusement and wonder at her burst of power.

"You bitch," he snarled, his wolf leaking through the words. His eyes were not human.

"I don't believe you were raised to speak to a woman that way." John Joseph Dooley strolled out of Salt and Pepper and right between Darrell and Katie Faith. JJ may have been in his eighties, but no one in their right mind would tangle with him and though Darrell was a fool, he wasn't *that* big a fool. He broke eye contact and took a step back.

Briefly.

"She used her magic on me," Darrell said.

"Self-defense," Aimee said. "I called the cops."

Which was evident as Katie Faith watched Jace unfold himself from the front seat of his truck and stalk over.

He was so angry it flowed from him like a furnace blast of heat.

"What happened?" he asked not JJ, but Katie Faith.

"She used her magic to assault me," Darrell called out.

"You shut the hell up, Pembry. I didn't ask you," Jace snarled.

"Way I saw it, you deserved all that and more," JJ said. "I'm sure most of the folks out here right now will tell you the same thing. You went too far, boy. Don't make it worse by lying now."

"Like I care what a Dooley has to say." Darrell sneered at the men and then looked around them toward Katie Faith. "This isn't over. You broke the law."

"I did not! You shoved me against a wall. I defended myself." Katie Faith shook herself free and moved around Jace. Not surprisingly, he reached out and touched her arm, looking toward her briefly with concern.

"We'll see what the mayor's office has to say about this." Darrell shrugged.

JJ shook his head, chuckling, but there wasn't a lot of humor there. "Are you stupid as well as foolish, Darrell? Get on out of here. Next time you try to scare a woman with your size, you best pick one that's not got enough magic to knock your butt out into the street."

"No. He doesn't leave yet." Jace turned slightly, never taking his attention from Darrell even as he spoke to Katie Faith. "Do you want to press charges? He threatened you? Did he hurt you?"

"I made my point," Katie Faith told him loud enough for Darrell to hear. "He doesn't mean anything to me now. I just want to be left alone."

"All right. If you're sure." Jace nearly growled it and that's when Aimee's father showed up.

Thank goodness because Katie Faith figured they were just a skosh away from a full-on street brawl.

"We saw the whole thing, Carl." JJ spoke calmly, firmly taking over. They'd been at the police station for less than an hour but Jace wanted them all to finish up so he could get Katie Faith home.

Jace hoped some of his anger would wear off by the time they were ready to leave the police station.

"Darrell Pembry blocked the way. He started talking to Katie Faith and Aimee. They tried to walk around him and he pushed her against that wall just next to the front door. I'd called Jace by that point because I had a feeling it was only going to get worse. But when he shoved Katie Faith, me and half the restaurant got up to rush outside to stop it. Can't abide a man using his hands on a woman. Turns out, that little lady's got a kick bigger'n most full-grown wolves." His cackle made Jace smile even though he hadn't planned to. "Knocked his ass right out into the street."

Katie Faith had been magnificent. Strong. Full of fury and power. However, she was also *his*. Agitation rushed through him again, filling him with rage anew at the thought of Darrell Pembry attempting to harm her.

JJ continued, "She used her magic, Carl. And yes, she knocked him back. Been a long time since I've seen that much raw power in a woman her age. But he was askin' for it and it was self-defense. You know as well as I do that you'll have twenty people all telling you the same thing. It ain't right to have her in a cell." JJ frowned.

Katie Faith and Aimee were currently hanging out in Carl's office, as far from a cell as could be. Hell, they'd probably ordered takeout while they waited.

Carl groaned, waving a hand at JJ's theatrics. "She's *not* in a cell. What do you take me for, JJ? I'm not charging her. I wanted to take statements and go from there. This is complicated business, as you well know. So I want to handle it right. By the book. I was convinced it was self-defense before I started talking to everyone and hearing pretty much the exact same story from a passel of people only underlines that."

In other words, the mayor was going to try to get his son out of the fire by tossing Katie Faith in his stead. Carl was going to protect her, which allowed Jace to relax just a smidge.

The cop part anyway. The wolf part would handle this business in his own way. And it *would* be handled.

One of Carl's deputies poked a head into the interview room. "Mayor's here."

Jace snorted and his grandfather squeezed his arm, hard.

"'Course he is. 'Cause this day ain't been bad enough." Carl shoved a hand through his hair but before he could leave the room, Dwayne barged in.

"Mind telling me what the sam hell is going on? I hear tell a witch used her power to harm my son," Dwayne yelled.

Carl didn't rise to the bait. Guardian witches had dealt with off-the-handle werewolves enough over the generations to know not to engage in this hysteria. "Sit down, Dwayne." He indicated a chair. "You really think that little old wisp of a girl, Katie Faith Grady, *just happened* to up and juice your son for no reason? You think all nearly seven feet of him didn't deserve it?"

Dwayne's jaw locked a moment but his spine soon lost tension. "Tell me."

Carl nodded, satisfied. "Boy shoved her against a wall. Wouldn't let her go. She knocked him on his behind. There were plenty of witnesses of all persuasions who back up her story. Even Darrell himself admits he was intimidating her. 'Course, he's saying he was merely walking by and she unloaded on him because she wants him back or some such. But we both know that's not true."

Dwayne sighed. "She got that much power in her?"

"Girl didn't even touch him with her hands, Dwayne. I felt the rush of electricity from inside Salt and Pepper." JJ looked smug and Jace, though proud of Katie Faith, worried at the expression.

"Damn."

JJ chuckled. "All that power coulda been yours. But it isn't because your boy couldn't keep his peter in his pants."

Politics. Jace groaned inwardly.

"You think, 'cause she's back in town, that she's gonna hitch her wagon to a *Dooley*? Darrell isn't the only Pembry male in town," Dwayne said. "Girl might be flighty, but she's got *some* taste."

Jace interrupted with a growl. "You'd best keep your tone respectful, mayor. Katie Faith Grady isn't some whore for your wolves to rut on." And if he couldn't, he'd find a fist in his face.

JJ eyed his grandson but Jace ignored it.

"She's in *our* territory. Ours to protect. Don't make the mistake of thinking you can just waltz in and grab her up to strengthen your house." JJ stood and Jace followed. "If we're done here, Carl, we're going to leave."

"Go on then." Carl shooed them out with a motion of his hand. Jace saw the twinkle in his grandpa's eyes and the answering set of the jaw on Dwayne's face.

This was not good.

And neither was the commotion out at the main desk.

"Is my daughter in there? You'd best get her on out here right this minute, Connie." Nadine Grady stood at the front window of the police station, arms crossed over her chest, looking every inch the guardian she was.

"Miz Grady, she's not being arrested. They just wanted to hold her until they questioned people. Let me call back and see what's going on." Connie smiled and grabbed the phone, all the while not taking her eye off Katie Faith's enraged momma.

Her momma who then said, "I'm gonna knock the pee-whining shit outta someone if they don't get my girl out here right now."

"Well howdy-do, Nadine." JJ approached Nadine with his arms open and there was nothing she could do but give him a hug.

Jace always did admire his grandfather's balls.

"Do you know what happened? TeeFay called me to say Darrell and Katie Faith got into it outside Salt and Pepper and she used her magic on him. She's on her way over, too, Connie. I don't think you want me *and* TeeFay out here on your behind," she called out around JJ's body.

Connie snickered. "She's on her way out, Miz Grady. Sheriff says to be nice and that he'll tell your daddy if you don't behave. Personally? I think Katie Faith shoulda fried his hair off too. Darrell Pembry thinks the sun rises just to hear him crow. Needs to be set back a few notches."

Nadine smiled all pretty-like at Connie, and Jace knew where Katie Faith got her mettle. Nadine had been through a lot over the past weeks and Jace sure as heck knew he wasn't gonna let the Pembrys hurt Katie Faith and her family. She was his and that meant her people were his too. That's who wolves were. Poor Katie Faith was never gonna see what hit her, but a Dooley man set his sights on her and there was no way she had a chance in the face of just how much Jace wanted her.

He smiled, both at the thought and the sight of Katie Faith and Aimee coming out front. It took everything he had not to step in and hug her. But he knew she needed to go to her momma first. It was enough when her eyes sought him out immediately.

They murmured back and forth as Jace and JJ both moved close. TeeFay came through the doors at full speed, her purse swinging as she stalked toward them. Lesser men would have run. TeeFay was a guardian through and through, much like Aimee, he supposed. But where Aimee's protective tendencies ran toward social work, TeeFay had been a cop in Diablo Lake for ten years before she had kids and now taught self-defense courses at rural schools.

TeeFay looked her daughter up and down and once she was satisfied Aimee was in one piece she looked over at Connie once more. "Where's Carl? I got something to say to him."

"He had to do his job, Momma," Aimee said. "It's fine. He had them bring in donut holes and decaf for goodness' sake," she added in an undertone.

Just then Carl came out with Dwayne and when he saw his wife he groaned. "Trula Faye, I was just doing my job."

"You put our daughter and our goddaughter in jail, Carl! You know as well as Mayor Hot Air there that Darrell deserved whatever he got."

Dwayne opened and closed his mouth a few times but in the end, he gave up and shook his head.

"Way I hear it, Carl, it's Darrell who needs to be in a cell. Or don't you get in trouble for assault if you're the mayor's son?" Nadine glared toward Dwayne for a moment and Jace almost felt sorry for the guy. "Why isn't he?"

"He's back there being questioned right now. Katie Faith says she doesn't want to press charges." Carl told his wife this, Jace was certain, to underline the politics of the situation and also to calm her down.

"Why would you do that, Katie Faith?" Nadine demanded of her daughter. "He hurt you. He should be in jail for that. Or at the very least, how about I get to hurt him right back? I know I'd feel better."

Katie Faith exhaled sharply. "It's dealt with. I'm sure he got the message and he'll leave me alone. If this goes any further I'll have to deal with him even more. Daddy is still recovering. I don't want this to stress him out any more than it probably has already." She looked miserable and worried and Jace didn't even think, he just put an arm around her and she leaned into him.

Carl's eyes went to them and one brow rose. "You sure about that, Katie Faith?"

She looked up to Jace's face and he smiled at her, torn between his need to comfort and protect her. He highly doubted Darrell would take what happened that night lightly, but she was right that Avery had had enough.

"Yes. I'm sure," Katie Faith told Carl.

"I want it on record, Carl Benton, that Darrell has threatened my daughter. Next time…" Nadine glared at Dwayne. "…next time he won't be so lucky. Rose Collins will be working with Katie Faith to hone her skill and manage her power better. You best tell the boy to keep away from her or he'll not only have Katie Faith to deal with, but every other witch in this town." She bristled and the metallic energy he always picked up from guardians pulsated from her.

"Now, Nadine, my boy messed up but you have no call to be threatening him." Dwayne put his hands up to try and calm her down.

The head whip Nadine gave Dwayne had Jace taking an involuntary step back. Dang that woman was terrifying.

Nadine's gaze narrowed as she curled her hip. "*No call?*" There was magic in the words. Power. Enough to make clear to the Patron of the Pembry wolves she was not to be trifled with and neither was her child.

Katie Faith made no move to stop her mother, which is what kept Jace at her side. As much as he hated the politics of it, Jace understood certain lessons had to be underlined. It was witches that kept the wild magic shifters used anchored and stable. Wolves and cats had teeth and claw, but witches had the kind of control to harness their magic no others did.

Darrell and Dwayne forgot that, Jace knew, because he did sometimes as well.

Nadine meant to remind them.

Dwayne made to respond but Nadine held a hand up to stay his words. "That was a rhetorical question meant to convey to you how ridiculous your statement was." Her tone was so patronizing and sharp it had Dwayne ducking his head slightly. "I'm not one of your wolves, so you be quiet because I'm still talking. *No call*, my fanny. The boy shamed her, cheated on her, dumped her at the altar and then three years later he threatened her on a public sidewalk. Assaulted her. Is that how you're raising Pembrys these days? Excellent job if you're working on raising up sacks of poop. As for my statement? I said it and I mean it. You cross my daughter again and you'll find out just what there's a call for." Nadine glared at the mayor.

"Not only the witches, but the Dooleys too. Girl lives on my land, surrounded by our wolves. She's ours." JJ's energy rose and filled the room, Dwayne's rose to match.

Jace looked to Carl, who rolled his eyes.

"Y'all need to quit it right now." Katie Faith stood tall. "I said my piece and made it clear. I don't live in *anyone's* territory." She looked at JJ, who didn't appear worried. "Nor do I need to be defended. It was a stupid thing brought on by a big giant ego. It's over and I'm leavin'." With that, she turned and stalked out and Jace strolled out after her. What a witchy badass she was.

"Need a ride somewhere?" he called out. She jiggled so nicely when she was moving fast and worked up.

"I need a ride anywhere but here. You going there?" she said over her shoulder as she kept walking.

He knew he could grin as long as her back was turned. "If you're there too, you bet I am." He held his hand out and she took it.

Chapter Eight

He led her to his truck, opening up and helping her in, though she didn't need the help. She took it anyway, liking the way he touched her. Moments later he got in on the other side and there she was, in a very small space with a man she'd been sort of crazy over for a long time. They'd been doing this hot for you dance for the last month and though the situation was serious, she let herself savor that bit of magic between them.

"I should go see my dad. Let him know I'm all right," she mumbled. "He's going to be all agitated by this mess."

He took her hand after he'd pulled away from the curb. "I can take you there right now, if you like."

She paused, looking at him. "You're being very nice to me, Jace. Thank you." She knew his impulse would be to defend and protect her. Knew, too, that he reined it in for her because that's what she'd needed at the time. It had been a *big* deal that he hadn't punched Darrell's lights out. She knew how much it must have taken to let her handle things instead of taking over.

"Are you all right?" he asked quietly.

"Yes. No. I don't know. Part of me likes that I sent Darrell's ass flying a few feet. I made my point. Another part of me feels like a jerk for making my daddy upset. My momma was taking names and kicking ass in there." She chuckled.

"Sometimes people tend to forget Nadine is a firecracker. It's good to remind them. The way she went off on Dwayne at the end? It was a struggle not to cup my balls in sympathy."

Her laugh was tired, but genuine. It was nice that he got what she needed in that way too. "I hope Dwayne can get Darrell to pay attention. He seemed pretty scared a time or two." Katie Faith allowed herself a snicker. "This is going to be all over town by morning. I hate that this drama might make Daddy upset."

Jace squeezed her hand as they turned up the long lane where her parents' house sat.

"You knew it would come up at some point. Darrell is too big an ass to leave it alone." Jace knew this wasn't the last from the Pembrys. "Dwayne already came into the Counter to warn you off. Darrell just saw that as an invitation to poke around too."

He keyed the engine off and Katie Faith spoke. "Darrell told me that just because he was taken, there were other Pembrys who'd consider me. No need to stoop to a Dooley. What a moron he is."

Jace growled and the hair on her arms stood up.

"You know where my interests lie, Jace Dooley, so stop that."

He made an effort to pull his wolf back. "You need to understand the challenge to my control right now."

She took his cheeks in her hands and kissed him. "*I do.* It means so much. Thank you for doing it for me." His begrudging smile drew downward into a frown when she opened her own door but she ignored it. "Come on inside. Every last light is on, he's up and chances are, my momma is racing back here with a story to tell."

He got out. "Next time, let me get the door for you."

She looked him over and snorted. "I can open a door."

He caught up to her on the front walk. "I know you can. But let's just pretend so I can feel manly and stuff. Unless you want me to go over to Darrell's and beat the stuffing from him. I'd prefer the latter, just in case you're curious."

He looked so hopeful she had to laugh. Without thinking, she hugged him and after a moment's hesitation, he wrapped his arms around her.

"You really okay?" he whispered against her hair.

"Are *you* okay? Hard to take, a wolf getting all up in your space that way." She wasn't going to pretend she couldn't see the way he'd stepped in and taken up a place at her side. Or that she hadn't allowed it, knowing what it meant.

"I hate domestic violence calls the most. They're pretty rare in Diablo Lake, but they're here, like with humans. We were raised up to take care of our own. To make sure they're safe and to not use our strength to hurt those weaker than we are. I wanted to kill him for touching you. I'm working on that now. I'm down to hitting him with my truck. Hopefully by morning I'll just be at using my fists."

She hugged him tighter for a moment. "I'm as okay as I can be. Physically I'm fine." She stayed there against him for another long moment before finally letting go. "I'll live."

She'd only gotten a few steps away before she caught his snarl. Katie Faith turned back to him, surprised.

"Don't talk like that, okay? It's not a joke to imagine you not living." He rolled his shoulders and it touched and amused her. He was a big ol' badass who also happened to be a freaking werewolf.

He did it for her. Was gentle when everything else called him to be vicious and hard. Made her laugh when she needed it or end up crying. He knew her in ways no one else did because he *looked*. He paid attention.

Holy moley. She needed to make something extra clear to him. Because he nearly shook with the need to harm Darrell.

She smiled and then dropped her eyes. That's when it all went sideways.

His wolf surged, bringing him to her side in just a breath. Her actions, the way she dropped her gaze meant she gave over to his dominance in the situation. He may not be a wild wolf, but he was still a wolf.

Need crawled over him, especially when she held very still, those big eyes of hers staring up into his after she'd dropped them first. Her heart beat wildly. He tasted it on the breeze, not fear but excitement, desire. She accepted him with her actions and that was a powerful thing. So powerful he nearly went to his knees with it.

All the other times they'd been intimate, kissing and touching, had been hot, but this, well this was her accepting what he was. Stepping fully into what it meant to be in a relationship with a werewolf.

He wanted to touch her, but didn't trust himself not to take her right there in her daddy's front yard.

"Katie Faith? That you, baby?" Her father's silhouette darkened the front doorway as he peered outside.

Jace forced himself to step back, but not before he tucked a curl behind her right ear.

She cleared her throat and stepped forward. "It's me. Jace brought me by."

"Come on in. Your momma's on her way back just now. Said there was a bit of a tussle. I'll let you cut me a piece of pie so I can relax just so when you fill me in." Her father held the screen door open and she went inside, Jace trailing behind, breathing her scent in deep.

The house was cheery, bright. Filled with shiny bits he knew witches seemed to love. God knew Katie Faith had enough of them in her apartment already. He'd been in the house once or twice over the years, but this felt different, more official-like.

Darrell Pembry was *such* a loser. He gave this up? Jace watched Katie Faith move, watched the light dance off the highlights in her hair, the curve of her very fine behind, and wondered what on earth got into Darrell to toss her aside for Sharon of all people.

The magic trailing in her wake slid over his skin as he followed. It felt so good he wanted to roll around in it. His wolf heartily approved of that idea so the man had to push that thought way far back. For the time being anyway.

Avery grabbed a pitcher and glasses, pouring out tea for everyone. "I just finished that tea so it's fresh."

"As if you'd serve anything else." Katie Faith paused, arching a brow at her father. She pointed the knife at the pretty peach pie on the table. "Am I going to get in trouble for cutting this?"

Avery laughed and hugged her before he sat with a happy sigh. "It's good to have you back home, baby.

Your momma is being nice to me. Too nice to get pissy about pie. I gotta take what I can get just now. Won't be recovering from a stroke forever. Aww, now, don't be stingy." He motioned at the slice Katie Faith had begun to cut for him.

"You are so bad." She shook her head at her father but gave him a huge slice of pie. "I assume you'd like a slice too?" Katie Faith asked Jace.

He nodded enthusiastically. Nadine had a way with peach pie.

She grinned at Jace, slid a slice his way. "Be back in a sec, gotta get the ice cream."

"Katie Faith Grady, there's no need for ice cream." Nadine stepped into the room and glared at her husband, then caught sight of Jace. Jace didn't miss the calculation on her features for a brief moment. "Well now, hey there, Jace." Her smile dimmed as she turned back to her husband. "*He* can have ice cream. You, on the other hand, nearly *died*. No ice cream for you."

Avery shoveled pie in his face at an alarming rate and Nadine groaned. "Avery! Slow it down. I'm not going to snatch it from you, for goodness' sake." She turned to her daughter, kissed a cheek and sent thanks when Katie Faith slid a slice of pie to her too. "Crissakes, Avery, a body'd think you were an eight-year-old boy at his birthday the way you're jamming that pie in your face. Gonna choke and I'll have to take you back to the hospital. Again."

Avery rolled his eyes but slowed down on the pie. "Now that I have the best pie ever made," he sent a waggled brow at Nadine who ignored him, "and your momma just spanked me, what happened?" Avery asked before forking up another mouthful.

"Tempest in a teapot, that's what." Katie Faith filled her father in, light on the worst of the details.

Avery laughed at the end. "I wish I could have seen that dingus's face when you sent him flying. Oh boy." He sobered quickly though. "You know this is going to be a problem. Those wolves are going to fight over you."

Katie Faith winced and Jace stretched his pinky out to slide it against the side of her hand.

"Had enough of that the first time around. I made it clear they all need to leave me be. We can all live here and not get into kerfuffles out on Diablo Lake Avenue. It's a whole bunch of hooey anyway. He doesn't even want me. I don't know what his problem is." Her anger seemed to push her hurt away. Jace could deal with anger, hurt just made him want to rip heads off.

"His problem is that you're a powerful witch who can bring any family you marry into some position in this town. Dwayne nearly beat the life out of the boy the first time he let you go. Even if he doesn't want you, he wants you anyway." Nadine harrumphed. "Pembrys always reaching above themselves. Darrell messed up big time and now you're back to remind him of that every day. To remind the town of that every day. That she's now living across the hall from this one," she indicated Jace, "means there'll be a turf war over it."

No sense denying it. "Avery, Katie Faith lives on Dooley land. You have to know how Dooley wolves are going to view that." Jace tried to be lighthearted about it, but it was going to be an issue.

It really just meant he needed to get moving and

make a claim. He was feared and respected enough that
once they figured out Katie Faith was his, no Dooley
would make a move on her. Since that night two weeks
before when she'd moved in and they'd kissed and talked
and laughed for hours, they'd both been circling 'round
the other. Teasing. He'd found her in the hall—because
he'd sought her out when he knew she was leaving—
and they'd ended up kissing one another breathless on
more than one occasion. And then the hike and those
stolen moments on the blanket under the sky.

It would happen. They were on the way. She knew it
and that was enough to keep his wolf calm. For the moment anyway. If his brothers messed with him and interrupted again right when they were just about to finally
get naked and busy, he might have to hurt someone.

And the way she'd dropped her gaze earlier? Yeah,
that was like dating a year in werewolf time. She'd done
it, knowing what it was. Which was exactly what he'd
been waiting for.

Katie Faith was his. Not the Dooleys', but his. As
long as she knew it, that was what mattered most.

As for how Pembrys would react? Jace *hoped* Darrell gave him guff so he could pop him one right in
that stupid face.

Katie Faith's voice grabbed his attention. "Good lord,
I'm a human chew toy between two gangs of dogs." She
rolled her eyes and Jace laughed because she needed
him to. Then Katie Faith sobered. "You know I was
ten kinds a fool with Darrell. It never even *occurred* to
me that he'd be after my power. I just... I thought he
loved me. But it wasn't that at all. It was about adding
me to the game as a power piece on their side. I hate

that I didn't know. I feel more stupid about that than being stood up on my wedding day." Tears threatened and every cell within his body readied to go to war to save her from hurt.

Nadine took a deep breath, looking quickly to Jace. He didn't quite know whether he was supposed to take it up then or if he should wait for her to.

"Of course you're more than that." Jace finally spoke, taking a chance. "So much more. But you know this town. You know our history. Like long legs or pretty eyes would be an attractor outside, power is here." Not that he didn't love her legs and those eyes of hers too.

Nadine nodded at him—apparently he'd passed a test—and looked back to Katie Faith.

"I don't want to talk about it anymore. I need to go home. I have work tomorrow. First day with the new espresso service." Katie Faith stood and her father did too.

"Honey, come here." Avery opened his arms and Katie Faith stepped into his embrace. "You know, it's not a bad thing that you're powerful. Not just that it makes you a great catch, you already are that, but it keeps you safer. You come from a long line. If I can make you stronger, if the combo of your momma's and my genetics makes you into a woman to be reckoned with, it's better than a woman to be pushed around."

Katie Faith really looked adorable when her face scrunched up that way.

"Fine, go on and be reasonable then. See if I care," she mumbled. But it was clear her mood had brightened a little.

"That's my job, baby. It's what good daddies do. Go on home. I'll see you tomorrow." Avery kissed her forehead.

Nadine followed up with a hug and a kiss. "Oh hey, I've got some of your books, ones you left in the attic. There's a box in the front room. Oh and your coat. It's in the hall closet. Don't forget. It's getting chilly at night now."

Jace started to respond that he'd get them but Nadine's fingers dug into his arm so he shut his mouth.

When she disappeared around the corner, Nadine turned to Jace. "This is going to be a problem. Dooley wolves have my daughter on their land and Pembry wolves aren't going to like that. I expect a call, you hear me? If any of those dumbasses show up, I want to know about it."

"Jace, I'm standing here at the front door pretending you aren't talking about me with my momma. It's time to go," Katie Faith called out.

He wanted to tell them he had it all in hand, but that was Katie Faith's story to tell her parents. Instead he went with, "Your girl is a handful. Darrell will know that." Jace kissed Nadine's cheek and shook Avery's hand.

"And that won't sit right with him," Avery said.

Jace hated it, but he knew Avery was right.

"No. But it doesn't have to. His opinion doesn't matter to me, or her. If he does anything other than have an opinion, he and I will come to an understanding. Any lesson he needs to learn, I'm happy to help with." Jace showed enough teeth to make it clear where he stood on the issue.

Nadine gave him a long look until she patted Avery's arm. "You were right."

"I'm also right that ice cream goes great with peach pie," Avery muttered.

"Before the pie wars begin anew, I'm going to get Katie Faith home. You take care." Jace double-timed it out of there before he got embroiled in that argument.

Chapter Nine

Katie Faith wanted to kick something, but instead she fumed while watching the town go by. Which took less than two minutes.

"My condo in Chattanooga was so pretty. I lived within walking distance from five different restaurants that were open past nine at night. Another few blocks there were two movie theaters. Clothing stores. A cupcake shop. God, I miss cupcakes."

Jace made a sound, torn between confusion and annoyance. She couldn't help but smile.

"You can make cupcakes. Hell, Katie Faith, you can hop on down to a bake sale in a few weeks and buy dozens of them. There's a movie theater here. Plus, if you want to see movies, I have that big screen TV."

He pulled up behind the mercantile and parked. Feeling nice for the time being, she let him come around and open her door.

"Never seen Mabel Peterson make pineapple upside down cupcakes," she said as he helped her out.

"They make those?" He carried the box of her books up to her door so naturally she invited him in.

"They do. You can't even imagine how many flavors of cupcakes there are." She paused. "Come on inside and shut the door. I'm going to have a beer so unless you want everyone in town to know it, close your mouth and the door."

She sashayed from the room, hanging her coat up in the hall closet. "Make yourself at home. I'll be right back."

In her room she pressed a hand to her belly and struggled for breath. The entire day, heck, the entire time she'd been back home everything had been catawampus. Her father's health, running the Counter, all this crazy stuff with the Pembrys.

Without a doubt, the man in her living room was a huge part of what sent her reeling. A month before he was the guy she knew and crushed on.

Then he'd been her neighbor and her friend and now…well now he was more and though she'd tried not to look at it too closely, the fact was, she was well on her way to being ass over teakettle for him.

She wanted to be near him. So much she'd deliberately taken on the choice of living on Dooley land. Knowing it would be a pain in her butt. Understanding what Jace was.

But she hadn't really understood. Not until he'd kissed her that first time in the starshine and moonlight. He made every part of her vibrate. Like a tuning fork only like sex and attraction.

There was no halfway for them.

When she'd been outside her parents' house and lowered her gaze she'd done it on purpose. Done it understanding the step she was taking.

He wasn't just some hot dude she was going to be dating. It never could be that simple between them. He seemed to unlock her magic in unique ways and if she wasn't wrong, it was the same for him. Their connection was intense on several levels. Alpha to alpha. Witch to wolf like a key in a lock.

Without a doubt, given all the politics and history between the parties involved there'd be trouble over their involvement. Beef between the wolves, between wolves and witches, between individuals jockeying for power—all of that would toss obstacles at them.

And still, she also had no doubt the trouble he brought was the good kind. So good she'd felt confident enough to take this leap with him.

Maybe. Maybe it was more like she'd been *driven* to take that leap. Scared, yes. Because her judgment was suspect. Hell, she'd planned to marry Darrell! But at the same time, she knew in her gut—and her heart—that things were totally different this time.

He was the one. The. One.

She'd gone into her bedroom to get herself together and had rocked her own damned world instead.

And that was before she went back out to find him sitting on her couch, shoes off, wearing faded jeans and a very soft T-shirt. He must have run over to his place to change. To remove the armor of his uniform and be vulnerable because he trusted her.

He looked so damned good. All tousled and sexy, wearing a grin that told her he was very satisfied with his own appeal indeed. Her heart stuttered in her chest. She licked suddenly dry lips and nearly fanned herself.

"You are a hundred kinds of delicious, Jace Dooley," she said. Out loud.

She wanted to laugh or something, but he studied her so intently she got caught up in it. Stilled. Not sure if it was because she was afraid or thrilled. Knowing it was both for lots of reasons.

Her pulse thundered and she let it. Understanding he'd hear. Giving that to him. He pushed from the couch in one fluid movement, stalking toward her. Her hormones danced, swayed with his walk. His gaze locked on hers, she caught sight of the wolf that was his other half.

She took a breath and he was there, against her, the heat of his body washing over her skin.

Katie Faith wanted everything. With Jace.

Swallowing hard, she let her head fall back, exposing the long line of her neck to him. Against her body, his hardened, he drew her to him snug. He dipped slowly until he pressed his lips to the hollow below her ear and breathed deep.

He growled and she went weak in the knees.

"I think *you're* the delicious one." He licked up her throat, nipping here and there, sending goose pimples blooming from the point of contact. Little earthquakes of sensation rolled through her body and she just held on.

His lips landed on hers, she sighed and then gasped as his tongue wandered in. It was the kind of kiss a person read about in *Cosmo*. The kind of kiss women argued the existence of. His taste was just right, as it had been the other times he'd kissed her, but this was more.

Things were different and that was all just fine with her.

They'd be different still once they took this next step.

Oh, she knew she was playing with fire. He was a very alpha male. He wore a laid-back skin. Most of the time. It was part of his strength. His magnetism.

"Are you really all right?" Jace asked her again, locking his gaze with hers. "Because, I have to tell you, I'm not entirely sure I am."

Katie Faith pressed kisses over his furrowed brow and down his temple.

"I'm going to be honest with you and it's going to push all your werewolf buttons. But I want you to hold back until I get a few sentences in where the story turns and you know there's a happy ending. Okay?"

"I can't promise not to react. That's not a fair thing to ask of me."

He was so serious. She kissed him again on the spot between his eyes.

"You need me around to lighten things up, Dooley. Just know that." Katie Faith smiled quick and circled back to the topic. "At least promise to make your very best effort to be patient enough to hear the whole of it before you react," she demanded.

"You're bossy," he muttered. "Okay. Fine. I can promise that."

Katie Faith let herself be there with him. Let herself feel safe. Made sure he understood that as well.

"He scared me. And then that pissed me off. When I got mad and reached for my magic it was just right *there*. It jumped to me eagerly and then it whipped out and sent him up, at least two feet and then about six or so feet away from me. Into the street. He could have gotten hit by a car." Katie Faith shrugged. "But I don't really care at this point. He came at me and I held my ground." Then again, the wall had been at her back so she couldn't move anyway. She preferred to think on that as a minor detail. "You though, well, you may as well have worn a sandwich board on Diablo Lake

Avenue saying you and I are…dating? Whatever you guys call it."

He let out a trembling breath that got surer by the end. "I wanted to beat him bloody." Jace's voice had gone down an octave, roughened, wild at the edges. "We guys call it, '*you're my woman, Katie Faith.*' Period."

She allowed herself a satisfied smirk. "That seems like it would suck if your name wasn't Katie Faith, though."

He snorted before leaning in to nip at her throat. "My ability to be amused is seriously impaired at the moment." Tipping her chin up with a fingertip, he caught her attention. Giving her his in return. "I'm not Darrell. I want you and once we take this step—together—things will change. This isn't some fun, casual thing we'll do until the other gets bored and we move on. This is forever."

Her pulse seemed to boom in her head. Jace said nothing, only looked at her, waiting patiently for a response.

"I guess that means you like me, like me." She aimed at a tease, but it wasn't. Not really. Because it was true and it was awesome.

"It also means I come with politics and they'll be yours too."

She nodded. "I know. But, truth be told, it'd be politics no matter what. No matter who I choose. Or who you choose for that matter, there'd be someone with something to say about it. It may as well be you and me against all that."

She dove in for more, giving, taking, falling into the rhythm they made with their chemicals. Swarming all around them, filling the air with heady magic of fur and energy. It was so sexy she had to moan, arched into him to get more because there was simply need she had to fill and he was the man who could give it to her.

Fuck. This woman fired every damned circuit in his body. He wanted to take her to the carpet and strip her bare to his touch. He wanted to lick every inch of that pretty skin. Her mouth on his was like a dream, a dream he'd had over and over for years and he realized, damn it all, that she'd been the one, the reason he'd held back with other women. Lovely women all, but none of them were Katie Faith. It was that simple and whoa Nelly was that something he'd have to parse over later.

He managed to maneuver them back to the couch and he settled her on his lap, facing him. All without breaking the kiss because she held on and apparently wasn't going to let go without a fight.

She fit against him perfectly. Her body was made to be against his.

The heat of her through her jeans drove him. Her softness, the cushion of her breasts against his chest brought him higher.

"This is your last chance before I get to ravishing. Once that happens there's no turning back."

She grabbed the hem of her sweater and tossed it over her head, leaving her bare except for her bra. He gulped like a cartoon character and began to sweat like one too.

"No turning back why? Because you're so amazing in bed no one wants to leave?" A smile played at the corner of her mouth.

What it meant that she teased him the way she did! He'd never had that sort of ease with a woman before. She knew what he was, respected that, but trusted him to tease and play. Trusted that he would never hurt her.

A gift. "'Course. But I meant once I'm in you, you're mine. I may have entered into, erm, casual-type relations with women before and all, but I suck at sharing. And I don't want to share you and there's not a casual thing about the way you make me feel."

Need crawled through him like broken glass, but he wanted her to understand the choice she was making and to make it with no doubts. She hadn't had a choice before, hadn't truly known the stakes when she'd hooked up with Darrell. But those stakes were a million times higher at that point because there would be major problems and a shift in power dynamics between the packs once Katie Faith was considered part of the Dooley pack.

Especially now that she'd proven herself to be a powerful witch with the way she tossed Pembry's ass into traffic.

She tipped her head, sobering. "I do believe you're sweet on me." Then a smile, pretty as anything he'd ever seen, swept over her lips and she leaned in just enough to give him a happy, smacking kiss.

What else could he do but laugh? "You're gonna cause me some big amount of tribulation before this ends, aren't you?" he murmured against her neck where he'd let himself taste her pulse.

"Only the best kind of trouble, Jace Dooley." The happy, sweet smile turned sultry and he felt himself react to that siren song of body language.

He stood and she wrapped her legs around him like a monkey. As she kissed his neck, he headed back toward the bedroom.

"Jace, are you in there?"

The bellow came from across the hall, the pounding fist on his door. He growled in annoyance, but kept on going. She sighed against his shoulder. "You should see who that is."

"No." He dumped her on the bed. The pounding got louder. "I have plans for you that don't include any family nonsense. They've interrupted us enough over the last week."

Then the knocking sounded on Katie Faith's door. "I know you're in there, Jace," Damon called out.

"I don't care," he called back. "Go away."

Katie Faith just lay there, looking up at him. He wanted to gobble her up. He got one knee on the mattress before Damon started in again.

"The station called because your phone is off. They need you," he yelled through the door.

Jace slumped over with a groan.

"I guarantee this is Pembry bullshit," he muttered as he forced himself to step away from the bed and the gorgeous witch in it.

"If it is, punch Darrell extra hard for me, okay?" she teased. "I'm not going anywhere. Deal with your job. Come back when you finish so we can finish."

"I'm not even on call tonight. Hopefully it'll be quick," he tried to reassure her as he headed out. If he touched her again, even just to kiss her goodbye, he'd never find the strength to leave.

"I guess this is what it's like to be in a relationship with a cop, huh?"

He growled. "Better get used to it, darlin'. I'll be back." He underlined that with a look that told her just exactly what she'd get when he returned. She smiled.

"I'll be waiting. Be careful."

Katie Faith watched his spectacular butt as he hurried out, snarling and grumpy. He walked with a slight limp, which probably was due to his hard-on. She was frustrated too, but at least she didn't have to walk around with a giant cock all the time.

With a sigh, she rolled out of bed to wander out to the living room once more. It smelled like him in there and it made her smile. Even as she recalled the events of the evening before they started—yet again—to get busy, she let this thing with Jace stay in the forefront of her attention. It was better than any crap with the Pembrys and the gossip that most likely already burned through Diablo Lake like wildfire.

It wasn't quite nine, and when she looked at her machine, she noticed some messages. One of which was from Miz Rose.

Knowing better than to avoid, Katie Faith called right back.

"Hello, sweetheart. I heard you had some trouble earlier tonight," Rose answered.

"How'd you know it was me?"

Rose laughed. "I should tell you I divined it, but I have caller ID like everyone else on the planet."

Duh.

She told Miz Rose about what happened with Darrell and at the police station.

"Scarlett has everyone worked up. Yapping all over the place that you're on Dooley land. They're spoiling for a fight," Miz Rose said.

"So everyone keeps telling me. Where else am I supposed to live, for goodness sake! The way this town is, no matter where I moved I'd be somewhere some group got angry about."

The more she thought about it, the angrier she got.

Katie Faith didn't move back to Diablo Lake so her movements could be scrutinized as some sort of power play by people she didn't even like! If she wanted to make a power play, she'd do it on her own. Well, once she knew how to and all.

"Tongues are wagging about you and Jace Dooley too."

Katie Faith was silent a bit, knowing she couldn't avoid the question. Not from Rose.

"I like him. He likes me. We're liking each other in what is an increasingly serious way."

"Pembrys are going to want you liking them instead."

Tough. "I don't much care what they want. I surely don't like many of them and none the way I like Jace."

"It's like that, is it? Well, all right then. We'll be behind you on this. Back you up when you make your own choices. I'll see you tomorrow morning. After we work, I'll even make you breakfast." With that, she hung up.

"Okay then." Katie Faith put the phone down, shuffling into her kitchen to make herself a sandwich. If she couldn't have sex—yet—she might as well have some roast beef and cheddar on sourdough.

Chapter Ten

Jace rolled up on the scene with a growl of supreme annoyance. It was not his night to work. He had a hot, willing witch back at home and this wasn't the first time he'd been interrupted before he got to anything really good.

"I'm sorry we had to call you out," Carl said as Jace moved his way. "I needed the bodies."

Jace waved away the apology. Part of the job was being called out when you'd rather be doing anything else. "What's going on?"

They stood in the parking lot of the high school. A group of werewolves, a mix of packs, stood nearby, the agitated and embarrassed energy coming off them in waves.

"Pembry peacocking. Darrell got into it with one of your cousins. Started verbally, moved to punches. Both transformed but then some Pembrys jumped in, making it three on one. Which got Dooleys mad and some of them joined the fray. When I rolled up, a lot of them ran off, but there are still several out there near the field." Carl indicated with the sweep of his hand.

Smart man not to wade in to that mess. He could have gone in and used his magic to break things up, but if it had escalated further he could have been over-whelmed. Werewolves in the middle of a fight didn't take kindly to interference by anyone.

However, Jace wasn't just anyone. He'd been born to wade into fights and yank wolves out by the scruff of the neck.

"Where the fuck is the mayor then? This is his prob-lem. He needs to deal with it." Wolves didn't jump other wolves. It wasn't their way. In fact, it was considered the worst sort of cowardice to horn in on a fight between two other wolves unless it was to break it up and save a life. You came on face to face when dealing with an equal, especially when it came to the routine scuffling that let off steam.

Bloodshed and maiming were part of their world. Attacking while one's back was turned wasn't. Honor was as important as sheer strength. Wolves without honor were eventually killed or exiled by their packs. Dwayne needed to get his wolves in line. As did Jace and his grandparents.

"Dwayne's on the way I'm told," Carl told him.

"Whatever. Let's get this cleaned up because the lon-ger we leave it, the more agitated things will get."

A few steps from Carl and Jace let the force of his wolf come just shy of full transformation. Wolf showed in his eyes, paced just below the human skin. The scent of Prime hit the night air, rich and sharp, pine and rose-mary.

He didn't walk. Not as Prime. He prowled over the last few feet to the knot of wolves.

They were creatures bred and raised on hierarchy. Strength and power were their currency, the rules that made up the world that kept them all safe. So he let his wolf out to play, knowing the slap of energy would get the attention—and submission—he needed to break things up.

Because it was what he'd been raised to do.

"You!" He growled as he grasped the neck of a Dooley wolf, a kid named Royce, and tossed him away, toward the sidewalk leading back to town. "Get yourself home before I beat you bloody. Damned fool." Royce was barely seventeen. His mother was going to kick his ass.

Jace thought of the way his grandfather had been paler than usual except when he'd been plotting. JJ would be showing up soon enough so he wanted to get this mess squared away first to save him the stress.

Darrell came striding back down the field where he'd once been a star. He'd been a far less petulant quarterback than he was an adult. "What are *you* doing here?" He tried to hold Jace's gaze but in the end, he dropped his eyes and pretended he didn't.

"Dealing with cowards who jump into a fair fight because your daddy can't be bothered to police his wolves."

Behind him, Carl sighed heavily. Jace knew this was skirting a line. He was a cop. He should not have allowed this to get personal. But it was personal and once he took over as Prime it would be even more so. He would put his wolves first, which wasn't his job as a cop.

Something to think over and maybe talk to Katie Faith about. She had a way of seeing things that he may not have thought about.

"It's not your business, Dooley." Darrell's haughty expression went a little embarrassed. Good.

"Huh. Yeah, well, Darrell, when your wolves jump

my wolves it is my business. When wolves are fighting in the middle of a high school parking lot where other kids could get hurt it's my business. Lastly, don't think, it's not your strong point. One of us is Prime and it ain't you. Now take your mongrels out of here before things get heated."

"Before?" Carl choked out.

Jace ignored Darrell and focused on Carl. "A fight's a fight. I don't care about that. You take your punches and you move the hell on." Wolves dusted up all the damned time. It was a generally accepted and time-honored way to work off steam as well as solve disputes. "What gets me so riled up is breaking the rules we all agree to. Wolves don't act like cowards. We don't fight like 'em either. Not if we want to keep our place in the pack." Jace had zero intention of letting any of this slide. It was something to be dealt with by the Pembry Prime because it was his wolves who'd pulled the bullshit to start with but the Dooleys who'd been involved would hear about that within the hour.

As Prime, he was next in line to run the pack—the presumed Patron. Over the last years he'd slowly been taking over tasks from his grandfather, especially when it came to disciplinary problems.

"The law here's one thing, Wolf Law is another," he told Carl.

A slam of a car door alerted them to the fact the mayor had arrived.

Dwayne hurried over, grabbing his son by the scruff of his human neck in much the same way Jace had with the Dooley wolf earlier.

"What the sam hell is going on here?" Dwayne demanded.

"Dooleys reaching above themselves as usual," Darrell replied.

"Darrell and Ethan got into it. Went physical. Pembrys then transformed and jumped in. Dooleys jumped in to stop that." Carl did the talking then, but Dwayne looked to Jace for confirmation.

Jace nodded. "You got yourself a problem, Dwayne. I suggest you deal with it because this will be all over town by morning."

Which meant trouble if anyone felt Pembry wolves hadn't been properly disciplined.

"You know what this is about," Dwayne told Jace. "Katie Faith being back in town has everyone all stirred up."

Jace gave the other man a long, look. He shouldn't have kept his eye, but Jace didn't care. "You'd be best to keep her name out of your mouth, Dwayne."

Dwayne's eyes lit with understanding. He glared at his son.

"This is about poor discipline, Dwayne. Plain and simple. Witches have lived in this town as long as wolves have. Shame on you for making this about that girl and not a lack of control on Darrell's part." Carl looked angry enough to punch someone. Jace remembered Katie Faith and Carl's daughter were close as sisters and Dwayne should have done the same.

"She started this!" Darrell yelped as his father whipped a hand out to knock his son from his feet.

"You hush now. This is *your* problem, Darrell. You can't step into my shoes if this is how you act." Dwayne snarled, as angry as Jace had seen him in quite a while. He turned back to Jace. "What's Katie Faith's situation to you? She claimed she didn't live on anyone's land just a few hours ago."

Carl interrupted their byplay. "No. You both listen to me right here and now. Katie Faith is not some prize to be fought over. I will not allow it. Not a witch in this town will. That girl is like my own. You made your bed, Darrell. You too, Dwayne. Back off or you'll have her momma and Miz Rose on your ass and I won't do a damned thing to stop it."

Jace shuddered at the thought. "You're right, Carl." His next words were all for Dwayne and by extension, Pembry wolves. "She's her own person. Where she lives has nothing to do with that part. The rest I think we both know." Jace tipped his chin to underline that.

"She hasn't made any public claim to the same," Dwayne told him with a shrug as if Carl hadn't spoken.

Jace just stared at him. Like that mattered. And she had made a public claim when she'd allowed him to take her to her parents' house that night. And then when she'd taken him into her bedroom. Any wolf standing as close as Dwayne was would know he still smelled of her magic. She was his.

Not to be owned. Not to be possessed. She was, as he'd told Dwayne, her own person. But he'd claim her all the same. And if he was lucky, she'd claim him right back.

"We done here? I have a woman to get back to," Jace said.

Darrell groaned and Dwayne narrowed his gaze at Jace. "You keep your wolves on a leash, Jace, and I'll do the same."

"Hope you do a better job than you're doing right now," Jace called over his shoulder as he walked away.

Naturally, as he pulled back into his spot at home, his grandfather came out to greet him.

"Stop right there." JJ stepped in between Jace and the stairs he needed to use to get back to Katie Faith. Not that he'd actually planned to go back to her just at that moment. He needed to clean up this pack business first. Still, he did his best to wrestle his agitation back. His grandfather would brook no insolence. To disobey one's Patron could—and did—get your ass kicked. JJ might be old, but he was strong enough to hold his position and that wasn't just about respect. His wolves feared him too. For good reason.

"Come on up to the house. Your grandma's got banana cream pie waiting, along with some coffee. You'll need to tell me what the hell happened tonight."

Jace nodded, following his grandfather's already retreating form up the short path to the house he and his brothers were raised in.

Damon already sat at the big, scarred kitchen table with what Jace bet was at least his third piece of pie. He frowned, quickening his pace to get a piece before his brother devoured the whole thing himself.

"Sit down. I made more than one pie. I know how Damon gets when I make banana cream." Their grandma smiled, pleased that they loved her cooking so much.

Jace managed to get a few bites in before he told his grandfather what happened at the football field. Damon would head over to a few houses once they finished up there to deliver the Patron's verdict and punishment.

"You smell like her," Damon said with a shrug.

Jace snorted. He did, and yet, Darrell, supposedly Prime material, hadn't even noticed.

Darrell had never been meant to have a woman as fine as Katie Faith. She'd always been made for Jace. He'd know her scent for the rest of his days. If he caught it on another male, he'd damned sure have noticed.

He knew he smirked and he didn't care one bit. With a happy sigh, he leaned back. "He thinks he can come at me. Darrell, not his daddy," Jace clarified.

"I reckon Dwayne knows damn well you'd take Darrell down."

"If Darrell—or any other Pembry for that matter—gets between me and Katie Faith I will kick their sorry asses." He ducked his grandmother's narrowed gaze at the curse.

JJ Dooley chuckled, pleased and smug. Jace knew he should be annoyed, but his grandpa was at his best when he was tickled at getting one over on someone so he let it be.

"You best get to work. You're not the only wolf in town sweet that girl," his grandmother said.

"Maybe not, but I'm the only one who has a chance."

She snorted at him, chuckling as she swatted his arm with a tea towel. "Never did have trouble with your self-esteem."

"It's time. You're going to be taking over as Patron soon enough. Once you've claimed her, then we'll need to get moving on that too," JJ said.

"We're done on this topic for now." Though Jace said this, he knew it was futile. His grandfather saw Katie Faith as a way to strengthen the Pack. He appreciated her as a person, sure, but he was the Patron and he put Pack ahead of people when he thought it was necessary.

His grandmother would see it as Jace finally settling down and getting ready to take over. She'd see Katie

Faith as a ticket to grandbabies and would be just as big a steamroller as JJ, but in her own way.

Damon just smirked, Jace knew, happy that the focus was on Jace instead of the other Dooley brothers.

"The pie was great, Grandma. I'm going to head back upstairs now." Jace stood, rinsing off his plate and fork.

"Take a slice up to Katie Faith. I know she likes banana cream." His grandmother shoved far more than a slice into his hands.

"You're pretty sneaky. She does love sweets." He grinned at his grandma.

"It's not just men who love pie, sweetie," she told him, accepting his peck on the cheek.

Jace rushed out before they started to give him sex tips or something equally disturbing.

"Hi," Katie Faith said, opening her door wearing nothing more than a tank top and tiny panties.

He gulped, sucking in her scent as he kicked the door closed, locking it. "Well now."

"Everything okay in town?" Her mouth resisted a grin, but only barely. She knew what her state of undress was doing to him.

He thrust the pie in her direction. "I have pie."

Surprised pleasure skittered over her features. "Penis and pie? How lucky am I?"

She was so ridiculous he had to give in and laugh. No way was Katie Faith not exactly where she wanted to be. She'd made the choice to accept him and underlined it by coming to the door with all that pretty skin exposed.

"I had a sandwich though. So I can wait for one until after I get some of the other."

His laugh died on a gasp when she whipped her tank

up and off with one hand, while depositing the pie on the table with the other.

Naked but for a tiny scrap of fabric over her butt— barely—she sauntered into her bedroom, knowing he was going to follow.

He double-checked the lock, tossed his phone down and moved in her wake. Taking his time, drawing her into his lungs as her magic seemed to tickle his skin.

Katie Faith turned as he came into her room. He stole her breath with the way he looked at her. Dark eyes so serious as they took a long slow perusal from the tips of her toes to the top of her head.

He did meander a lot around the boob area, which was flattering, if she did say so herself.

"Everything okay?"

"Huh?"

She smiled. "The call you went on? You know? Your job?"

He toed his boots off and she watched carefully as he nudged his shirt up and then over his head.

"Good lord above," she wheezed out at the sight of all that tawny skin stretched taut over muscle. Katie Faith pressed a hand to her chest to keep her heart from bursting free. "You're!" She just pointed. Slightly accusatory. Mainly appreciatively.

He grinned. At first it was flirty but then. Well he did something, his gaze went all hooded and suddenly he was telling her with his mind or something just what he was going to do to her.

Her cells all swooned and dropped their panties.

"I'm?" he asked, but he couldn't have pretended to be innocent with that damned expression. He knew he was blowing her gaskets with his hotness.

Which made him even more alluring.

"You know what you are." She folded her arms across her chest, but under her boobs just right to keep the girls looking their best. "So? The thing that called you away from me earlier? Everything okay?"

"Oh. That." He bristled a little. Like the aura of magic and power around him grew brighter and then sharper for long moments.

Mesmerizing.

"It was stupid werewolf bullshit. Pembry wolves jumped a Dooley. Rules were broken. I don't want to talk about that right now because, damn, you're pretty without clothes," he told her as he unzipped his pants and shucked them and his shorts.

Katie Faith sighed happily. Truth in advertising, apparently. Jace's cock was every bit as impressive as she thought it might be.

She gave two thumbs up. "Excellent. You look pretty spectacular naked too."

"Now that we've gotten the compliments out of the way, let's get started with the good stuff."

"I don't know how I'm supposed to do anything but fall over faint when you talk like that while you're naked. Or clothed. I mean, the intent is big here."

Katie Faith screamed at herself to stop talking. She was off on a babble, which was erasing her cool points for opening the door in barely any clothes.

"You can use your mouth in better ways than talking." He crooked a finger at her, beckoning her close.

She got close enough for him to haul her all the way to his body, skin to skin as he managed to pick her up, turn and land them both on the bed.

"I can see having sex with you means I need to work

out. Damn it. I was hoping to coast on my good looks a while."

He rolled so she ended up astride him.

"I'll do the heavy lifting," he assured her.

"I'll let you know when I get tired," Katie Faith mumbled as she bent to kiss across his collarbone.

He smelled so good she paused here and there as she licked and nibbled to sniff him.

Every time she did he made a sound that sent a full body shiver of pleasure through her.

His muscles seemed to radiate power. She knew what it must have cost him to be still and let her roam all over his body, kissing, licking, sniffing, nuzzling and all that good stuff.

She learned what he liked, how he liked to be touched.

But then he whipped her to her back, looming over her as he settled between her thighs.

Before she could say a thing, his mouth was on hers, taking, taking and taking until she was breathless and trembly.

The kisses they'd shared had been pretty hot, but the ones he laid on her right then were so much more. He sipped at her, treasured, tasted, devastated and claimed her mouth with a skillful ninja-like dance of sex moves. Tongue, teeth and lips all working like a goddamn robot of pleasure.

Beep. Beep. Boop.

Okay, that made her nearly laugh, even as she was so turned on her muscles just sort of quaked and jumped.

He used that clever tongue on her right nipple. Some sort of sex trick that made her hips jut forward of their own accord.

"What was that?" she gasped.

"What do you mean?" he asked but he knew what he was doing to her. The clever, clever cad that he was. His stubble scratched against her belly as he kissed each rib.

She dug her nails into his shoulders where she'd been hanging on as he pillaged her, or whatever it was, something fantastic and totally devastating all at once and he hadn't even made her come yet.

But it was close. Building up like a storm on the horizon.

He hummed his delight as he spread her thighs with the width of his shoulders and then took a lick along the seam where her leg met her body. Then on the other side. His hands—really big hands—petted from her breasts down her sides to her hips. Over and over again until she was hypnotized by it. Soothed as he incited her in a dozen other ways.

He slid her open with his thumbs at long last and sighed so happily, so much like a dog after you gave it some of your scrambled egg it nearly made her laugh.

But she looked at him there, head bent over her pussy, those wide, sun-kissed shoulders, his hair, still streaked with summer gold here and there, one rebellious curl falling down over his forehead.

He looked at her as if she was the most beautiful and sexy creature he'd ever seen. And that stole her breath. Made her heart skip a beat.

He dipped his head and kissed her. Long and slow as he served himself her body. She dug her heels into the mattress with a groan of pleasure.

He was *so* good at that. She might have told him, but by the time it left her lips it sounded more like a bunch of pained breaths.

Jace did something to her clit with the tip of his tongue and the edge of his teeth that felt so good it nearly hurt. She writhed against him, wanting more. He gave it to her when he circled a fingertip around her as he slowly eased inside. Stretching her a little as he sucked her clit in between slightly puckered lips.

It was suddenly way too much and she overflowed with sensation as she came so hard her teeth tingled.

He held on, continuing to kiss and lick until she was boneless.

"Now I think you might be ready," he murmured against her belly.

Still reeling from the taste of her, the magic dusting his skin, the memory of what it felt to make Katie Faith come like that, Jace managed to heave his body up the bed to settle beside her.

"Ready for what?" she asked, cracking her eyes open to take him in.

"We've been interrupted right as I was about to get inside you on more than one occasion now. I've got lots of energy stored up. I wanted to be sure you were ready."

She snorted and gave him the okay sign. "When I can make my legs move again, I'll bc all over that."

Jace never thought he'd be a laughing while having sex kind of guy. But he loved her irreverence. She lightened his heart.

He wanted to take her in so many ways it was hard to settle on just how he wanted her right then. As he considered, he trailed a fingertip over the hollow of her throat and then down to one nipple, drawn tight against his touch, and then the other.

She was warm and soft, totally open to him as he

touched her, sliding his fingers over all the skin he could reach.

"Eventually, you're going to pet me to sleep," she told him, a smile on her lips.

"I'm boggled by all the options. Too interested in each and every way I plan to fuck you over the next sixty years or so to pick just one."

Her brows flew up. "Sixty years huh?"

"Well, that's an understatement, but I didn't want to scare you. I plan to have recovering from a very fine orgasm with you in my arms as my very last memory at a very ripe old age in the triple digits."

"Everyone thinks you're so serious. If they only knew." Katie Faith stretched out to kiss his chin. "Because we have at least six decades of sexytimes ahead of us, I'm going to get started."

With that, she clambered over him, straddled his waist and as he struggled to get breath, she'd grabbed his cock at the root and then he was right there, pressing up into her snug heat as she brought herself down on him.

"I think that was a really good choice," she told him around a kiss she'd bent to deliver.

"I agree." Though to be fair, he couldn't really see any situation where his dick was in, on, around this woman that he wouldn't like.

She hadn't bothered to turn off the bedroom light, a fact he was glad of as he lay back and watched his siren of a witch ride him.

Tenderness he hadn't been aware he'd been capable of rushed through him. His wolf approved of the look and feel of her. The strength in her inner thighs, the way her hair tumbled around her face.

His woman looked well pleasured. Lips swollen from kisses, skin still flushed from orgasm. Her eyes were heavy lidded. So pretty. All his.

He wanted to roll around with her in this bed until it smelled of them. She brought all his alpha tendencies to the fore. He wanted to claim and rut. Wanted everyone in a fifty-mile radius to know she was his.

For those hours it was just the two of them. The following day the gossip would be in full swing. Everyone would know what happened, right up to the point that Jace drove her to her family and then home. Across the hall from his place.

Katie Faith kissed him again, nipping his bottom lip. "Stay here with me. All the politics will still be there in a few hours."

Of course she knew he'd been thinking about wolf crap. He grinned. "Don't you worry, darlin', I'm not going anywhere."

To underline that, he cupped her breasts and thought of yet another reason why this position was a favorite.

She quaked and tightened all around his cock and they both moaned softly. She added a grind and a swivel each time she took him all the way inside. Pleasure tore through him, digging in.

There was only so long he could deny himself. He wanted to last hours and hours, but the depth of what she made him feel drowned him. So delicious and sticky sweet he had to gorge and gorge instead.

He stretched his fingertips out to brush over her clit each time she ground herself into him. Each stroke she was hotter inside, wetter. Her skin sheened with sweat, the scent of her desire laced with her magic rose between them.

She let her head fall back as she began to climax around his cock, as her inner walls grabbed him so tight he had no other choice than to follow, coming in what felt like wave after wave for ten minutes.

He still saw stars as they managed to untangle and settle on the bed as they caught their breath.

"Wow," Katie Faith croaked.

He managed a nod of his head. Wow, indeed. He got to his feet, pulling her up after himself. "Pie, beer and round two."

"You're really handy."

Chapter Eleven

Katie Faith surely hated the alarm when it went off at six thirty. She purposely had the base on the dresser so she'd have to physically get up to turn it off. She'd fallen back to sleep enough times to be late for things and get in trouble. The lesson was she had to make herself start moving to overcome her deep and abiding love of sleep.

Jace's eyes came open and she snarled when she noted they were clear and ready for the day. "No way are you a chipper morning person."

He grinned, stretching as he rolled from bed.

"Oh god. You are. You're one of those people. You love to watch the sunrise, I bet. Not because you haven't made it to bed yet, but because you're up and jogging just to watch it."

He laughed, looking ridiculously gorgeous as he sauntered toward her bathroom. She knew she had bed hair and morning breath and he looked like a cologne ad designed by horny ad execs.

She'd have bought five bottles of it immediately.

Instead, she had her own exclusive supply right there.

Though. She cringed when he started peeing. "Close the door!"

Laughing, he did as he finished. Gross.

"I draw the line at using the toilet with the door open. Just so you know," she told him when he came back out.

"My face was between your thighs right before my cock was inside you and you draw the line at hearing me pee?"

She tried not to look too devastated that he put a shirt on. It helped that he referenced something so happily true.

"Yes," she said, closing the door. "As you can see," she called out, "I will also close the door when I pee. It's just a service I provide. I also expect you to put the seat down."

She brushed her teeth quickly, groaning when she remembered she had a lesson at Miz Rose's. Getting the shower water started, she grabbed a towel and jumped in.

"I guess I had you figured for a morning person," he said, sliding into her tiny shower along with her.

"Stop that!" She rerouted a questing hand at her nipple. "No time for morning sex. Miz Rose doesn't tolerate tardiness or any other foolishness when it comes to her lessons."

He pouted and she told him to stop that too. And then he gave her a saucy little smirk when she wagged her finger at him and realized he'd do whatever he wanted because he was a werewolf.

And a really dominant man. One who was confident enough in his own power to give her space to fight her own battles—though he might have frowned a lot while he did.

Which, as it had turned out, rang her bell. Like school was out.

"I can smell when you're turned on," he said, sliding his body against hers.

"I can only take so much sexy from you. You're going to fry my circuits and then what good will I be?" Laughing, she held her hand out as she finished rinsing off and left him to finish on his own. "Anyway, you were getting dressed a few minutes ago. Or was that a fake out?"

"I was going to head back to my place to shower but then when you turned the water on I knew you were in here naked and slick and why would I not come in here? Where else on God's earth would I be but right here to look at you all slippery and grumpy."

"I'm not a morning person. I hate mornings. But that's when I have to get up to work. And since this whole stupid crap between me and Darrell happened, I'm sure every single person within a hundred miles of here knows by now. I'll do some brisk business at the Counter. It's already warm so I'll be selling a lot of vanilla Cokes and milkshakes."

He got out, crowding her as she finished slathering on lotion. Of course, he followed her as she got dressed, leaning in to kiss her. Or take a sniff.

Once she'd pulled her hair back into a braid, she tip-toed up to sniff Jace right back, happy enough to hug him as well.

His arms encircled her and he hauled her close with two hands on her ass. "When you smell me it makes me want to strip you right where you stand and fuck you."

A thrill ran through her.

"Oh?" She'd aimed at nonchalance but it totally came across as oh-my-god-take-me-now. Probably.

"Sugar, you can't look at me like that. You have to

go to Miz Rose's. She'll be mad at me too, if you're late. She scares me," Jace told her as he flicked open the top two buttons of her blouse before leaning in to rub his face all over her cleavage.

Straightening, he rebuttoned her and stood back.

They both sighed wistfully.

"I'll be in on my lunch hour. You'll eat with me," he said. "Lock your door." He pointed as they left.

"Why? Who the hell is going to chance coming up here to steal from me? Darrell might be aiming for a confrontation of some sort, but he's not suicidal."

Jace kept staring at her until she rolled her eyes and did it, tossing her keys in her pocket.

"Things are going to be crazy for a while. You have an appointment to get to. But at some point, we need to discuss what last night—" he gave her mouth a long look "—means. To you and me and to wolves and witches and all that stuff. For now, expect foolishness from all and sundry with a cock in this town. You know that."

She sighed. "I do know that. I'm still smarting a little, I guess."

He brushed his thumb over her bottom lip. "That Darrell was a fool?"

Katie Faith laughed so hard she nearly choked on her spit. "Oh no. Yes, it was embarrassing and hurtful at the time. It's pretty humiliating to be that woman who got stood up at the altar. But that's past and I can tell you honestly I don't have any feelings for him and haven't for years. Well, disgust. Which is only natural."

Jace took her hand, kissing her wrist.

He thrilled her to her toes.

"To deny that your power is part of what I love and desire about you would be a lie. It would fail to accept a basic fact. We're not humans. We're not all that different, of course. But a few of them are pretty big. Your power makes my dick hard. Like the way your tits jiggle when you slam your trunk closed."

"Yeah?"

He nodded slowly as she blushed. "Absolutely. Your dorky sense of humor too, for whatever reason." He tried to look severe, but she saw right through him.

"So it's okay to admit it makes me wet that you're Prime? That you're so strong and fierce, so feared and respected you only have to unfurl your power occasionally? And when you do it makes it hard for a girl to get a breath?"

He cursed under his breath.

But he'd made his point. Because he got that she was bothered about being thought of only for what her power would bring to a family.

And he helped her see it as something beautiful that he cherished.

"Thank you," she told him before kissing him goodbye and dashing to her car. "See you at two."

Thankfully, she was ten minutes early. Which meant she was exactly on time for a cup of coffee and something sweet they always shared before a magic lesson.

She'd stopped by her parents' yard to clip some roses and dahlias so she headed straight into Miz Rose's kitchen to grab a vase and put them in water.

"Your daddy is so good with anything and everything green." Miz Rose breathed in the flowers Katie Faith had placed on a table in the bright kitchen, before sitting down.

"I hope cinnamon rolls are all right. I was in a hurry so I just had to toss them together this morning."

Katie Faith knew the rolls had been kneaded, left to rise and then kneaded again. Knew, too, that the cinnamon sugar dusted over the top was the very same kind her dad kept in their kitchen in a saltshaker to pour over buttered toast.

"You should get right to telling me exactly what happened last night," Miz Rose ordered her.

Katie Faith gave her a recounting of what had happened out on the street. "And then Jace got called away to some Pembry/Dooley foolishness sometime after that."

"You don't like being the center of this mess."

"Heck no! I didn't come back here for that. I left here because of it."

Miz Rose shook her head. "Foolishness then and now. You can't pretend away your power."

"That's not what I did! When I left here I didn't think I had much. Now all the sudden it's the topic on everyone's tongue. I wish I was just a regular person."

"Hush yourself." Miz Rose paused to put another cinnamon roll on Katie Faith's plate because she was the most awesome and majestic creature on the planet.

Katie Faith took a big bite. She didn't want to be rude after all and the nap she'd have to take later that day would be worth it for how good these cinnamon rolls were.

"You're not a regular person. You don't live in a regular place. You aren't a regular anything and the male I assume you've hooked up with nice and permanent isn't regular either. Stop pretending like you have any other choice but to be who you are. I don't abide a whiner and that's what you're dangerously close to doing." Miz Rose narrowed her gaze at her a moment.

Katie Faith drank some more coffee to help the cinnamon roll down, naturally, as she waited, knowing Miz Rose had more to say.

"This power you seem to think just popped out of your back pocket the day before yesterday has always been yours. Each of us, as we grow up here, comes to our full potential in her own way. Your daddy, for instance, was in his late thirties before he really found his place. Your mother, she had it early on. Maybe ten or eleven? She just always seemed so confident in her magic."

Katie Faith nodded. Never had she seen a witch more comfortable with her connection to the earth and her magic than her own mother.

"You were always a smart girl. Quick to learn your basics like control and such. But you never wanted to push much past that. When you left here, you tried on being someone else for a time. But that wasn't you. It never was you."

"It sucked being me for a while."

Miz Rose chuckled. "I imagine it did. But you were counting off time when you grew up. One thing to the next, but you didn't really live them. Not all the way. And when that faithless turdbrain Darrell threw a wrench into your very well thought-out life itinerary, it was the best thing to ever happen to you. You ran off, sure you did. And you pretended to be a young woman living in the city for a while. But your magic was always there, waiting. When you came back here, you had to confront all that stuff and you realized you'd left it all back in the past where it belonged. That's why your magic has been so strong since you've come home.

You're in love. For real this time. But you're confident now. In your appeal as a woman. It's hard for you to accept that you were important to the Pembrys for the power you'd bring them."

"I've been thinking about that. A lot. I didn't know how to feel. Not entirely. But Jace said something to me, put it into perspective in a way I hadn't really considered. I was just tripping myself up."

"Took you long enough to get there," Miz Rose muttered.

"I hate that I was blind to it. Not that they did it. Not that Darrell didn't want me after all. Truly I can sit here and tell you I am so very glad to have dodged that bullet. I hoped that he'd be happy with Sharon and grow up."

"Well, he's always been spoilt. You know that. He won't grow up. First he's going to have a tantrum. I expect his momma will be the one to finally teach him the lesson he should have learned a long time ago. He does love Sharon. Their kids are dumb as rocks, but cute. He wants his daddy to say good boy and pat his head. You being back is a reminder of his failure. It's going to get worse before it gets better. Which is why you need to work on pulling up more power quicker and then how to control it when you use it right after. I want you working on storing some power. A reserve. You can use a necklace, bracelet, what have you. I use the opals in my wedding ring."

As a witch, Katie Faith had a well of power and energy, but if she used a lot at once, or got very tired, she'd have a harder time with spells or defending herself if she had to. Keeping reserve power in an object a witch carried on her person, or kept close, was a way to have a spare battery of sorts. For emergencies.

She frowned. "You think I'm going to need to defend myself? I don't want to start a war. I just want to live my life in my hometown and be left alone."

"I think you're going to be one of the most powerful witches this town has seen and it is always better to be safe than sorry." Miz Rose shrugged. "You blasted a full-grown werewolf out into the street yesterday. They're going to go crazy over you now. So you be as strong and as capable as you can be. That's the way to be left to your own choices. It's also a hell of a good reason to be grateful you're far more than regular. You have choices, Katie Faith. Choices are power. You have the magic to make a lot more of them than most women. Being strong means I make my own damned life even now that I'm old and my kids want to help more."

Katie Faith laughed. "I'm sorry. I shouldn't laugh."

Miz Rose waved a hand. "You know what I mean. My sons and daughter are all good children. They want to help and do things for me. My grandchildren are the same. All you kids who grew up around my worktable show up and ask if you can drive me places. People bring me food so often I rarely have to cook anymore. My freezer is full. No one can stop me if I want to go to Nashville to see my boys."

Her "boys" meant country singers Brantley Gilbert and Luke Bryan, both of whom were on constant rotation in Miz Rose's musical choices. When they came near while on tour, she made a production of it. Shopping, eating at all the restaurants she researched and seeing a few concerts.

A long time ago, Kenny Rogers was one of her boys. But he'd done something to push her buttons, offended her somehow. One day all her Kenny Rogers record albums, 8-track and cassette tapes so lovingly cared for and enjoyed for decades disappeared.

No one spoke of it. Which Katie Faith had always thought was pretty cool.

"I hope to be as strong as you, so when I'm your age, everyone is afraid of me like they are you," Katie Faith told her. "What is it you have up your sleeve?"

Miz Rose's eyes twinkled a little, clearly pleased and complimented. Which, thank goodness, because she had just blurted it and blurting sometimes got her in trouble.

"I aim to train you so you're stronger than I ever was." She paused for a moment. "Over the last two generations witches in this town have given up too much of their power. We used to have a greater say in how things worked around here. It's our magic that keeps the shifters safe. You're what we need to underline that."

"I don't want to be anyone's pawn." That she was certain of.

Miz Rose just rolled her eyes at Katie Faith. "Didn't I just tell you I wanted to help you be as strong as possible so you could make your own choices? Young people today. Lordy. This silliness between Dooley and Pembry wolves has been in the making for years now. Since before I was born. We aren't here to make one pack stronger than the other. We're here to make Diablo Lake a safe place. A haven. They've all used us like chess pieces. Not just shifters, but our daddies too. Foolishness."

"I guess we better get to work making me super witch." Katie Faith grinned.

Ninety minutes later she unlocked the front door at the Counter for Miz Rose. "I'll get some coffee brewing,"

Katie Faith said as she headed inside, turning on the lights and the sign in the front window.

"Merrilee Tanner is stopping by soon so keep an ear out at the back door," Katie Faith told her while she set up the front bakery case. "I finally talked my dad into letting me try some baked goods."

"Merrilee really can use the money right now, what with her Mandy off to college this year." Miz Rose patted Katie Faith's arm.

You came from a small town, you pulled together. It was just how she'd been raised. Diablo Lake was an extended family. Even the Pembrys were part of that.

"I don't want to get here at three in the morning to bake everything myself but I wanted food. I picked up one of Merrilee's better than sin cakes and thought maybe she'd be willing to do some baking for me. I figure we can start with a few things and see how it goes."

"When I was younger, Merrilee's uncle Pete had a restaurant in his carport. People could walk right up, get served off plates they returned a few days later."

Katie Faith started laughing. "Well. That sounds… uh, colorful. What kind of food?"

"I used to think it was roadkill, but he never would say. Said it was all a secret family recipe. Yeah, for raccoon."

Ew.

"Huh. What happened?"

"There was a big fight between Pete and some of his friends. Spilled out into the street. Carport caught fire and his wife made him close up after that. She left him about six months later. He was a decent cook, but a lousy husband."

Katie Faith clucked her tongue. "This town has some stories, I tell you. Oh, hey, Merilee just pulled up."

There was a special kind of magic around Merrilee Tanner. Nearly six feet tall. Sturdy. She spent a lot of her life outside and it showed. There was a solid strength to her that Katie Faith loved.

She had long hair she kept in a braided coil that ended at her butt. Except for when she worked magic. Then it was free like a wild river of gold. She baked like an artist and played the mandolin and could chop wood and change her own oil. Her husband had died a decade earlier and she'd raised up four daughters, two of whom were now off in college.

She was one of Katie Faith's heroes.

Immediately the scent of warm blackberries filled the space as Merrilee came inside with several big bakery boxes in her arms.

"Morning! I'm not going to fib, I'm in a fine mood today. Probably because school is back in at long last and my house is quiet for the first time since May."

They all laughed as they unloaded the muffins, loaves and bar cookies. "Went berry picking so I figured I might as well make something for you with them. I'll come by later to see how things are going. I have a few ideas for tomorrow."

"Great! I'd love to hear them. Thanks again, Merrilee," Katie Faith called out as Merilee headed out.

She brought out a few things from the kitchen. "I found these cake plates in the shed behind the house. Daddy said these were around when he was a kid. I thought they were pretty. A good thing to have here in the shop, don't you think?"

Miz Rose's face lit at the pretty stands. Some were

porcelain while others colored glass of some sort. Katie Faith had used a lead testing kit on those before using them with any food. She arranged them all artfully with all the baked goods and the little cards with prices on them.

"What's that? Can I buy one of those to eat?" A handsome man stood at the counter. A cousin of Darrell's if Katie Faith remembered correctly. Four or five years older than they were. Three other men his age stood with him, all Pembry wolves.

"This here muffin is called blackberry cobbler. I've got some peaches and cream loaf, a dollar a slice. Chocolate chip cookie bar or butterscotch chip." Katie Faith rattled off some prices she'd been toying with and given the way he said he'd take one of each along with a cup of coffee she had made a good guess.

"I can't believe that boy just spent all that money on some stuff that he could make at home for under a dollar," Miz Rose whispered after he'd left.

"Convenience and a sweet tooth. Wolves love cake and pie and all that stuff. I need to work chocolate into more things. Which I think is a good, basic life goal. Chocolate in all the things."

As she'd figured, the news about what had happened the night before had spread and led to a steady flow of customers into the Counter. Sure, they came to gawk, but she'd make them pay for the privilege.

"Hey, Katie Faith. Miz Rose." Carl came in with TeeFay. "We just wanted to check in on you. See how you were."

Everyone else in the place eavesdropped unashamedly.

"It's a nice day. Sun's out. Got some new baked goods in to go along with your soda, shake or coffee."

Katie Faith appreciated them coming in. Knew part

of it was to stand behind her and let the wolves know they'd best leave her be. Part of it was because they were like her own parents, she and Aimee had spent so much time in one another's homes.

Still, she wasn't going to get into what happened the night before in front of half the town.

"We just had breakfast with your mom and daddy," TeeFay said. "He said he'll be coming in later so he expects a malted to be waiting for him."

That made her laugh. "As if he could sneak one past Momma."

"It keeps his mind busy, trying to figure out how to cheat on his diet when your mom isn't looking." TeeFay winked.

"Which is never. I can tell you that for sure. My mother doesn't not look. She always looks." Katie Faith knew it firsthand.

They chatted some more before each one headed off to their jobs.

A gaggle of good-looking Pembry wolves came in, all straight white teeth and really great hair.

They greeted her good-naturedly. She didn't blame them for what happened with Darrell, though that jack-wagon would be banned from the Counter for life.

"You remember me, Katie Faith?" one of them asked.

"Uh, you're Danny, right? Your momma and Darrell's are cousins."

He grinned. "Yeah, that's me. So, you want to go out to dinner or something?"

"I'm pretty sure I babysat you, Danny. Are you even a legal adult?"

Miz Rose chuckled in the background but Danny blushed. "I'm twenty-one. Legal and then some."

"Ah. Okay. Well. Thanks for the invite, but I'm going to have to say no thank you."

"Why not? Are you with someone? I have older cousins," he blurted.

Katie Faith gave him a raised brow with enough severity behind it he bent his head and broke eye contact.

"That'll be three dollars even for the soda and the slice of peaches and cream." The day she let some kid she wiped snot off make her feel like she had to give him an accounting of her life was the day she gave up entirely.

"Thank you. Nice to see you. You should come by the theater. We're always happy to find you a pair of tickets. My dad says."

"I'm sure I'll see him to give him my thanks. There'll be plenty of movies to see once the weather turns."

Not that she'd be taking free movie tickets, though she'd get a kick out of sharing this story with Jace.

She shifted her attention to the next wave of customers coming in.

And one of them was JJ.

"Afternoon, JJ. How are you today?" Katie Faith called out.

"Just thought I'd come by to see how you were feeling. And maybe also get a cherry Coke."

Sure, that was all he was up to. Not that he couldn't have just asked Jace.

"I'm always good when business is good." Katie Faith turned to make his soda, placing it in front of him with a smile before she headed over to deal with other customers.

"I told Damon to mention this, but I bet he hasn't yet. We'd like to give you the friends and family discount on your rent," JJ said all casual-like as she came back down to his end of the long counter.

Ha! As if.

"I appreciate the gesture, I surely do. But I can't do that," she said quietly and respectfully. He was trying to get her allegiance, she understood the why of it. But that wasn't how she was going to play this whole situation.

"You're the gal our grandson wants. You're back here in town taking care of your family like you should be. Least we can do," JJ insisted.

"The pie Jace brought me yesterday was payment enough. Patty sure does know how to bake a mean banana cream."

He sized her up. She knew people didn't take her that seriously, that guys like JJ thought she was dumb but pretty and easily manipulated because she was female.

He'd learn eventually. That was her resolution for living back in Diablo Lake. Stand up for herself and not take any guff. Even from her boyfriend's grandpa.

Her dad came in, her mother at his side, which got people focused on something else and made her dad's face flush with pleasure. People cared about him and it was nice for him to see it in their faces.

"Where's my malted?" he asked as he came around the counter.

"In your imagination, Avery," her mother said calmly as she escorted him back to the other side of the counter at a barstool.

Her mom gave her a kiss on the cheek as she passed. "You go on home now, Miz Rose. Your ride is here."

"I'll see you day after tomorrow for your next lesson," Miz Rose called out as she left.

"Glad you're here, Mom. We've been crazy busy today."

"I bet every rubbernecker in town was over here today." Her mother narrowed her gaze at JJ a moment.

JJ toddled off after leaving her a ridiculous tip and repeating his offer of a rent discount. Her mom rolled her eyes when Katie Faith explained what all had happened.

"We got two dozen calls at least today. Scarlett is suddenly very interested in having me down at the Presbyterian Church lady lunch things."

"You think she wants to cook you for dinner?" Katie Faith teased her mother.

"If anyone could, it'd be her."

"I figured I'd find about six dozen people in here," Jace said as he came in holding a large bag.

Everything inside lit up at the sight of her handsome man.

"We just had a lull. Everyone will be so bummed they missed the moment you came in here. I'm sure if you wait five minutes half the town will be back."

He kissed Nadine's cheek and shook Avery's hand before turning his attention back to Katie Faith. "Ha. Not interested in anything but our late lunch. I brought sandwiches, chips and some soda."

"You two go on out and enjoy the park bench for lunch. Avery and I know how to run this place while you're out," Nadine said, making a shooing motion with her hand.

Jace opened the door for her and they headed a block up to the green space that was the town square. Picnic tables dotted the grass under the big oak trees.

Jace laid out all the food while she set about unwrapping things and opening sodas.

"I didn't know what all you'd like, so I made you a turkey as well as a ham and a tuna fish. Or you can eat them all."

"You made me a sandwich?" She blushed.

"Three." He preened a little, making her laugh.

She grabbed the ham. He'd eat the other two sandwiches for a snack and not even break a sweat.

"Thank you."

They ate as people stared at them while trying to pretend they weren't.

"Had a Pembry offer me free movie tickets and your granddaddy offered me a rent break. I'm getting all sorts of stuff these days."

"I've seen you naked. Totally worth free movie tickets." He kept his tone dry but she laughed so hard she nearly choked.

"Am I worth some popcorn too?"

He nodded, expression still serious. "A premium sweet treat like a big bag of M&Ms too. Or a slushie."

Katie Faith snorted and then coughed because she got embarrassed about the snort.

"You'll turn my head, sir," she managed to wheeze as she got her breath back.

He looked at her, taking in the details of her face, the play of expression across it as she shared a meal with him. Eating the sandwich he'd made and brought to her.

"JJ came by to offer the discounted rent himself, huh?" Jace shook his head. "Damon tried to talk him out of it yesterday. I told him not to do it and that you'd say no if he asked. I also said I didn't plan to get in the middle of it."

She took him in carefully. The afternoon sunshine seemed to glint off bits and pieces of her magic as it floated around her like dust. He caught her anise scent with a happy sigh.

Ever since she'd been back—especially since their first kiss—his life had been a series of amazing moments.

Right then was one.

He'd tuck this picnic with her into his memories, remembering the glory of falling in love with her.

"You're fucking beautiful. You know that?" he asked her.

She smiled, quick and genuine. He loved her smile. The one she used only on him. "Thank you. That's very nice to hear. I do love you in your uniform. Especially the pants because they hug your butt perfectly."

He really couldn't imagine anyone else saying that to him. He grinned her way. "I'll keep that in mind. We haven't used my handcuffs yet. We should pencil that in."

Her blush brought more of her scent his way. He breathed deep, sucking in as much of her as he could.

He hummed. "You still smell like me," he told her slow. Teasing.

Her blush deepened as her eyes flew wide and then narrowed. "I took a shower this morning. I should know, you came in and hogged all the space."

She wasn't complaining, though. Her tone remained that husky sex voice she had. There were no lies either. She said the words and they pleased her. Her expression caught between sexual attraction and romantic teasing as her mouth formed each sound.

He wanted to lean in and sip them from her lips.

"You know how much I like it when you're wet." He let that hang a few seconds. "Before you left I unbuttoned your blouse and rubbed my face all over your tits. Remember? I had a little scruff so your skin was pink. Your heart pounded too. Like it's doing now."

She swallowed hard, licking her lips.

"It pleases me that my scent is on your skin. I'm happy to know every single wolf who sniffed around you today got a snout full of *me* all over you."

Though it galled him to no end that any Pembry would offer her free anything. *Katie Faith is mine.* Those little sniveling shitheads trying to sniff around Katie Faith were lucky he was more amused than offended.

Her scent changed for Jace. Delicious and sticky sweet. No one knew that side of her. No one knew that alluring combo like nothing and no one else but her.

"That was so hot you had to pause to imagine sex with yourself, right? I know the feeling. Happens to me all the time when you talk all sexy like that. Thinking about sex with you is nearly as good as the actual having. But I'm going off on a tangent now."

"I'm pretty much always thinking about sex with you. Do you imagine sex with me? Or sex with yourself? Because for the record, I'm up for both as long as I can watch the latter. Come to think on it, I'd be okay watching the former too." He waggled his brows. "But I was also thinking about how these pups can sniff around but you only change for me. Bloom for me." He tangled their fingers together. "I was thinking that you're all mine."

She really should be annoyed by all that bravado. But she really liked it. Like a whole lot.

He was always so laid-back. Until he wasn't. When

he turned up his intensity his smolder was nuclear. Even as he was bossy or went all alpha male *you're mine*, she got swoony around him.

Because it was him. Anyone else but Jace and she'd have tossed something at his head by now. But the way *he* said and did all that he-man alpha wolf stuff *to her* just totally worked.

He was so sexy and so dirty and wow, she was so lucky.

"I guess you'll just have to buy me tickets for the movies in the future," she said. As for being his, there was nothing to argue about. He made his declaration, she accepted that. None of those things seemed to be at issue.

She could go out in the middle of the street and declare him her boyfriend, lover, whatever. She could say it like, "oh Jace, that's my boyfriend" every five minutes for a day or two. Or she could live her own damned life without having to verify her relationship status when here she was having lunch with Jace. In public like relationship-type people did.

"This is going to be crazy for a while," he said quietly.

"*A while*. I never figured you for an optimist. It's going to be crazy forever because this is Diablo Lake. I can't take a rent break from JJ. I need to pay my own way."

"Eventually we'll live together, right? Because you know, wolves, we have a thing about that."

"I know you all have a thing about that to get girls to let you sleep with them. This is very fast." She gave him a raised brow.

"Well, sure, that part's true too. The sex part. But, you're not living in Nashville or wherever. We aren't *dating*. We've been dancing around one another for the last month. And before that a few years. We were always coming to this point right here." He said the last with a smug expression. "I've known you since we were kids. Fast." He sneered and still looked sexy doing it. "I like sleeping next to you. I want to continue doing that. Eventually we can do it in the same house. I'm not going to pretend otherwise."

"We'll deal with potential rent issues then."

He started to argue and she realized being in love with this lunkhead was going to be a full-time job.

"Don't argue, for goodness' sake." She held a hand up. "Some things you won't win and this isn't even a big deal. Jeez. Save it up for when it's important."

He made a strangled sound but she smiled at him instead. "What are you up to tonight?"

"Shift's over at six thirty. I've got football practice with my brothers until eight thirty if you want to meet up after that for a late dinner?"

"I'll be at Aimee's watching reality television and that show where the women compete for the pretty but awful guy who claims he wants a marriage when he just wants a career selling pants or toothpaste. She loves that shit. I should be home at nine or so."

"I'll get a pizza. I've got beer already."

They cleaned up their lunch and he walked her back to work. Plenty of people saw them, hand in hand, heads close together as they spoke. She wouldn't have to yell it from anywhere.

Then he kissed her. Right on the sidewalk, in the middle of the afternoon right as the kids were getting out of school, Jace laid a kiss on her lips that zinged and pinged through her system like a pinball until he stepped back, satisfied he'd underlined what they were to one another.

"I'll see you tonight, darlin'." He gave her a secret look that said all sorts of dirty, thrilling things.

He waved toward her parents before he took off down the street at a long, powerful lope.

"Hot damn," her mother whispered.

"I know! I try not to think about it too hard or I get so nervous I panic."

"Well now. I suppose that boy just told all and sundry exactly what was what." Her dad just shrugged and went back to the Coke float he'd been making.

Chapter Twelve

"First up, I say we catch up on *Date the Dolt* while you tell me about that kiss your man apparently laid on you in the middle of town in front of God and everybody."

Aimee handed her a cocktail and they settled on the couch.

Katie Faith gulped it down in three swallows. "For Christmas you're getting bigger cocktail glasses. These things are tiny."

Aimee poured her another from a nearby pitcher. "I made plenty. Act like a lady." She snickered.

"Boring. Anyway, yeah. He totally did. Well, not in the middle of the street, I think my mom's behind that one. On the sidewalk outside the Counter. Kids were heading through town. Middle and high school just got out. My parents were right inside. Thank god they couldn't see the sex look he gave me after making out with me in broad daylight. Shew." Katie Faith fanned herself with a napkin and then put a few snacks on a plate.

"I'm having pizza with him later. I should take it easy on the frozen spring rolls. But we both know I won't." Katie Faith clinked her glass with Aimee's.

"Girl. Hang on and let's see who he gives the wrist corsage to and then I want to hear about the kiss."

They watched Gabe, the hunky single dad and widower who owned a landscaping empire stand in front of a table full of the fugliest corsages Katie Faith had ever seen.

"What the fuck are those? I bet it's one of those flowers that smells like rotting meat. It looks freaky. How's that sayin', *hey girl, I think I want to keep you around a week more to see if I can't get to third base on camera*?" Aimee asked, shaking her head.

"It looks like the saddest prom date ever. Meat flowers and desperation. Damn, Candy's eyes get wider and wider each week. The whites are so…obvious." Katie Faith leaned back a little.

"Like a spooked horse. Maybe Gabe's cock is ginormous and she's having second thoughts. I mean, enough is a feast and all."

"The thing I like best about you is how you're so genteel and such." Katie Faith watched as Gabe's flat, empty doll eyes pointed at Candy as he said he liked how she scuba dived and tried new things on their date.

"Do you think he means butt stuff?" Aimee asked. "You know with the trying new things comment?"

"Maybe that's why she looks like she needs to be hosed off and brushed down. If Gabe has a big peen— not overrated, I'm just saying—and there was butt stuff." That dissolved into incoherent laughter and coughing as Gabe anointed his meat flowers on four more ladies and they were off to the next staged opportunity for intimacy.

"Not overrated, huh? So you finally achieved consummation?" Aimee asked, turning the sound down while Brittni and Gabe painted pottery and talked about childhood.

"We did indeed achieve consummation. Twice for him. Three times for me. Damn, that makes me cheerful!"

They fist bumped like awkward white girls but didn't further embarrass themselves by attempting fireworks or jazz hands.

"We did get interrupted. Again. But he came back and it was well worth waiting for. That's all I'm going to say. Ha! I'm a liar. It was awesome. Like fireworks and a live symphony orchestra climax awesome."

Aimee nodded, approving. "And he's packing some heat?" She indicated her crotch as if Katie Faith didn't know what she meant.

"Monstrous. Well, not scary, but it's a serious penis. It means business. Girth and length. And excellent recovery time. That extra orgasm for me was from a most excellently talented mouth. Damn, I'm a hussy. I wonder if this is what Sharon and Darrell had and that's why he couldn't go through with our wedding. Ugh, I don't want to understand him and maybe feel a little bad for him though."

"Whatever. He's a dingus. I do think you were badly matched and yeah, you're doing the sex with a werewolf so that means there's all that imprinting when it's the real deal. All joking aside, it's really different?" Aimee asked.

"It's different than everything else. Not just that it's mind-blowing because he's really good, but it's me and him. Something about us." Katie Faith lifted a shoulder. "I'm not a nun. I've been with werewolves and human men. I've been fortunate to have had partners, even jerkwad Darrell, who always made sure I came too. But with Jace it's more than skill and size, it's magic. Mine and his." As she said it, she realized she hadn't really understood it until then. Her mother told her that connection with the right person could be this electric and wonderful, but she'd always thought love was love. Happiness was something you worked for. And she would have to because Jace was a handful.

"I haven't felt anything earth-shattering yet. Or mind-blowing. Mildly pleasant, sometimes really pleasant." Aimee refilled her glass. "My parents have it. Yours too. And now you. I don't want it right now. I have stuff to take care of that I don't want to have to negotiate around another person. But I do want it. I want to grow old with someone. I'm glad to know it's out there."

"Well, watch out for the bossy ones who'll kiss you in public so all the wolves in town know not to give you free movie tickets." Katie Faith explained about the Pembrys who'd come into the Counter earlier.

"Bossy or not, it sounds sort of romantic in that werewolf way."

"It was because he's not usually like that. But I had hoped to keep it to ourselves for a while. Now everyone knows for sure."

"Everyone knew for sure already. When he took you home from the police station. When he nearly lost his job and assaulted Darrell. That would have been so cool though. Not nearly as cool as you doing it." Aimee cackled. "Boom! Flying dirtbag."

"I'd be lying to say it wasn't enjoyable. I can still see the look on Darrell's face. For a bit there, I was scared."

"I hate that he made you scared. He's going to be in so much trouble with his daddy now."

Katie Faith snorted. "Makes it worse in some ways because I'm a scapegoat either way."

"We won't let you be."

"I love you, Larnamae."

"You're fucked up." Aimee shook her head.

"I know. So, guess what? Miz Rose is giving me lessons, right?"

Miz Rose gave a lot of lessons to the witches of Diablo Lake.

"Yeah?" Aimee refilled the chip bowl.

"She told me today she's sick and tired of all the bickering between the Dooleys and Pembrys and thought the witches around here needed to stand up to them more. Keep them on an even keel."

"Lemme guess, she thinks you're the chosen one to lead us to the Promised Land."

Katie Faith made a face. "Well, yeah, duh. Also she mentioned you being powerful and smart too. Just so you know, she's on the hunt for you to be in her army."

"Awesome. I bet we'd have the best snacks of any army ever."

"Right? I was thinking the same thing."

Aimee cocked her head. "I think she's right, you know. About the wolves? The cats have their own issues, but my dad was just saying it's our job to keep the peace here, to guard that balance of the multinatured living here in Diablo Lake."

Katie Faith sighed. "Yeah. I think so too. I can't deny how fun it was to use my magic to defend myself and that balance when Darrell came at me. But it means drama. Problems and complications."

"Yep. Basically, a day ending in Y. Not like you'd have some normal life elsewhere. What were you going to do? Marry some human? Never tell him you're a witch? Bring him here once a year, maybe twice? Your life is what it is. You were meant for more than just living day to day. Stop being bitchy to fate. Don't matter either way."

On the television Gabe had unhinged his jaw to swallow half of fiery redhead dental assistant Lacey's face.

Katie Faith recoiled. "Ugh! I can't believe Lacey is letting Gabe kiss her. With tongue. She could get a cold sore!"

"Especially after he kissed Brittni as their vases fired after their ceramics date."

Katie Faith grabbed a licorice whip, using it to underline her point. "Brittni and Lacey need to dump Gabe and run off into the sunset."

"Take his meat flowers and say good day, sir."

She finished her licorice with a wrinkled nose. "He can keep the meat flowers, though."

Jace met Major at the football field. Contrary to what Katie Faith assumed, it was his brother who coached the team. Jace and Damon just lent a hand. It gave the teenagers a chance to run and be rough but with rules.

And it allowed Jace and Damon to hang out with their brother and model adult behavior for the young people. Which meant there was always some sort of break up of at least one fight between wolves but the teens didn't step over the line. Shifters healed fast. They lived in a very physical world so fighting was part of what they did to handle beefs from minor to serious.

But while sneakiness and predatory behavior were prized, stalking and watching for prey had to be strictly

defined so it never crossed into harassment. It was wolf
and cat business, not human business.

A black eye from the defensive end who got sick of
you wasn't the same as a shifter using their size to harm
a weaker being, especially one he or she was supposed
to protect like a child, elders and romantic partners.

"Hey." Jace handed Major a bag with his dinner in
it. "Grandma came by the station just as I was leaving. She made us fried chicken." He handed the other
off to Damon.

"Probably to make up for JJ offering Katie Faith a
rent discount." Damon rolled his eyes.

"Probably treated with some sort of mojo to make
him extra fertile so he knocks Katie Faith up and they
have great grandbabies," Major added with a shrug before demolishing his dinner.

"Don't you have kids to push around and make run
until they throw up?" Jace grumbled.

"Indeed I do once my dinner is finished. Lots of
spectators tonight." Major tipped his chin toward the
bleachers.

When it wasn't freezing or raining, they had parents,
grandparents, girlfriends, boyfriends, whatever, in the
stands watching practice. As long as they didn't distract
the players, Major didn't make a big deal of it. But that
night there were easily twice, maybe three times the
normal amount of folks up there.

"Funny how many women live in this town all the
sudden, no?" Damon smirked. "Jesus. It's like everyone from sixteen to eighty-six who isn't attached is up
there."

"What are you looking at me for?" Jace demanded.

"You kissed Katie Faith in front of God and everybody. In front of her parents. Half the women up there want to make sure you're going to not treat her bad. Her first go around with a wolf didn't go so well. The other half, well some of them want to make a run at you before you're off the shelf for good." Damon put his empty Tupperware back in the bag, tucking it with his things nearby to take home.

"Y'all better get running!" Major hollered at the boys, who quickly complied.

Jace tried not to look back over his shoulder at the stands as he jogged out to get the tackle dummies set up, but he knew they were there. Watching.

Thirty minutes later, one of his grandmother's sisters, Alice, waved Jace over with a bellowed *yooo hooo* and an imperious wave of her cane that sent two other people scrambling to avoid getting knocked upside the head.

He grumbled, determined to wave her away, pretending not to know what she meant, or that he was too busy. It was that or tell her to mind her own business.

"You know she's only going to get louder. Why punish the rest of us?" Major said. "Go on. Be nice. Grandma will skin you if you're rude."

"Aunt Alice is scary enough on her own. She's wicked fast so stay out of her reach," Damon joked as he guffawed. Like a dick.

Jace put on his best cop dealing with old people face but she just gave him a long look. "Sure is dry out tonight," she said once he approached.

"Feels like rain might be coming soon though."

She blinked. "That was my way of letting you know I was thirsty and needed you to bring me a soda."

"I'll be right back, Aunt Alice." He turned to jog off,

but she called out to him that he needed to bring a lot of sodas so she could share.

Out on the field, they ran drills, both his brothers studiously avoiding his gaze.

He took an armful of sodas over to her and the rest of the female elders in his family.

"So." Alice cracked her soda open and took a drink. "Hits the spot. Thank you. You moved Katie Faith Grady in across the hall from you. Right smack dab in the heart of Dooley territory."

Another one of his great aunts, Carmen, held out a clear plastic container his way. "Cookie?"

He took several with his thanks.

"You two have been flirting up a storm since the minute she got back," Carmen said.

"And dating for, I'd say three weeks? Four?" Alice asked.

Jace just gave them a general movement. Not really a full-on agreement, not a denial either. He didn't know where they were going with this so he wanted to be careful about what he revealed until he knew more.

"Most folks have noticed it over the last two weeks especially," Deidre added. She was one of his third or fourth cousins. She and Alice had run together since they were kids. "And if they didn't, they surely did hear about that kiss this afternoon. You declared yourself loud and clear. What are your intentions then? Rose Collins would be very unhappy if you weren't taking what you did seriously."

Jace willed his blush away, setting his jaw carefully. His energy changed and the women all gave him raised brows.

"You mind telling me what you're doing, boy?" Alice asked in a very calm voice.

"I'm not Darrell. I'm not him." Jace meant more than just Darrell with the last. He didn't need to bring up his father for them to understand, though.

Her face lost its calm facade. Instead she frowned and before he could move, she'd latched on, pulling him into a hug as the others clucked and awww'd over him. That would teach him to let them get close enough to hug up on him.

He managed to disentangle himself in enough time to see one of the aunties give a glare to one of the younger women who'd been trying to catch his eye.

"This is for real and forever. Things are changing. We just needed to make sure you understood that." Alice nodded her head once to underline.

"Like I said, I'm not anyone else. And you don't know Katie Faith very well if you think she'd stand for any foolishness from me or anyone else. She's a big girl now." Jace let himself smile at the memory of her distinct hatred of mornings.

How it was that Katie Faith being grumpy made him all hot and bothered, he didn't know. But there he was, struck stupid by the way she scrunched up her brow and her hair went all bristly as she'd stomped off to the bathroom.

"You all have a good evening." He bowed slightly, totally done with their test and the conversation.

"Thanks for the Cokes, Jace," Alice called out as he headed back to where practice was beginning to wind down.

"It's really gross how many moms are up there scoping out your butt," one of the kids waiting his turn to run told him.

Jace shrugged. Wasn't like he was going to complain a bunch of folks found him attractive. He wasn't unaware of his looks or of his position. He'd grown wary over the years after getting burned by people he thought truly cared about him.

Katie Faith didn't give a shit about any political stuff. She respected his position and his power, but she just seemed to find her way around anything she didn't want to do.

Yeah, he knew she liked the way he looked. He loved the way her scent changed when he took his shirt off, or when she stared at his forearms and hands as he was drying dishes.

Compared to that scent—just for him—what was the temptation?

Still didn't mean he was going to let a seventeen-year-old pup bust his balls. "Give me thirty push-ups," he tossed out as he turned his back and focused on the rest of the kids practicing.

The brew pub had a pretty decent take-out pizza business going so he ordered two different kinds of loaded combos and asked them to set aside a few bottles of the Diablo Lake Porter.

He jumped in the shower, changed and before he ran up the road to get the pies, he checked in on JJ to have a little chat with him about offering discounts and such to Katie Faith.

It was just his grandmother in the kitchen though, when he came through.

"Alice called over here a while back," she told him as he bent to kiss her cheek.

He grunted. "Is Grandpa around?"

"He'll be around when he wants to be. And he doesn't just now."

Jace withheld the sigh he knew she'd be annoyed by. "I'm sure he knows I'm looking for him. I'll check again soon but I need to grab my dinner just now."

"No one thinks you're Darrell."

He did sigh then. "Hard to think otherwise when half the town thinks I'm going to get Katie Faith in a family way and then dump her. I'm not *him* either."

She flinched slightly, getting his point about his dad. "He wasn't all bad, but he was weak. Some people, no matter how much they were loved and raised right, are broken."

Jace didn't say aloud that he'd spent his whole damned life trying to prove to people who should know better, that he was better than that. Better than the male Jace had no memories of.

But he was eternally sick and tired of carrying Josiah Dooley's bullshit around.

"You don't have to be stoic every minute you know." She pointed to a chair at the table and he obeyed.

"I have a pizza order waiting," he said to her, trying to be patient.

"Use that thing to tell one of your brothers to go get it then. I have some things to say and I won't take no backseat to pepperoni." She pointed at his phone.

Knowing there was no way around it, Jace texted Major, who said he was on his way to the pub anyway and would drop the food by when it was ready.

"Everything would be so much easier if you all just

obeyed me like this the first time." With a sigh, she sat across from him. "I sometimes forget that Josiah's mistakes weigh on other people's shoulders too." At Jace's surprised look she waved a hand. "What? That's the bull's-eye, ain't it?"

He *really* didn't want to have this conversation. He had pleasant things to look forward to, like pizza, beer and his woman. Talking about his father was only going to make his life less pleasant and it wouldn't change the past in any case.

"We loved Josiah. Same as we did the rest. He never seemed to settle or be still. Nothing satisfied him. You're a Prime. He never was. Not even potentially." She shrugged.

"Why's everyone in my business then? A bunch of aunties show up at practice to give me stink eye and make me cart sodas to 'em?"

"Pack business is their business." She lowered her voice. "If you were truly like him, or like Darrell for that matter, you'd be surprised by the fact that your kiss this afternoon was as good as you getting down on one knee. But you know what you're doing. You do *everything* with a reason. That's why you're Prime. Why you'll be Patron soon enough. Katie Faith and that kiss mean things will change now. For everyone in this town. The question isn't *are you a womanizer layabout like Josiah*. It just isn't an issue with you."

"Am I worthy? Is that it?" he burst out.

"I think that's part of the question, and you and I both know it's more important to you than anyone else. The answer for your family is that they took a long look and liked what they saw. A man ready to lead. A man ready to dig deeper roots and a stronger foundation for the future. What is it you see?" his grandmother asked him.

That was a hell of a question, wasn't it?

"It was a point needed making," he said, avoiding the other question. He'd wanted everyone to know Katie Faith was his. That they were together. Wanted to extend his protection to her in a way she'd accept and one that meant something to them both.

"Okay then. Since she hasn't burned the place down, I take it she's all right with you making your point on her lips in front of her mom and daddy?"

He cracked a smile then. "No one hit me or used magic to toss me in the street on my butt. I guess so."

"You're worthy, Jace. You've been ready and now you have someone to be ready for and with. But it's going to be rocky awhile. I expect you know that too."

He nodded. "Things are already unstable. It'll come to a head, some bones will be broken, some blood will be spilled and we'll move on. It's how things work here and we sure aren't moving down to Chattanooga."

"Show some respect for your elders. Don't make it a big deal if she sleeps over or if you sleep over there." She gave him the stink eye.

"It's respect for Katie Faith too."

His grandmother beamed. "I taught you right. Okay, go. I heard your brother pull up. Katie Faith just got home too."

She had a good ear still. The same hearing that always caught Damon sneaking out. Though never Jace because he wasn't a dumbass like his brother.

He hugged her tight. "Thank you for the pep talk."

She kissed his cheek and smoothed his hair back the

same way she had since he could remember. "I'm your grandmamma, that's my job."

"I'm still looking to have a word with Grandpa so when he's ready to be found, send him my way, please."

"He's eighty-four years old. He does what he wants. Go on now." She waved him out.

He followed his nose as pepperoni and sausage guided him to his door, where Major stood, chatting with Katie Faith.

"Hi!" She turned a goofy smile his way. "Gabe made out with Lacey and then he didn't even give her a corsage. Can you believe that guy?"

Someone'd had a few. Jace kept that to himself as he took the pies from his brother and opened his door.

"I invited him to eat pizza with us but he's going back to the pub. Lots of women out tonight I noticed on the walk back from Aimee's."

"I'll see y'all later." Major hugged Katie Faith and ducked out.

"It was very nice of him to pick up our pizza. Is everything all right?" She tossed her bag on the floor next to his couch.

"I just got caught up in a conversation with my grandmother and rather than run out on it, I asked Major if he could grab the pizza when it was done. He was supposed to call me to see if I'd finished, but he clearly didn't bother to wait for that."

Jace put the pizza down and then pulled her close. "Evening, Katie Faith," he murmured into her hair.

"Hi." She seemed to melt against his body. This was coming home.

"Who's Gabe?"

She laughed and told him about some reality dating

show thing she watched with Aimee as they plated up the pizza, grabbed beer and he took her out his bedroom window to the roof where he'd put a blanket earlier.

"From here we can see the stars but no one but the stars can see us."

"Sneaky. I like it."

"How was practice?" Katie Faith asked. She didn't go for nonchalance because she'd gotten a call from her mom telling her how many aunties showed up at practice that night and also how many single folks sniffed around too.

She figured it was better to just get it out of the way before they had sex. Because she had plans for that and they didn't include any deep conversations about nosy elders.

His expression was adorable though. Panicked and annoyed all at once. She was going to hell for that too probably, but she loved to poke at him. Ruffle him up and make him laugh.

He had so much on his shoulders she craved easing when she could. Also, he needed someone not to take him so damned seriously as Jace Prime Alpha Wolf. Grr.

"I should have known you'd hear about it. I figured tomorrow first thing, but apparently this relationship of ours is the most weighty topic in the whole fucking town's mind."

Katie Faith snorted. "Stop. I hear you had a legion of lady fans who fed you cookies after you hauled sodas for them."

"Carmen made her oatmeal chocolate chip cookies."

She nodded, totally understanding. "I don't suppose

you saved me one." He ducked his head and she gave in to her desire to give him a quick hug. "I'm joking."

"I have a dump cake. Aunt Alice sent it home with me after practice."

"Another reason to keep you around. You have excellent connections for baked goods on the regular."

"The kiss this afternoon got everyone riled up," he said.

"Like you knew it would."

"I knew you'd figure it out soon enough," he muttered. "You said you hated that people kept asking you. Now they won't have to."

He was even more handsome when he jutted his chin out defiantly. Ridiculous.

"So, you did it for me?"

"I can't tell if I should be scared or if you actually get it."

"You should always be scared, Jace. I'm not mad that you kissed me. If I was, I'd have told you right then instead of locking lips and hugging up on you."

"So what's the problem then? Everyone knows we're together so they don't need to talk about it all the damned time."

"It's cute when you're so clueless. But right now you know exactly what's going on."

He nibbled on her fingertips a moment before grabbing another slice of pizza. "By kissing you today I told everyone you were mine. Is that what you mean?"

Warmth burst through her. "That's a start. A really good one, but don't let it go to your head. You got all riled up about the whole offer of free movie tickets. From a boy I babysat, by the way." She rolled her eyes.

"Boy's got taste, I'll give him that." He gave her a

pirate's grin. "Like all the others have been boys. Let's get that straight."

She shifted closer to him so she could nibble on his earlobe. He exhaled, a little shaky.

"I don't have anything confused so there's nothing to get straight, buster." She grabbed his bottom lip between her teeth and tugged slowly until he moaned, relaxing, giving in to that essential need to be touched shifters came with.

"I warned you. Back in the early days, what it would be like with me."

He got up quickly, gracefully, and hustled her back inside, closing the window once they'd brought food in.

"Better?" he asked.

"Huh?"

He was on her in two steps, sliding his body against hers as he then embraced her, rubbing his hands all over her upper body.

As if that was going to make her more coherent? She fell into his touch, the strength of his hands as he touched her.

"I saw you shiver outside. Getting cooler at night. Now that there's a witch in my life I need to remember things like getting cold."

"I like it when you pet me," she confessed. "And I like it that you got jealous. I mean, you didn't do anything I *absolutely* wasn't on board with. Enthusiastically so. Now. You were reminding me of some sort of warning you gave me?"

He tugged her to his gigantic recliner, tucking her against his body. He gave off enough warmth that her muscles relaxed and she snuggled in.

"I'm not a boy. I'm not even a man. I'm a Prime.

Other wolves bringing you flowers and thinking they can sniff around? For what? They don't know you like I do. Don't see every beautiful, wonderful, weird as hell thing about you like I do. And I don't like it one damn bit. Not only because you're mine so they can all fuck right off."

She snickered as she patted his chest a few times. "I don't like it either. But it's not going to make any difference in the choices I make. In the one I made when I let a gorgeous werewolf I've been half in love with since I was seventeen kiss me and touch my boobs."

He rumbled. A sound of contentment from deep inside his chest.

"They're great boobs. I'm mighty glad you let me touch them."

"Where did you hide this sense of humor back when we were teens? You just brooded all around like the hottest older boy crush ever. Frowning."

He frowned just then and then deeper as he realized she'd seen.

"I'm well known for my wit, I'll have you know."

Truth was, he did have a really great, dry as a bone humor.

"You make me laugh more than anyone I've ever known." He looked a little surprised at his admission, but recovered quickly. "I can't for the life of me imagine what you and Darrell talked about. You dated him for a long time."

Darrell had rarely laughed at her weird comments. She couldn't poke fun at him or be lighthearted because he'd been really sensitive and who wanted to upset the person you thought you loved?

"I don't really remember. A lot of time on what he

wanted or thought. His opinions on all things, especially Darrell. Like any shifter boy I've ever known, he wants his parents to be proud of him. Why?"

"Just hard to imagine him being dumb enough to not see you for the treasure you are and smart enough to get your sense of humor."

"I guess it takes a Prime to know what a goddamn national treasure I am."

A surprised gale of laughter came from deep in his belly as he picked her up and carried her into his bedroom.

She loved the way it smelled in there. Totally him. Delicious and sexy Jace Dooley. Yes indeed.

"Get naked while I light some candles." He set her on her feet with a kiss before turning to deal with candles he'd situated all around the room.

She whipped her sweater up and off before shucking her shoes, pants, tights and panties. The last thing, the flick that undid the snap between her breasts, she waited for his attention to land on her again.

Jace hissed as her breasts sprang free and she let the bra fall to her feet.

"You got candles for me? Or are these all-purpose seduction sconces?"

"Seduction sconces? You're not all the way right, Katie Faith. You know that."

"Lucky you."

He nodded slow. "Yeah. Really lucky."

Jace had been about to get his clothes off and order her pretty little butt on the bed when she dropped to her knees and looked up at him through her lashes.

"Go on then," he told her.

Within a few moments she'd gotten his pants opened and his cock out, licking around the crown.

He had to lock his knees to keep from falling over as a bolt of lust swept through him. His sweet, pretty, quirky witch there on her knees, her mouth wrapped around his cock as she looked up at him was the hottest thing he'd ever experienced in his entire life. He hadn't even known it was possible to feel that sharp, dirty, dark sort of pleasure until right that moment.

He sifted her hair through his fingers before tugging her a little closer. She made a low sound, a ragged moan that seemed to wrap around his balls and squeeze slightly.

Unable to stop her, not wanting her to, he let her draw him closer and closer to climax until he was so very close he had to wrench himself away several steps.

"That wasn't very nice. I wasn't done."

"Damn what you do to me when you make that face. So hungry for me." He shoved the rest of his clothing off and was back against her, skin to skin, moments later. "I'll always happily put my dick in that pretty mouth of yours. But right now I want to fuck you."

He slid his hands all over her body, breathing her in, bending to kiss here and there, to taste or nibble.

Then he spun her so she faced the bed and using his body, bent her over. Her heart pounded so hard he easily heard. He scented her honey, knew it was all for him. Loved that.

He reared his upper body up, keeping his hips pressed to her, holding her in place. There were no words left, just sensation.

Her fingers flexed in the comforter as she thrust

back against him, reminding him she was an alpha in her own right. *Demanding* his full attention.

He gave it to her, licking a trail down her neck and over her shoulder. Her contented sigh echoed through him.

She pressed back again. No mistaking the order to get inside her. He smiled against her neck as she reached between them to get him lined up.

He took that place where neck met shoulder, breathing her in, testing the tendon there with the edge of his teeth.

A delicate shiver passed over her as her pussy superheated around the head of his cock. One arch of his hips sent him deep as he bit, hard, holding her as he thrust hard, deep and fast.

Little earthquakes of sensation echoed through him as her inner walls clutched him. So damned hot he nearly lost his mind.

That feral part of him, the wolf, had been watching their witch, admiring her strength and ferocity. Now the wolf coveted her beauty. The earthy sensuality she emanated was irresistible.

She brought out that need to protect in both aspects of himself. The need to spoil and incite. The need to delight and satisfy. Pleasure that she was so perfect and strong.

His.

He reached around her hip, between her body and the mattress, finding her clit already slippery. At the first touch of his fingertips she gasped, body rippling around him.

She tightened impossibly more, heating, so wet and slick he was nothing but the movement of his muscles, the taste of her skin, the way her climax seemed to catch them both in a greedy fist.

He joined her, gasping as his muscles ached, as he came hard enough that he could only manage to lunge a little once they'd both gone still, dragging her along with him so they were mostly on the bed.

"Damn. You fucked me stupid," she mumbled. "And I think you gave me a hickey."

He managed to drag his eyes open to see he'd left a pretty obvious love bite on her neck. "I may have."

She giggled. "You must have fucked me stupid because I'm not even mad. Tomorrow I will be. Probably."

"Get used to it, Katie Faith. Wolves like to leave marks."

She shivered again. "I guess I'll have to." But she smiled as she said it.

Chapter Thirteen

Katie Faith stopped by to see her parents after she closed up one afternoon two weeks later.

"I'm going to the grocery store so I thought I'd see if you two needed anything," she said as she entered the living room where her dad watched television at an alarming volume and her mom attempted to read a book.

"Hey, baby." Her dad held his arms out and she gave him a hug.

"How'd it go today?" He had a doctor's appointment first thing that morning so her parents had spent the night near the hospital and had come back a few hours ago.

"I'm looking great."

"Did you have them check your hearing? Jeez, Daddy, this television is so loud I could hear it from the porch."

Her mother snorted as she stood to kiss Katie Faith's cheek. "He claims there's nothing wrong with his hearing."

"Uh." Katie Faith didn't want to get in the middle of this argument, that was for sure. She just hoped Jace wouldn't watch TV that loud when he was an old guy like her dad.

"Anyway, he's telling you the truth. The doctors said

he's doing fantastic." Two of them were witches, so they had taken into account Avery's sped up metabolism and healing, so it was even better to hear her dad was doing great from people who knew his whole story.

"That's a relief." She hugged her dad again. "So anything from the market?"

Her mother made a list of some basics. "Thank you, honey." Her mother walked her to the car. "Not just for this grocery run. But for everything. For putting your life on hold to come here. For being so loving and helpful. We sure are proud of you."

She hadn't realized how much the words would mean until her mother gave them to her. Tears welled up. "Every single time in my life when I've needed help, you and daddy have been there. Of course I'm here. And you know what? I'm glad. I have a good life here. I see Aimee every day. I see you two every day. The Counter is doing great. I just got two contract jobs for some basic bookkeeping so I can easily cover the snow tires I'm going to need soon enough."

"That boy is nuts about you." Her mom patted her hand. "You two come for dinner this upcoming weekend. We want to know him better. Oh, and I saw Patty in town a few days ago. She and I thought it would be nice to have a unified Thanksgiving. What do you think?"

"It's not even October yet."

"There's no call not to be prepared then, is there?"

Her mom was seriously good with the disapproving tone. "You're totally right. Of course I'm in. I'll talk to Jace about dinner this weekend. I have to check with him to see what shift he's working."

"Let me know the best time. That's easy enough to work around."

"You should make a roast. You know, for company and all," her father added.

"I'll make roast beef. You can have trout. Your brother brought some over yesterday so it'll be perfect. And good for your heart."

Avery's grunt of annoyance that his younger brother had brought over fish made Katie Faith laugh.

"I'll be back in a bit." She took the list from her mom and when she hugged her dad as she passed by, she told him she'd bring him back a treat.

This was the reason she'd come back. To help lighten the load on her parents. It pleased her that she could. Pleased her that she was able to have them back in her life on a regular basis too.

The parking lot at the small market in town was full, but she found a place a ways from the doors. The building was one of the oldest in town and one Katie Faith remembered going to from a very early age. It was a nice thing to have those memories and those roots. Small towns had their drawbacks. There wouldn't be forty types of jam on the shelves and they closed at 10:00 p.m. If she wanted anything rare or exotic, she'd have to venture out of the mountains and head to a big city, or order online.

But the roots? The way she waved at friends and family as she grabbed a wobbly cart and headed inside were firmly in the plus column.

She was still smiling as she picked up a flat of peaches and slid it on the shelf on the bottom of the cart. Maybe she could con Miz Rose into making some cobbler for her if she brought over the raw ingredients.

"I nearly didn't recognize you, Katie Faith."

Katie Faith, however, would recognize that voice

anywhere. She straightened and turned to face Scarlett Pembry.

"Hello, Scarlett."

"I've been looking for you in town, but now I realize, I may have seen you multiple times but didn't recognize you."

Wow, that was a world class backhanded compliment.

"Well, the years have been kind to some of us." Katie Faith smiled bright, loving the way Scarlett's smirk fell off her face right quick.

Katie Faith added some plums and nectarines, hoping Scarlett would wander off.

"I haven't been able to welcome you back to town in person. I did ask your momma to come down and have ladies lunch with us, but she's so darned busy."

"Thanks. This upcoming weekend it'll be two months now. We'll see how happy I am when the snow comes." She gave Scarlett a quick smile. "As for Momma, she's still working at the Counter and of course Daddy needs someone around as well. She's got a lot on her plate just now." And she doesn't like you because you're terrible.

That last bit she kept in her head.

"I thought you came back so she wouldn't have so much on her plate. I know you have this budding romance with that Dooley boy but you should mind what's really important."

Katie Faith just gaped at Scarlett's words for long moments. Instead of ramming her cart into the other woman, she steered around her.

"Huh. You and I must have different approaches on the meaning of things like what's really important."

Scarlett put her hand on the cart, stopping its progress. "I wasn't done."

"Oh, I think you are. If you want to stand around here and insult me, more power to you. But I'm here shopping for my parents so I need to get back to what's really important."

"There's no need to be so hostile."

"You're right." Katie Faith pushed the cart harder to underline that point.

"I want to ask you to move to a different part of town," Scarlett said.

"No." She won free of Scarlett's hold on the cart and kept rolling herself toward the dairy section.

"You're tipping the balance living in Dooley territory. Just because you've lowered yourself to being involved with one of them, doesn't mean you have to destabilize the whole town."

"Anything available in the Pembry part of town?"

Scarlett's smile went very catty. "Yes, as a matter of fact. We'd be able to help you with the costs of moving and give you a break on the rent."

"That's what I figured. You can take your offer and stick it where the sun don't shine."

Scarlett, struck still by shock, watched as Katie Faith kept going. Once she turned the corner, she hustled her steps, wanting to be done and get the hell away from Scarlett Pembry.

This was short-lived as she caught up to Katie Faith as she put the milk into the cart.

"We weren't done speakin'."

Anger that'd been simmering began to boil. "Oh, we were. Trust me on that."

Again, Scarlett grabbed the cart. "You're not going to take the balance between Pembry and Dooley into account? It's your damned *place* to do that." Scarlett's expression told Katie Faith just what she thought about witches.

"I think, between the two of us, it's you who needs to mind your space."

"You think a few years in the city makes you good enough to take me on?" Scarlett's mean, narrowed gaze honed in as she let her wolf get alarmingly close to the surface.

Katie Faith's power rose in response. Sharp and hard enough that Scarlett's indecision showed in her gaze.

"I *don't* think about you at all unless you're in my face. Where I live isn't your business. And don't tell me it's about balance when you'd be just fine with me living in your territory."

"Lay down with dogs you gonna get fleas, girl. You're choosing the wrong side. Your job as a witch is to rein them Dooleys in."

Katie Faith was beyond boiling and fully into volcanic rage. Instead of louder, she went quieter, all her power focused on her words. "I have *had* it with you and your family. Don't you dare tell me what you think my job is as a daughter, a witch or a citizen of Diablo Lake." She looked Scarlett up and down. Utterly and totally sure she could, in fact, take her. And without a sweat.

In the time she'd spent with wolves when she'd been with Darrell and most definitely since she'd been with Jace, Katie Faith knew how she had to deal with shifters as powerful as the one she faced.

She used her magic to push her cart hard enough to overpower Scarlett's hold. "Don't think I'm going to allow you to push me around," Katie Faith said as she walked past.

People had paused to watch the whole scene. Scarlett may crave all that attention, but Katie Faith wanted none of it.

"You know how dirty them Dooleys are." Scarlett had given up trying to block her and was walking alongside now, barreling through anyone unfortunate enough to be in her way.

Scarlett's country showed a lot more when she was pissed off.

"Ask me, Jace will turn out just like his father. Blood will out they say. And then how will your daddy be? When you're abandoned?"

"I don't know, Scarlett. He handled it fine the first time." Katie Faith's smile was saccharine sweet and totally fake. "Which is the last time I'm going to allow you and yours to harm my father. It happens again and you'll have me to deal with."

"You're just a hole with some magical power to Jace Dooley. Don't think you're anything more."

Oh how she wanted to slap the spit out of Scarlett Pembry!

"Oh you have a mouth on you, don't you. I can see where Darrell gets his manners."

"Hey girl!" Aimee rushed over and pulled Katie Faith into a quick hug. "What on earth has you over here on the bargain aisle?" She looked Scarlett up and down.

Thank god for friends.

Katie Faith laughed as she pushed her cart once more, leaving Scarlett standing there.

"I don't want to talk about it here," she said in an undertone to Aimee as they checked out under the scrutiny of at least a dozen people. "I have to take groceries over to my parents' house. I'll talk to you later."

Aimee walked with her to her car and helped her load the bags before Katie Faith hugged her friend tight.

"Thanks for having my back in there. She said some pretty nasty stuff."

"She's out of line. And she's wrong. You want to spend the night at my house? We can watch movies and eat junk food and gossip about how good Jace is in bed."

"That sounds really good, actually. But I have some stuff I need to finish first." She needed to process everything. So many things weighed on her mind right then that she really just had to be alone for a while.

Aimee told her to call if she changed her mind and headed back to finish the shopping interrupted by having to step in and escort Katie Faith from the store without getting into a brawl.

She delivered the stuff to her parents, unloaded it, put it away for them and after hugs and kisses, she headed off. She didn't tell them about what happened at the market because it would only upset them and it was something she had to figure out herself. She'd do whatever she could to protect them.

There'd be a few calls, if Katie Faith knew this town, and she thought she did. But she had some time, most likely until the morning. Anyway, if she didn't mention it now, her parents might believe it wasn't a big deal. She'd tell them *after* her father had a good night's sleep. She'd be damned if she let Scarlett mess with his health.

Tomorrow morning. No need to interfere with his sleep.

Ha.

She needed to tell them. But she didn't know how. Especially because she was still so upset she knew she'd lose her composure, which would make things even worse and she was sick of things being worse.

She needed to think and if she went home, Jace would be there and she wasn't ready to talk to him about it yet either. Especially after Scarlett had said all that poisonous stuff about the Dooleys and Jace's dad.

The batting cages sat on the outer edge of Robby Cuthbert's land. Just two cages with pitching machines you loaded yourself. Nothing fancy, but they'd been well used by the last three generations of kids in Diablo Lake.

Everyone in town kept it up. She knew Jace made a habit of checking the machines on a regular basis and doing maintenance. Before him, others had done it.

Katie Faith's dad had brought her out here when she was four. A lifelong Braves fanatic, he'd had her at his side watching games with him for as long as she could remember. He gave her a bat and a mitt for her birthday. And since that day, whenever she needed to think or blow off steam, she made the trip out to hit some balls.

At eight on a Tuesday night, it was abandoned, which was the way she preferred it. She put her headphones on, hit play, and Ellie Goulding's "Army" began.

She hit the release on the arm and let her magic free.

Jace knocked on Katie Faith's door but no one answered. Seven already and he knew she'd closed up. She'd texted him earlier to say she was going grocery shopping and would see him later that evening so hopefully she would be returning soon.

It was odd, missing her the way he did when he saw her daily and slept at her side every night. But he'd gotten used to her in his life all the time. He liked it that

way. Her scent was all over his stuff and he knew damn
well she used his razor on her legs. But he didn't care.

He went home, made himself some bacon and eggs
while catching up with an old episode of *Homicide
Hunter: Lt. Joe Kenda.*

When she hadn't texted him back by eight he began
to get a little concerned. It wasn't that she didn't go
out and do things with her friends and family. She was
a busy woman, after all. But they touched base often
enough that he was restless enough to text Aimee at
eight thirty.

His phone rang immediately and he picked it up.

"I didn't want to type out the whole thing in a text
message," Katie Faith's best friend said.

"I don't want to bug Avery and Nadine. I don't want
to inadvertently worry them by calling to see if Katie
Faith is over at their place. It's not that big a deal, but
she and I had some plans and she hasn't texted back."
He rubbed a hand over his face, feeling like a fool. But
she'd called instead of texted, which meant there was
something up.

Then she told him about the scene with Scarlett.

"I didn't hear it all because I was trying to get from
the doors to them and Scarlett actually stalked Katie
Faith all through the place. But for sure it was mean
and gross. She said a bunch of hurtful stuff. Katie Faith
was so angry. I'm pretty sure that Scarlett wanted it to
go physical."

He growled. Those fucking Pembrys.

"Anyway," Aimee interrupted his growling, "she said
she had groceries to take over to her mom and daddy's
place. I figured she'd go home and hang out with you."

He wasn't worried for her safety. Not exactly.

But that unsettled feeling grew and it would, he knew, until he found her. Because being his meant a whole new level of concern and protectiveness between them.

He sighed: "She'd want to keep this from her parents if she could."

"Definitely. He just had a check-up so it's on her mind even more than usual. And Scarlett brought that up."

"That bitch brought up Katie Faith's daddy nearly dying? This is a new low, even for her." He'd have to deal with that at some point. For now though, he just wanted to be sure his witch was okay.

"Katie Faith's not here, which is one of her places. And with you is another. Uh. Let's see…" Aimee thought it over.

"Wait. I think I know where she is. I'll text you once I check," he told her as he grabbed his keys, stepping into his shoes on the way out the door.

He finally relaxed once he saw her car parked at the side of the dirt road next to the batting cages.

All those years ago he'd found her and she'd done something to him. Planted a seed of want so deep he'd never get enough of her. Today she was a woman hammering ball after ball as she sang at the top of her lungs.

He grinned so hard it hurt his cheeks.

He moved into her line of sight slowly, especially when he noticed she'd been wearing headphones. For long moments he just stared at her, loving the ferocity on her face.

And the jiggle of her tits.

But mainly the ferocity.

The machine spit out the last ball and she let herself

relax and get her breath. He waved and she jumped, her vision, which had been blurred as she puzzled over something a million miles away, sharpened on him.

And she smiled.

"How did you know?" she asked him as she walked around the chain-link gate and into a hug.

"How did I know where you were? This isn't the first time I've found you down this way." He kissed the top of her head, pleased she was so happy he'd shown up.

"Not that, though I'm glad you remembered. How did you know I needed you?"

He breathed her in as they stood, hugging, the scent of wet earth—he bet Mrs. Cuthbert had done some work out in her massive garden—and a river off in the distance. All around that was Katie Faith. Her magic.

What odd things truly made someone happy. He smiled against her hair. "I'm the one who needed you."

She hugged him tighter.

They'd gotten back and had settled on his place where he'd gotten her a glass of wine, something to eat and tucked her in next to him. He'd given her the time to change into her PJ bottoms and quickly text Aimee that things were fine and she was home. They'd driven by her parents' house but the lights had been off and all was quiet inside. She'd left a message for them both that she needed to speak to them when they woke up and to call her then.

And now it was time to deal with everything else that had happened that night.

"You ran. The first time we met out at the batting cages," she said before he could speak.

He hadn't expected that. He opened his mouth to explain.

She shook her head. "No, don't apologize. I brought it up to say tonight was different in all the ways that count. That means more than anything I can say. Thank you for coming to find me and thank you for standing with me."

She brought him to his knees in so many ways.

"I will always come for you. I won't be in your face when you need to be alone. I respect your independence. But I want to make you happy. I want to protect you. I want you to know I love you."

She blinked up at him, surprised as he was at what he'd just said aloud. He'd been thinking it for a few weeks, but right at that very moment he tipped irrevocably into forever-love with her.

"I was going to say it first." She made a face and then put her stuff down to hug him.

"So that means you love me too?" he asked, amused.

"Duh." She settled back at his side.

"You want to talk about what happened with Scarlett?"

"She brought up my dad's health. She held my cart! Like to stop me from going anywhere? This was after she followed me all over the store trying to start a fight. Told me what my *role* was as a witch here in Diablo Lake. The stuff…she said some things about your dad. Her tone when she did was vicious. Worse even than in the days after the wedding got called off and she was telling everyone I was whoring out all over the eastern seaboard."

Shifters had a physical advantage over witches and humans. They were stronger, faster and had quicker instincts and reactions. Living in a mixed community meant shifter parents had to instill control in their children from the start. A fight between two shifters was a lot more violent than one between a shifter and a human. That the Patron of the Pembry wolves didn't mind her manners made him so angry he had to focus on the feel of Katie Faith's skin against his where their arms touched. Letting her draw him back from the brink.

But there would be a bill come due at the end of this.

"She's taunting you. That bit with the offer to give you a rental break and pay your moving costs? This is going to be trouble."

"It already *is* trouble, Jace. But she's gunning for more. I got the feeling she wanted me to say no so she'd have an excuse."

She'd have to talk with Miz Rose about it. Because Scarlett was trying to use her like a pawn in her dumb power play and that was just what Miz Rose had been talking about. And she was trying to push Katie Faith around. Turns out, she was done being pushed around.

"All this politicking is making me so grumpy. Also hungry."

"Lots of things make you hungry."

When she'd turned to find him standing there at the batting cages earlier that night it was like everything she'd been ruffled by and scared of flitted away because Jace was there.

In his bossy pants way, he made everything better just because he'd been there.

"Are you saying I'm fat?"

The horrified look on his face was enough to have her laughing and throwing her arms around him again.

"You're really mean, Katie Faith."

She kept laughing.

"I'm going to need to take this to my grandpa and the rest of the elders," Jace said.

"Do you think they'll make me stop teasing you?"

He groaned. "Har."

"I have to talk to all the witchy folks too. This isn't just about this particular situation anymore. There are a lot of unhappy people in town when it comes to how the wolves are fighting back and forth and using the witches as their bargaining chips. And that is most definitely *not* our role in Diablo Lake."

He sighed. "I know. But I'd be lying if I denied how much it amuses me that you're mine because they let you slip through their fingertips."

She glared at him. "Really? So, like the cool holiday toy? You and Scarlett are going to grab the last Katie Faith on the shelf and beat each other bloody to see who gets it?"

His chuckle died. "That's not how I meant it."

Of course it was. Oh, she knew he loved her for lots of reasons, but this whole being fought over stuff was really annoying now.

"I could lie to you. Pretend we don't care about it. I'm trying here, Katie Faith. But if I hide stuff that's important, it's worse, don't you think?" He shrugged. "I'm Prime, I'll be Patron soon enough. I have you, this gorgeous, smart and talented witch who also happens to be powerful."

"Like when the housecat brings home dead birds?"

He winced.

"I don't want to talk about it anymore right now. I have to tell my parents about this tomorrow. You're going to have to have some sort of wolf meeting thing and life goes on, I guess. I'm just dreading how far this is going to go before we find equilibrium."

"It's a long time coming. This is how it goes when two packs live so close to one another." Jace shrugged. "It works here because of the land and the witches. Mainly, Dooley and Pembry get along, work and play side-by-side. But this isn't playing by the rules. They're pushing and pushing to see how far they can go. It's not going to end easily."

"Great."

"Don't get me wrong, darlin'. We'll get there. Eventually. How about a massage, another glass of wine and some sex to make everything better?"

Chapter Fourteen

It hadn't made everything better, but, as always when it came to sex with Jace, it certainly helped her get a decent night's sleep.

In the morning, he headed to the big house to have breakfast with his family and to tell them what had happened, and she drove over to her parents' place where she'd asked Miz Rose to meet them.

Her mother answered the door and by the look on her face, she'd had a call already.

"I think you have some stuff to tell us, huh?"

"I didn't say anything last night because I didn't want him upset before bed," she said to her mother quietly. "And because," she sighed, "I just didn't have anything left to deal with it last night and it would have ruined your sleep and I just couldn't."

"Okay. I understand. But we worry about you. Next time, just tell *me*."

"Stop whispering in there!" her dad called out from the kitchen.

Her mom rolled her eyes and led Katie Faith through to where her dad, Miz Rose and TeeFay already waited. Katie Faith simply launched into the story, not wast-

ing any time, editing it the best she could to give her
parents the information but keep her dad calm.

By the end though, he was red-faced and clearly
pissed off. Katie Faith snuck looks at her mom to follow her lead on how to proceed with this.

"Maybe you could all fill me in on some history. Miz
Rose, you've said this situation has been going on for
decades now. What do you mean specifically?"

She had a hard time believing that if she went to Jace
with the facts, he'd listen to reason. But she needed to
understand all the facts better first.

"Yvonne Johnstone."

Yvonne was one of the Pembry elders by marriage.
Goodness knew all the ways they were kin to one another, but she was a witch married to someone in Darrell's granddad's generation.

"One of the first witches from my generation to essentially be traded off to the wolves in what they call
a dynastic sense. She'd been set to marry a witch, and
after a meeting between her parents and the parents of
a werewolf she ended up engaged to him. Her dad got
more business and the pack got themselves a witch."

Katie Faith looked to her mom. "Momma! I can't
believe no one ever told me this story."

To be fair, every time she'd ever seen Yvonne and
Dean together they seemed happy. Their kids, unlike
Darrell and some of his brothers, made Katie Faith be-
lieve not all Pembry wolves were elitist jerks.

But they were a powerful family in the pack.
Yvonne's magic most surely was one of the reasons.
Having a witch in your pack, especially a powerful
one meant your alphas could change forms far more

quickly. It meant you could manage your own hunting ground and family.

She'd always considered it a beautiful sort of synchronicity, but this was something else entirely.

"I know we're up here in the woods and all, but this is Middle Ages stuff," she told her parents.

Miz Rose chuckled. "The more power the shifters gain, the less they see us as an independent power and partner in this town. We're the boys and girls they marry to keep their packs strong enough to rival one another. It used to be that we all lived here and worked together. Our magic was complementary."

"Now it's all wolf dominance displays and silliness. Like they're the only voices that matter," her father said.

Katie Faith sighed, shaking her head. "I want you to know Jace isn't like that. He doesn't treat me like that. Heck, his grandma makes me pie! His brothers carry my stuff up the stairs if Jace isn't around. In all my interactions, especially since I moved in, his family has been very warm and lovely to me. And sure, part of it is my power, but I just can't see the next generation of Dooley wolves acting like this. I certainly can't be part of it if that's the case."

"That boy is cow-eyed over you. Patty raised him, along with his grandma on his momma's side. He respects women," Miz Rose said. "But JJ isn't as modern in his thinking."

"And there's bad blood." Everyone turned to Katie Faith. "What? It's no secret. I know what the rumors hint at, but nothing specific. So, tell me why Scarlett said all that about Jace's dad. I know he was repudiated. I've felt weird asking Jace but I know he's forbidden from discussing it and he's a Prime so the rules are extra hard on him."

"I can only tell you what I know, which is based on some personal knowledge but mainly gossip because the wolves closed ranks and no one spoke of it. Josiah was here one day and the next he was gone and no one ever said his name in public again." Miz Rose settled in the way she did before telling a juicy story. Katie Faith already felt bad for Jace.

"Josiah never was much for rules. Or manners. He was one of those men who was so handsome they were pretty. Sweet talker. He got into trouble on and off all his life. He had a taste for too much liquor and other people's wives. Scarlett is walking a very fine line here by bringing that up to you."

"She had venom in her voice." Scarlett was going to try to hurt people Katie Faith cared about. She'd *already* done it with her antics so far.

"That woman has been nuttier than a fruitcake since she was knee-high. You told Jace about it. It's a private matter, a pack issue. When you're married, I expect you'll be part of those discussions, but you've done all you can at this particular time." Avery rapped his knuckles on the table.

"I think we all need to keep ourselves sharp. Katie Faith and the others need to keep training too. She's not the only talented witch in this town I work with. We need to stand together here. I'm not dying knowing our children are so vulnerable."

"Rose Collins you stop that right now. You're not dying any time soon." Her mother sent the older woman a censorious look. "But I agree with the rest. We should all meet more often. Just to keep our community connected. Keep folks strong, but also let 'em know they're not alone. And in that, let the shifters know we're done being played with too.

"Things are going to keep on this way for a long time to come. Even after we fix this current situation," her mother added. "You've gone and hitched yourself up not to just any shifter but a Prime. It's going to be tough sometimes."

"He's a handful, but he leaves me alone when it comes to the important things." She hadn't realized what an important quality it was until Jace. Or, probably to be more accurate, until she was ready to demand it and had a man who respected her independence. "I need to get to the Counter to open up," Katie Faith told them. "I'll talk to you all soon."

Jace had asked Damon and Major to meet him for the talk with their grandparents. They all sat at the table already when he came inside.

"Hey, y'all." He grabbed a seat and began to fill his plate. "Let me tell you what happened down the A&P last night."

Once he'd finished, his grandmother sighed. "I will say that sweetheart of yours makes me like her more by the day. Takes a strong spine to stand up to the fury of a woman like Scarlett."

"Katie Faith is an alpha through and through." Jace didn't hide his satisfied expression. Sure she was little and had a weird sense of humor, but damn she was badass and sexy. "She's not really the issue anyway. Pembrys are over the line here and the witches are going to be mad about it."

He watched his grandfather's face darken, not sure if

he should tell them about the way Scarlett had brought up his father or not. But if they found out—and of course they would—and he hadn't told them, it would be worse. It was his job to share things with his family.

"She brought up *Jace will turn out like his father.*"

"In the middle of the grocery store?" Damon's astonished expression was nearly comical.

"Not the first time they've mentioned the repudiation and his reputation." The set of JJ's mouth told Jace his grandfather wanted to punch someone bloody. "It ain't none of their business who you're like or not like. They're just burnt up their sons are all knotheads and dimwits. You pay them no mind, you hear me?"

"JJ, you need to keep yourself together here," his grandmother warned. "Nothing they say changes a damned thing. They don't matter."

Major said, "But they do. And this is just another in years' worth of rule breaking from Pembry wolves. I can't say shit about my own father, but the Patron of a pack can? In a public place? And this is already all over town. I heard about it about ten minutes after Katie Faith left the store."

Jace sent his brother a glare. It wasn't doing any good to get their grandfather any more whipped up.

Major hardened his jaw, glaring back. "This is about her. They're pissed you snagged her up."

"This has been building for years. She's part of it, sure, but it's more than that."

His grandmother interrupted. "This has always been about strength. Who has it. Who doesn't. Katie Faith being with Jace means she'll lead this pack soon enough."

"Katie Faith has her own perspective on all this.

The witches are stirred up. Last night's events make it worse."

"You need to be sure to tell her to keep them calm," JJ advised.

Jace and Damon snorted while Major shook his head.

"One does not simply tell a woman like Katie Faith what to do," Damon said, imitating Boromir's speech from *Lord of the Rings*.

"You really get her," Jace told his brother.

"She's not just going to let Jace pat her on the head and tell her what to do." Damon laughed along with Major.

"If she means to be at your side, she has to toe the line. That's how it works." JJ's chin jutted out just the same way Major's had a few minutes before.

Jace had absolutely no intention of running anything about his relationship with Katie Faith past his grandfather. It wasn't up for discussion. "This is Dooley business. Right now she's not a Dooley. She's something else entirely and that'll be between her and me." He'd never make her choose her allegiance that way.

JJ rocketed up from his chair and then swayed slightly, the high color from his anger drained away, leaving him pale and shimmering with sweat. He righted himself quickly, wiping his brow with an ever-present handkerchief.

"This is a breach and it should be answered," Jace told his grandfather before he got any more worked up. "I'm Prime, let me handle this."

His grandmother got up under the pretext of getting something from the fridge, but on her way she took a long, careful look at her husband before meeting Jace's eyes for a moment.

His grandfather suffered from Roame's Disease. An illness that struck only werewolves. Little was known about it, though certainly more than even a decade before. Though he was much better, stress could cause flare-ups resulting in debilitating abdominal and chest pain.

"Yeah, you handle it. I'm available if you need me," Damon told him and Major echoed that offer.

"I appreciate it." Jace stood, clearing his dishes away. "I've got to run now. I'll check back in with you later or if anything else changes."

Thing was, he realized as he drove in to work, *everything* had changed.

Chapter Fifteen

"Well, no one is ever going to accuse me of having a green thumb," Katie Faith told Miz Rose as they worked side by side in the big flowerbeds in her front yard the next day.

"You have a deep harmony with the earth, but your talents lie—like your mother—with defense. With protection and management. It's why you do so well with numbers. You can't make your roses bloom like your daddy can, but you can manipulate energy incredibly well."

She beamed under Miz Rose's compliments. That she respected the commitment Katie Faith had and the hard work she'd put in to train meant a lot.

In the two months she'd been back, Katie Faith had gone from thinking of her magic as something she only brought out on special occasions—like the good plates at Easter—to using it like another limb.

It wasn't even a matter of calling it anymore. All these lessons had really worked because now it was always there, ready. It had been such a simple revelation, but it had shaken her to realize all her potential had just been waiting for her to take the reins.

There was a great deal of joy in that discovery. It wasn't like she could shape shift or fly, magic didn't work like that for witches. But she had her own talents. Though she couldn't get green things to love all over her like her dad could, she used her magic to dig into the soil, to loosen and move it out of her way.

Magic was in a sense, physics. It was the ability to use energy to make other things happen. Moving them, like with big dumb werewolves. Pouring energy into other things to make them grow, heal them. Aimee's magics could soothe and calm, for instance.

No love potions or death spells. No, learning to be a witch was about letting her magic flow through her just right. It took control she had to learn. Gardening was Miz Rose's way to teach using something relatable. And a sneaky one to get some free labor from her students.

Whatever the cause, she got it in a way she hadn't with other lessons on the same topic. From a trickle slowly to a waterfall, Katie Faith and her magic learned each other as they became more and more enmeshed.

"Up until two months ago I had no idea I could feel like this. My magic fits like my favorite pair of jeans. Thank you." She rocked back to her heels, her knees popping as she stood.

Miz Rose had been sitting nearby in a chair after telling her it was too cold to bend in the dirt. She directed Katie Faith to put the tools away and how to clean up the area.

Though she actually knew how to clean. Apparently not good enough for Miz Rose's standards.

She withheld a snort of amusement.

"Now," Miz Rose said to her as they went back inside, "before you go back to work, or your young man, or wherever; you don't have to thank me. Your magic is yours. It's always there, you simply speak its language now."

"See but when you say it like that it makes perfect sense to me. But I hadn't thought of it that way. You help me so much because you give me perspective."

"Well, you're welcome then. I'm glad you're back home where you belong."

Katie Faith headed over to the Counter to help close up. Her parents had been on in the afternoon, insisting Katie Faith take the morning off to help Miz Rose with her bulbs and to spend some time away from the drama that had seeped into everything since that horrible scene in the market between her and Scarlett.

It had helped remind her just exactly why staying in Diablo Lake was worth it.

Community.

Family.

Smiling, she parked her car out front and as she headed toward the doors, the sound of shouting, howling and then a scream caught her attention as she turned toward the west where the high school and junior high kids walked when they got out at three.

"There's some kind of fuss over at the stump," Aimee said as she came up the sidewalk toward her.

"Don't tell me. Wolves?"

"You told me not to tell you." She shrugged.

Katie Faith sighed. "Should we call the police? What sort of fuss?"

More people began to come out of the storefronts to stare up the street.

Her dad came out. "Katie Faith, you and Aimee get inside right now. Heaven knows what's going on but you don't need to be in the middle of it. I'm going down to have a look."

Both Katie Faith and her mother scoffed as Katie Faith hustled her dad back inside.

"You're the one who needs to stay here. It's a fight at the stump. Isn't the first. Won't be the last."

The stump was a small open area that served as a hangout and park. Unsurprisingly, there was a big, flat stump in the center of the glade where kids hung out on weekends and after school. The trees lining the glade had formed a magical space in the center. It was on that spot where there'd been a tree that'd towered over the rest, filling with power and magic over hundreds of years.

It had to be felled right when Diablo Lake was founded after a lightning strike left it leaning and dying. Timber from the tree made up part of every home in town, posts lined Diablo Lake Avenue that'd been cut from the heart.

Silly shoving matches were a fact of life when there were young people around, especially shifters. But real violence in a spot that was held in such honor by the citizens of the town could very well fracture the community.

"I'm heading over there," Katie Faith told her parents. "If there are any witch kids involved we need to handle that." And chances were this stupid fight was probably about her in some way, so she felt responsible.

"Don't get in the middle of this," her dad replied.

"I'm already in the middle of this. Everything is okay. Just a bunch of dumb kids. But someone has to be the adult."

And he was not in any sort of shape to be that adult, though she'd never say such a thing out loud.

Aimee took up at her side as they hurried up the street, following the noise.

Jace jogged over from his truck, waded into the melee, grabbed shirt collars and started yanking kids off one another.

"I said, everyone knock it off right now!" he bellowed in his best Prime/cop voice.

The principal came rushing over, along with several teachers and parents. Jace eyed the onlookers, giving them his best disappointed-dad face.

"What is wrong with y'all? Kids beating each other silly and you watch instead of step in to stop it? Act like you got some sense! Jim Bodine, don't you dare run off. I know where you live and if you make me chase you down, I'll kick your butt."

The kid stopped with a groan.

"What exactly is going on?" he demanded.

He felt Katie Faith's magic before he caught sight of her as she and Aimee approached. He smiled a little at the edges before he put all his attention back on the group of teens all yelling now about Dooleys and Pembrys. A whole lot of dumb bullshit about bumping shoulders or side-eyed looks got them all het up.

He scrubbed a hand over his face before drawing all his power around him and yelling out, "Enough!" That magic whipped them all into silence and once they obeyed, everyone else calmed down too.

Once they'd given him their attention, he spoke again. "We all live in this town. And we all need to work *together* instead of at cross-purposes." These shifter boys needed a fucking dressing down and as a Prime, it was part of his responsibility.

"Y'all are wastin' my time, making me come over

here to break up a bunch of fights that had gone too far because you were too busy thinking with your dicks instead of your brains. We're neighbors and friends. We're family and this is silliness you're too smart for. Even if some of the adults in this town aren't."

He didn't look at any one kid specifically. "*None* of this is worth truly hurting someone over. You want to be known as that guy who nearly killed someone over a bumped shoulder? That make you tough? That don't make you tough, that makes you a coward. Every last one of you shifters has a responsibility to use your strength wisely and appropriately. You think this crap is appropriate?"

Every head hung low by that point. As it should have. But kids made mistakes just like adults did and he wanted to encourage better control, not beat them up forever. "Get your butts off to wherever they're supposed to be right now. Don't let me catch any of y'all in a tangle again. You hear me?" Jace added a growl at the end, which sent them all scrambling, even the few witch kids who'd been watching the goings-on.

Jace looked for Katie Faith and once he'd noted her speaking to a small knot of witches, he turned his attention back to the situation at hand.

The principal shook Jace's hand. "Nicely handled. Been a bit more agitation in the last few weeks. Mainly along the usual lines." He didn't need to say Pembrys and Dooleys, everyone knew it. "The kids are usually better at policing themselves and breaking things up before it comes to violence."

As well they should. That pack-enforced behavior was an important lesson most shifters grew up with.

How they created lasting bonds with their peers and elders.

"Gonna need to reinforce control and discipline over the next little while within the packs," Jace said as he caught Katie Faith's smile as she made her way over to where he stood with the group of adults who'd gathered.

"This isn't the first time we've had a rough patch." Jace's Uncle Talmage tipped his chin. "Won't be the last, either. There's no call to get worked up because this is how it goes. You gave 'em a spanking. They needed one. Things'll even out soon enough."

Uncle Tab was the smartest of his generation. He'd have made a great Patron but he wasn't interested. Told Jace he could get a lot more done from the background than in the leadership seat. Because of that, his grandfather had focused his attention on Jace and his brothers.

His grandfather underestimated Tab's strengths, but once Jace was Patron, he wouldn't make that mistake. His uncle was a huge asset with an encyclopedic understanding of their history. Not just Dooleys. Not just werewolves or shifters, but Diablo Lake.

As a teacher at the high school, he had special insight on how the younger generation viewed things. Young people weren't as silly and dumb as his grandfather thought. If Tab wasn't alarmed, Jace could allow himself to worry a little less.

He nodded his thanks to his uncle, giving him a respectful tip of the chin.

"I'll keep checking in with you," Jace told the principal. "Make sure things are all right. Give me a call if you have anything you want me to know or you need me to come out. I know both those boys; I'm doubting either family's going to call to complain, but if they do, send them my way as well."

If they were smart, they'd back Jace up and go about their business. If not, he'd smack them down too.

Everyone dispersed, including Aimee, leaving Jace alone with Katie Faith.

"Hey there, Officer Dooley." She kept her hands tucked into the front pockets of her jeans and he knew it was to keep from touching him.

He couldn't help but send her back a look that told her he felt the same way. Every single part of his being screamed out, *mine* each time he saw her.

"Afternoon. How was bulb planting and witchery with Miz Rose?"

She laughed and he held a hand out. She slid her fingers through his and they set off toward the Counter. "It was good. It's not so much that she shows me spells or whatnot. She explains it to me in ways I can understand. She says I'm learning to speak my magic's language. I think that actually sums it up pretty well. So I'm feeling quite witchtastic."

He chuckled. "Witchtastic? Is that even a word?"

"It is now. What are you up to tonight?"

"I'm off shift in an hour then I promised Damon and Major I'd help them out with a construction job later."

He'd much rather be with Katie Faith snuggling and having dinner, but the more money he saved up from side jobs, the more he'd have for their future.

"Come on by when you're done if you aren't too tired. I have some side work of my own and then I think I'll hang out with my parents a while. My uncle is in town a few days so I thought I'd have dinner there. I'll bring you home some leftovers."

He kissed her. A quick one, suitable for the public. She didn't get on his case about stuff, which he liked.

"I'll text you when we're wrapping up to touch base."

"Third base I hope," she murmured as she sashayed back inside with a wave.

Chapter Sixteen

Damon waited for him outside the squat little city building. "Darrell showed up at the Counter under the guise of looking for you."

Jace saw red as rage flooded him. His skin burned and itched, the magic of the transformation beginning to gather.

And then he heard her footsteps rushing up the street.

"I'm guessing she just heard about what happened from her daddy," Damon said as he planted himself between Katie Faith and the door.

That's what enabled him to get it together. She needed him to be under control. His pack needed him to be under control. And so did Diablo Lake.

He turned. "Hold up, darlin'," Jace murmured as he caught her up in his arms. "Let me get to the bottom of this. I promise you I'll handle it."

"Is he in there? Hiding under his daddy's desk, I bet. He got *my* father all worked up, Jace! I'm going to twist his nuts off."

He and Damon both cringed and sucked in air.

"He's not inside. I'm going to him now, as he says

he's looking for me. Go back to the Counter and keep an eye on your folks," he told her.

"I came back to Diablo Lake to take care of them. That scumbag came into my place of business and got my recovering father upset. I'm not just going to let him get away with this." Her chin jutted out and he was torn between annoyance and admiration.

"I understand. He *won't* get away with it. I'm asking you to let me do my job as Prime and as a cop. Please."

She looked him over carefully and finally let out a breath. "I expect a full update very soon. If he comes anywhere near me and mine again I'll handle it."

He sighed. "Okay, I get it." Jesus she was hot. Also, trouble. So. Much. Trouble. "You and yours are me and mine. You understand that? Go on back to work, now. I'll check in with you soon." He risked a quick kiss and she allowed it before turning on her heel and stalking away.

"Damn, boy. You got yourself a keeper there," Damon drawled. It was a joke, but they both knew it was true.

"She's a goddamn handful, that's what she is. Is he inside?" Jace asked his brother.

"No. Dwayne shuffled him out right quick. She was right about that. Darrell may be looking for you, but his daddy don't want him found."

"Darrell and I have unfinished business." That he'd gone to Katie Faith's family business to stir trouble was a direct attack on Jace. And it got his woman all riled up. He found himself hating seeing her upset more than anything he'd ever hated. He just wanted to fix it for her. Make her smile.

"I imagine so. Scarlett is laying low after that stunt she pulled at the market day before yesterday."

"It's not over. But for now, I have to give Carl a quick update on that stupid fight down at the stump and go find a shithead who needs his ass kicked. Dwayne's been ducking me so I haven't had a face-to-face with him about her yet so I guess that's two shitheads."

"Don't do it without backup."

Jace curled his lip. "If Darrell can't handle me, he needs to be taught the hard way. I don't need a posse to go with me."

"He's normally not the brightest, but as of now he's backed up against the wall. He's acted like a total jack-wagon in front of everyone. His momma broke Pack rules. His daddy sure as hell can't step down and let *him* lead the pack. He's not even Prime yet and this makes it even less likely that he will be. Desperate people do desperate things," Damon warned. "I'm your enforcer. Let me or Major come along."

"The day a wolf comes at me from behind is the last one that wolf draws breath." He'd learned that at seven years old. It wasn't something he was prepared to be merciful about ever again.

Damon grinned, nodding. "Good. Okay then. Still, I think you should have me there. Another witness will be useful and most likely keep things from exploding into violence. Though if anyone needed some violence in their lives, it's Darrell."

"Give me twenty minutes to handle this other stuff first and I'll meet you at the house," he told Damon, who agreed, ambling off.

Not quite twenty minutes later, he and Damon drove over to Dwayne's, but parked on the next street over.

Before he got out of the truck, Jace turned to his brother. "This isn't just pack business. This is about the treatment of Katie Faith."

"Which *is* pack business. She's your woman. Which makes her ours too. He'll probably avoid answering the door but if we come around and enter from his back gate it might be better." Damon got out before Jace could argue and they headed to Dwayne's place where they found him on his back deck.

Before he stepped into the yard, Jace held his right hand up, palm out. A gesture letting Dwayne know he wasn't out for blood. Just yet.

"What are you doing here?" Dwayne demanded.

"I'm here because several wolves in your pack have been causing problems in Diablo Lake. I've tried to engage you on this in your office multiple times but you've been out every single time I called or dropped by. Imagine that. Your Patron came dangerously close to spilling pack secrets to a witch in the middle of a crowded grocery store. She also used her size to intimidate Katie Faith."

"You need two wolves to make that clear?" Dwayne taunted.

Tedious given the presence of two of Dwayne's cronies sitting on the deck with him and the others inside the house. In any case, Dwayne Pembry didn't pull his strings.

"And this afternoon a bunch of wolves got into it down at the Stump. There were witches involved though lucky for you, none got hurt. To top it off your son has attempted to harm and intimidate Katie Faith and her family."

Dwayne's derisive snort had Damon tensing up at Jace's side.

"He showed up at the Counter less than an hour ago, directly after that mess at the Stump and claimed to be looking for me. Avery was there and between that and Scarlett's behavior at the market, his health is jeopardized by all this stress. You must know that as Prime of the Dooley Pack and as Katie Faith's man, this can't be tolerated."

Ah. *That* Dwayne hadn't known about Darrell going to the Counter. Jace could tell by the way Dwayne jerked ever so slightly at the mention.

"Scarlett was feeling protective of the girl. She was once like a daughter to us. You can't fault her for trying to warn Katie Faith about what she was getting into with you and yours," Dwayne said.

"Revelation of proceedings held by repudiation tribunals is a violation of pack law. Using shifter strength and speed against nonshifters is also forbidden. It's not like you can claim not to know the law, Dwayne. You have a pack discipline problem and it's spilling out into my pack and into this town. As Prime, as a cop, I'm here to tell you to fix it or others will do it for you."

Dwayne stood but Jace didn't move a muscle. "I don't take orders from a Dooley."

"You need to deal with your ego so you can get your house in order. And since I'm here, why doesn't Darrell come say hello? Since he's looking for me and all," Jace said.

"He's not here. I'll tell him you came by and I'll tell you to be going now." Dwayne had gotten some of his composure back.

"Of course he isn't. Remember what I said, now. Get your pack in check while you still can and stay the fuck away from Katie Faith and her family." Without another word, he and Damon walked out the way they'd come in.

Chapter Seventeen

It turned out Jace didn't need to find Darrell because the dumbass came to find him first as he and his brothers finished up their construction job, loading debris into the dumpster when Darrell came screeching up in his car.

"Well now." Jace jumped down from the bed of the truck, tossing his gloves on the bench seat. "Look what the cat drug in."

"I been looking for you," Darrell said as he tried to look tough. Not tough enough to have come without four of his wolves for backup.

Jace rolled his head on his neck, undoing all the kinks as he widened his stance a little. Taking up more space. Showing his dominance and power. Then he tipped his chin, lip curled to show his teeth for a moment. "And here I am. Brave of you showing up at the Counter. Gold star at being a stupid prick with his head up his ass."

Jace didn't take his attention from Darrell. Every single bit of his focus was on the other wolf.

Darrell growled at him, snarling a little. But Jace held his ground, not giving even the slightest flinch.

The wolves Darrell had brought with him began to inch back and show physical signs of submission.

No matter how hard they fought it, if Jace was truly a dominant wolf, their physical reaction, their body's need to submit to his will would show and only the strongest like another Prime could hold out if he truly pushed it.

But Darrell wasn't Prime material. No matter how much his momma wanted him to be, he wasn't the son capable of holding the pack together. Jace let that show in his eyes, the utter disdain for Darrell and his weakness.

"I came here to tell you to keep your complaints about my mother to yourself. Loser." Darrell looked like a big baby right then.

"Your Patron was out of line. Handle it and there'll be no reason for her to get called out." Jace kept his gaze on Darrell but knew his brothers had fanned out to be sure they didn't get flanked.

Tension hung heavy in the air as Jace showed his teeth. But not in a smile. "You done crying at me now? Because I've got a few things to let you know."

Darrell's eyes widened. "You got a mouth on you."

By that point, several more wolves from both packs had shown up, gathering around. Though dark was just beginning to settle, none of them needed the outdoor lights that would flicker to life soon.

Being a shifter meant fantastic hearing and vision. Enough that everyone standing around heard and saw the whole thing. Jace could have been diplomatic, but that wasn't what this situation called for. Darrell had been pushing and pushing and now that they had an audience, a public lesson had to be doled out which would handle a lot of other business at the same time.

He'd be Patron soon. He'd be married as soon as he could convince his witch to do it. There was no way he'd live the next stage of his life dealing with petty bullshit like this, much less anyone harassing Katie Faith or making her unhappy.

Jace tipped his chin to look down his nose at Darrell. "What's so important that you've made your pack look bad? *Again.*"

"Don't worry about what Pembrys do. Know your betters. Y'all can barely manage being Dooleys." Darrell sneered.

Damon snickered because the big dumb asshole was more funny than ferocious. And because part of what made his brother so scary was that he could be joking one moment and breaking bones the next if he got pushed too far.

It was mocking and provocative and the perfect response.

Darrell's face darkened as his normally handsome features turned vicious. He rounded on Damon. "What are *you* laughing at? Your momma got around and your daddy shamed your entire family. Your brother's new lay is my *leftovers.*"

All of which had been a miscalculation on Darrell's part. One he might have realized right as Jace leaped at him, fist connecting with his nose to a chorus of *ooohh-hhhh* from the bystanders on both sides.

The man let the wolf fuel his strength, but kept back. *That* was control.

Newly disgusted, Jace let himself use the force of the punch to let his body connect with Darrell after his fist had. They hit the ground in a tangle of limbs as Jace kneed him in the side, getting astride his opponent's chest, Jace's knees impeding the fists flying in his direction as he punched Darrell's face again, and twice more.

Bone crunched. Blood spilled hot and slick, the sticky-sweet scent of it rising on the air. Inciting.

"Piece of garbage!" Darrell finally got himself together to launch a counterattack, landing a fist to Jace's gut.

Jace didn't bother with words as Darrell threw him off and he landed in a crouch before standing slowly. Astonished dismay stamped itself all over Darrell's face as Jace so easily got his balance again, ready for more.

"Son of a whore."

The angry shouts of reaction from the bystanders turned, sharpened back in Darrell's direction as Jace plowed into him at high speed, his shoulder to Darrell's gut as he straightened his legs and heaved the other man up and over his back to the pavement.

Moments later the heavy thud was followed by all the breath exhaling from Darrell's body as he hit the ground.

Jace watched Darrell try to stand on shaky legs. "You didn't know a Prime could move like that, did you? Because you aren't one and you never will be. Just you know it was a Dooley who bested you just now. And who always will."

It was then Jace noticed that his grandfather stood, his arms braced across his chest as he'd been watching the fight. He'd shown up with Uncle Tab at his side. The crowd had grown to about two dozen. If Jace wasn't careful—no matter how much he wanted to grind Darrell into dust—a full-blown riot might break out.

"You're trash. The whole lot of you barely fit to do

more than clean up after the rest of us. Pump the gas and do the yard work. Lazy and shiftless. Your daddy done got hisself killed because—"

"Shut the hell up!" Dwayne came into the circle of shifters, aiming his command at his son. "Get your ass in that truck right now, boy." He pointed to the running Ford not too far away with a Pembry cousin at the wheel.

Jace turned to Dwayne, pointing. "This isn't over. You can't just run in here and intervene. He bought himself every single blow. You can't pay his bill."

"He's upset."

"After decades of making excuses for Darrell that's all you have left?" JJ demanded. "You heard what he said. He's out of line. Now he's going around starting fights, inciting witches—who're pissed at us anyway case you haven't noticed—and you're going to step in because of this *mysterious upset*?"

"You made your point, Jace," Dwayne said, avoiding JJ's questions. "No call in putting him in the clinic."

Werewolves healed most injuries quickly enough. But they weren't immune to pain, and the more damage they took, the longer the recovery would be. Darrell would most likely need to shift when he got home and spend the rest of the night as wolf. He'd wake up in the morning just fine, maybe a little sore.

"And what was my point, then? If I made it, that is." Jace left his hands at his side. The stance still ready to spring at any moment. He let that show to Dwayne too.

"What is it you want out of this?" Dwayne asked, clearly wary.

Jace didn't bother hiding his sneer. "We already talked about that not even six hours ago. You have discipline problems in your pack that are involving the rest of this town. What are you going to do about it? Because we both know, just like everyone here, that your fuckup of a son isn't going to listen to you and you're not going to discipline him hard enough to be sure he won't go shooting his mouth off. I *want* Pembry to stop stirring shit up in Diablo Lake and I *want* you, as Patron, to guarantee that."

Carl rushed up, bulling his way through the crowd. He took a look at Darrell sitting, still bloody and dazed in the truck and then straight over to Jace with his battered fists. But Jace didn't care. He *couldn't* care about that because right then he was the Prime of the Dooley wolves and this wolf had broken rules and threatened Katie Faith more than once.

"I can promise to do what I can to keep everyone calm but only if Dooley does too." Dwayne spread his hands out, palms open in some trumped up gesture of goodwill.

"Not what I need from you. We're past *do what I can*. They're your wolves. Be a leader. If not, others are going to handle the things you won't. You're going to tell your wife to keep her mouth shut about closed disciplinary hearings. And she's going to keep her distance from the Gradys. As will your son. You hear me, Dwayne? He gets Katie Faith this upset again and his daddy won't be able to save him."

"This is all Katie Faith's fault," Dwayne said with a snarl. "We were all doing just fine before she came back."

If Damon and Major hadn't been there to grab him as he went for Dwayne's throat, Jace wasn't sure what would have stopped him from beating the other man unconscious.

"You keep her name out of your mouth too, Dwayne."

"Think with your head. She's the problem."

"After years of total peace and harmony, a young woman returns to her hometown to plot the demise of your pack? Really now? *You're* the problem. You and your lazy, coward of a son. You leave her alone. She don't want none of y'all."

"This isn't over," Darrell shouted from the car.

Jace looked to Dwayne. "You remember what I said here today. Just so there's no misunderstanding later when he gets caught out for all the shit spewing from his pie hole."

"You can't talk like this," Dwayne said. "I'm Patron of the Pembry wolves. You have no authority with me and mine. Who do you think you are?"

There it was. That holier-than-thou, shit-don't-stink attitude. He stood there even after everything that'd been happening and still thought he was better than any Dooley.

Jace moved fast enough that Dwayne couldn't prevent his step backward and gasp of surprise. He leaned in, owning the other wolf's space. "I'm Joshua Carron Dooley. Prime. I'm telling you because it's your job to lead or to get out of the way of someone else who could. So go on and make me prove you wrong, old man," Jace whispered.

He let his wolf get so close to the surface it showed in his eyes. His wolf didn't respect Dwayne Pembry at all.

He blew out his breath to be done with Dwayne's stink.

And then turned his back, walking across the pavement of the parking lot to the truck where he'd been dealing with concrete debris. He put his gloves on and returned to work.

"Unless any of you plan to pay my light bill, get the hell home and let us do our job," he said as he hopped up into the bed of his truck.

The crowd in the lot began to disperse, get in cars and drive away. Once the scene had calmed down some, JJ hobbled over as Major finished tying down the load.

Jace told him about the conversation he'd had with Dwayne at his house earlier and JJ sighed at the end, even as he smiled faintly.

"You handed his ass to him. As for what he said… Your mother was a good woman who had the misfortune of falling in love with my son." His grandfather's voice was quiet, but the three brothers heard him just fine. "You've done her memory proud. All three of you. As for your dad getting himself killed?" JJ's pain washed over his face. "You know that's true. I wish it wasn't. But if it hadn't been then, it would have been some other time for the same type of reason. The more you show them how they can push your buttons with talk about him, the more they're going to use it against you. Don't."

Their grandpa mopped his face while Jace and his brothers shared a concerned look. He was pale. Too pale. Too out of breath. Suddenly Jace saw him, not as the hearty and hale man he'd been all of Jace's life, but as a man who was getting older. A man fighting poor health during a crisis in the pack and in the town.

"We've got this handled. There's nothing to be concerned over."

"Hey, Grandpa, why don't I drive you home? You're on the way," Damon said.

"I'll follow along in a few minutes," Jace told them, knowing he had to face Carl.

"You're a cop here, you can't just have battles in the street." Carl's stance was less than confident. Jace knew he probably agreed with what'd been done, but he couldn't have his cops disobeying.

"He came at me. I defended myself, my woman and my pack. I did it in my off time. I'm not wearing a uniform or on duty. I work for you, yes, but I don't put aside who and what I am. Not totally. I did what had to be done. To prevent even more nonsense. And I'd do it again. I know this puts you in a hard place, but I have to do this."

"If he complains I'm going to have to put you on paid administrative leave." Meaning Dwayne. "You're a public employee."

"Go ahead on." Jace shrugged. "Seems to me if Dwayne can be mayor, I can be a cop. But whatever, I have responsibilities and I won't shirk them. Now. My grandfather's health is shaky and I want to check on him before I get back to my other job."

Carl sighed heavily. "Call me before you come in tomorrow. Let's just keep updated on what's happening. And off the record? Darrell is a punk for getting Avery so upset. He deserved a punch in the face." He spun on his heel and headed out.

Chapter Eighteen

A few days later, Katie Faith and Jace worked together to finish up a planter box that ran around the front of the mercantile. She liked working with him, making things pretty. He was big and strong and it was surely a pleasure to watch him at it.

He just did it to keep his grandmother happy—which made Katie Faith go all gooey—but no matter the cause, he was shirtless and sweaty and all was right with the world.

He hadn't said much about the fight he'd gotten into with Darrell and she hadn't pushed for details. Heaven knew she'd heard all about it before he'd even come to her door that night.

It had been, in part, about her. But she also knew it was bigger than that. So she figured he'd come to her with it when he was ready.

Until then, she'd watch his grumpy ass—shirtless, sweaty, gorgeous—haul stuff around and dig in the dirt.

"How's Avery?" Damon asked as he dropped off several plants for Katie Faith to place.

"I think I've managed to talk them into going to Nashville for a week. He's got a bunch of doctor's appointments coming up at Vanderbilt and things are so stressful here for him." She shrugged, guilt swamping her. "His blood pressure has been high and so he'll agree, most likely, because he knows Mom's right about him ending up in the hospital again if he's not careful."

Damon knelt as he gently tapped the bottom of one of the containers to free the plant. "This isn't your fault, you know."

"It is. But I appreciate your saying that."

"Goddammit, Katie Faith, stop that right now." Jace picked her up from her crouch, kissed her hard and set her back to her feet. While she still reeled, he got in her face again. "As much as I think you're a miracle, you're not the reason for all this. If it wasn't you, it'd be someone else. Something else. This is about power and balance. And leadership. I won't have you beating yourself up over it."

He was so stern and sweetly concerned at the same time she couldn't bring herself to argue with him.

His hands on her shoulders anchored her, gave her a safe place.

"Don't try to change my mind with that face either."

That made her laugh and throw her arms around him even as he told her how sweaty and dirty he was.

"Believe me, buster, I know just how dirty you are," she said in his ear before letting go.

"Don't try using *that* to change my mind either," he murmured before kissing her.

"Aw jeez, every time I see you two you're all over each other," Aimee said as she approached.

"Disgusting, right?" Damon asked her.

"I guess it's okay if you like to see two gorgeous

people making out all the time. Usually it keeps her stunned enough that she barely notices when you steal food off her plate."

Damon nodded. "That's an excellent tip. Thankya kindly."

"If you're done mocking, Aimee, can you please bring that watering can over here and soak this bed?" Katie Faith pointed at the work she'd just done before she moved to the boxes lining the front railing. Even in the coldest part of winter, many of the trees in town would still give fruit. The geraniums she tucked into the freshly turned potting mix would be brilliant red and pink into the spring now that Katie Faith lived upstairs. Her presence there had begun to fill all the spaces around her with magic.

The earth in Diablo Lake gave back to her people. Generations of witches had tended it, nurtured it and protected it. Generations of shifters poured magic back into the air each time they took the change.

Synchronicity.

"Guess who I just saw on my way over?" Aimee asked, trying to sound casual and failing miserably.

"Elvis?"

"Wouldn't that have been cool? Macrae Pembry just narrowly escaped tapping my bumper when he pulled down his parents' drive back out onto the road. He looked mad."

"But still really good though, huh?" Katie Faith asked. Mac was the second oldest Pembry brother. She'd barely had contact with him when she dated Darrell because Mac had been in the army.

She'd had enough to remember how totally gorgeous he was.

"I heard that," Jace muttered, but went back to his work, though he did hammer a little harder than he had before.

"What's he doing back, I wonder?" Damon asked.

"Where's he been gone to? Still in the army?"

"He got out of the military and then went to school in London." Aimee went to refill the watering can.

"He's got to be back for damage control," Jace said after he killed the poor wood he'd been hammering. "Of those boys, Darrell is the biggest jughead, but not the only one. Mac was smart. He got out. But he's trained and he's stronger than Darrell. I'm going to wager he's been called home by Daddy."

That's what Jace would have done in Dwayne's place. His oldest son Billy ran the Pembry freight company most of the folks in town used to special order large items. He worked hard but he'd never be Patron. He lacked ambition as well as intelligence. Samuel, the youngest son, was a dumbass who'd gotten himself arrested and tossed in jail for eighteen months for assault on a visit to Atlanta.

Since he'd been back, Dwayne and Scarlett had kept him on a very tight leash.

"Maybe this will be for the best," he added with a shrug.

"Sure and calories you consume on your birthday don't count." Aimee rolled her eyes and Katie Faith laughed along with her. The two had a back and forth that kept Jace cracking up.

"I don't remember much about him. He was already in the army when I started coming around the Pembry house. But he wasn't a jerk to me. Then again, Dwayne always was nice to me too. And we know how that turned out." Katie Faith dusted her hands off as she stepped back to survey her work.

The front of the mercantile, the place everyone in town bought their nails, hammers, tents, fencing and other dry goods, looked much better with the addition of the new plants and flowers.

"My grandma is going to like you even more now." And she would. Katie Faith had just made the place nicer. Had added her magic and her touch to the area and it worked.

A pretty, sunny smile was his reward.

"I was thinking that old cart out behind the shed would be really pretty if we sanded it down, stained it and then used it out here to put plants in," she told him. "Then I could help with a display of whatever's on sale."

"That sounds like a lot of work for us—meaning me—to do." He frowned and she rolled her eyes. He'd do it because she suggested it. Because it would please her and he liked making her happy.

"It'll be good for business. You like that part. Now's time for lots of gardening projects. Look at you here with these starts and bulbs on sale, just waiting to be bought. Gonna need a new rake I bet. I could work that into the display."

Her energy was infectious, which made him smile before frowning again.

"Halloween's coming up. We can sell pumpkins out here on the grass. Have some hay bales, leaves, you know, all festive and pretty. Merrilee's been doing the baking for the Counter and she mentioned she sells kettle corn at the middle and high school games. I bet we can sell some here, you know with the pumpkins. Tie it in with Founder's Day celebrations as well."

The bump to business would be a good thing. His future as a cop was uncertain, especially once he took over as Patron. He needed to start thinking about where he'd get the work to earn the money to pay his bills.

She walked through the big grassy yard that sprawled from the wide front porch to the street, talking about what she'd do and all the different ways she could make it look nicer and catch a customer's eye.

All the things she'd plant there would say loud and clear that a witch lived there. It also said she was his and part of his family and her magic was theirs and the pack's.

As he watched her, his anxiety bled away, replaced by certainty. Everything was going to be just fine. Better than fine, it would be fantastic.

He knew how to fix things. His life would go on after he left the police department. His witch loved to make money and plans and she knew how to do both successfully. Jace had little choice but to love her utterly and totally.

As she approached him, she cocked her head and he knew she'd figured out exactly what he'd been thinking. He'd also been thinking about sex with her, but that was a constant.

He didn't argue. Instead he said, "Your wish is my command." He bowed low, taking the opportunity to check her out as he did. She looked really cute and sexy with all that hair in a messy ponytail, dirt smeared on her chin.

"I'm super lucky," she said with a grin.

When she hugged him, he managed to say, "You'll get even luckier later tonight," into her ear.

"More than once?" she asked as she went back to her feet.

His heart lightened. As she'd intended. He allowed a smile just for her as he kissed her as long as he could in what was essentially their front yard in front of a whole bunch of people. And then he swiped his thumb over the smudge on her chin.

"The sacrifices a man makes to keep you around," he teased.

"We still on tonight?"

They had a real date. A movie and then beer and wings at the pub.

She deserved to be taken to dinner. Deserved a normal night out from time to time and he'd be damned if he let anything get in the way of that or the sex he'd just promised her.

"I'll meet you back here at six. The movie starts at six thirty."

"Okay. Now get back to work." She swatted his butt before starting to clean up the mess they'd made with tools and lumber.

Some women would have pushed him to share all the details of the fight between him and Darrell. Katie Faith had simply pulled him into her arms when he'd stumbled into her bed that night after spending several hours installing a hot water heater.

The next morning she'd simply told him she'd be there when he wanted to talk about it. He'd tell her after he figured it out himself. Because it wasn't the punching that had left him reeling.

His father had been a specter all Jace's life. Each

time he thought Josiah had been put away, something he did or said would always come back to hurt those he'd left behind.

That Darrell and his mother thought to use those things to slap at Jace and Katie Faith galled him far more than they'd humiliated him.

The whole story was going to spill out at some point. Such things rarely stayed a secret forever. Jace had a good idea of the outline of what had happened, but he wouldn't tolerate the idea that his grandparents couldn't talk about their son but Scarlett felt like she could.

He'd spent years knowing he'd take over at some point and that *some point* seemed to be approaching at a high rate of speed. His grandfather's health had been declining for years, even after he'd gone into remission. Usually a werewolf in his mid-eighties would see at least another twenty years of fantastic health. But JJ had been weakened first by an accident he'd had fifteen years prior, and then the succession of tumors he'd developed in his GI tract had hit one after the next. He'd been in remission, but as a result, he was a lot more frail than he would have been.

All the stress of this nonsense with Pembry, as well as the resurrection of the drama about the death of Josiah had sent JJ teetering after a reasonably long decent spate of health.

Another thing that made him furious with the Patrons of the Pembry wolves. His grandpa didn't need this bullshit.

"Imagine if your face froze like that, Jace." His grandmother frowned at him as he walked into the kitchen at their house.

He smiled, more automatic than genuine, but the hug he delivered was genuine.

"Just thinking about work. How's Grandpa?"

She blew out a long breath. "He's out at the lake today with Russ. They won't catch a thing, but he'll be out on a boat, away from the drama for a little while. He'll stay out at Russ's place and they'll run. That'll be good for him."

Jace nodded. It would be. Russ was JJ's brother. He'd be sure JJ got some relaxation in and would keep him away from town for a few days to get him feeling better.

"Good. You're all right?"

She snapped her towel at him. "I can still take you in a fight, mister."

She probably could. Her path had been here on the home front, raising kids and keeping the house and the pack running while JJ was the muscle.

But that didn't mean she was weak. He'd seen her in action more than once and knew she was lightning quick and strong. Vicious when she needed it.

"You know it!" He held his hands up in surrender, his smile real this time.

"Where's Katie Faith?"

"She headed out with Aimee. There was talk of hair color and nail polish. She did a nice job out front."

His grandparents' house sat just to the north of the mercantile so he knew his grandma had checked out their progress through the big front windows from time to time.

"Looks bright and sunny out there. Even on a cloudy day. 'Course, that's sort of what she carries around with her. It's good she's taking an interest in the mercantile."

"She's got all sorts of plans for pumpkins and kettle corn and hay bales out there." He shrugged as he filled his grandmother in on all the stuff Katie Faith talked about. It was their business and he knew Katie Faith would want him to emphasize they were seeking permission, not making a decision without asking.

"Clever as well as pretty, that one." She waved a hand at him. "You and your brothers need to take a more active hand around here. I'm pleased to see it. She already looked at the books for us. It must have taken her forever and a day but she organized our accounting from your grandpa's scribbles."

"She did?" he asked, surprised.

"Her way of checking on your grandpa, I think. She charms him. I figure if she can handle JJ, she can handle you."

"I think it's the other way around, Grandma." He snorted. "That witch of mine is trouble with a capital T. But she's so cute doing it I can't hold it against her."

She laughed, hugging him quickly. "I like to hear that." After a long pause, she spoke once more. "You and your brothers are going to have to handle this business with Pembry. JJ can. He can do it and he'll win, he always does. But I'm afraid of the price he'll pay. I'd rather be happy and proud that our grandsons are leading the pack with your grandpa at my side. Alive."

"This is going to get uglier. I just have a feeling."

She sighed out. "Scarlett is off her rocker. Darrell is stupid, but yearns for some attention from his daddy. He's got it."

"Mac is in Diablo Lake. Aimee said she saw him earlier today. There's some hope with this if he's still the smartest of the brothers. I can deal with him. Even Dwayne if Mac can keep him in line."

"If not, you're going to have to teach them a lesson. I'm sorry about that. But it's still true. But at least you'll have Katie Faith at your side. She's good for you and this family."

He agreed with all of that.

Chapter Nineteen

Halloween was a pretty big deal in Diablo Lake. Partly because it fell within two weeks of Founder's Day, celebrations everyone in town loved and participated in. Partly because you can't have a place full of witches and shifters that didn't love the pageantry of Halloween.

It suited Katie Faith to see everyone excited by the preparations for events to come, culminating in the Founder's Day dinner dance. She'd decorated the front windows of the Counter the week before with pumpkins as well as setting out displays of nuts and berries. As Samhain approached, she'd add a loaf of dark bread each day for the three days prior.

Three major cultural events that held the community together happened within two weeks so it was collectively referred to as Collins/Hill Days, after the witch and shifter who built what is modern-day Diablo Lake.

This would be her first Collins/Hill Days in four years.

Her first Samhain with Jace. That was sort of weird to think about. Would he know what to do? Think she was weird for it? Darrell had never wanted to participate and she hadn't really cared one way or the other.

With Jace it all mattered.

With this new magic coursing through her it all mattered.

She'd been about to lock her door and head home when Mac Pembry came in, hesitating on her doorstep.

He'd been back in town a week at that point and his presence had coincided with a general easing back of hostility from the Pembry wolves. She didn't know for certain if he'd been the reason Dwayne had declined to make an official complaint about the fight between Jace and Darrell, but she was pretty sure that was the case.

"Hey, Mac." She waved at him. "I was just locking up."

"I was hoping to talk with you a bit," he said.

"I'll let you walk with me. I'm headed home now. That work?"

He nodded, stepping back so she could lock up and meet him on the sidewalk.

"Please don't tell me there's some sort of drama coming my way from y'all. I'm tired and I have plans to work on my dress for the dance," she told him as they began to walk.

He laughed, a little embarrassed at the edges. "I can honestly tell you I'm not here to report on any drama coming your way. I wanted to check after your dad's health. I figured it'd be easier to ask you than call over there and risk upsetting him more."

"I appreciate that. He and my mom are in Nashville this week. He's got a bunch of doctor's appointments and it's been so stressful here I thought it would be good to send them out of it a while."

"I'm sorry for that. Darrell had no call to come to your place of business. Not with you there. Not after what he did and how he's been acting. It won't happen again. I respect you and your family. I don't want bad blood."

"What kind of school did you go to? In London I hear?" she asked because she wasn't sure what she wanted to say to him about wolf business just yet.

"London School of Economics."

"Ah! Now it makes sense. You're good at this whole diplomacy bit."

He stiffened beside her a moment, but they kept walking. "My concern for Avery is genuine. As is my annoyance at my brother for his clumsy, petty slap at Jace through you."

"There we go. See, I can deal with that." She stopped, turning to face him. She wanted to see his expressions as they did this. "Y'all are pushing a lot of buttons in this town and I'm not the only one who is tired of it. Your brother is a dullard, but your momma has got to be kept under control. I won't let you or anyone else use me or my family to hurt Jace. I will react with whatdo-youcallit? Extreme prejudice. You got me?"

He watched her a while, his head cocked to one side.

"I do believe I got you, yes. However, you're smack dab in the middle of this. Not because you're the bad guy but because your allegiance is to Jace who's the Prime of the Dooley wolves. You can't pretend that away any more than the way you've made the front of the mercantile fairly scream a witch lives here."

"Oh really? Please do, near stranger, tell me what I can and cannot do." She narrowed her gaze and he broke eye contact. That was better. "I'm not an idiot. I'm well aware that my being with Jace means I'll be considered part of the Dooley wolves. When the time comes. However, my allegiance is to my family. Always. To the other witches in this town. Don't presume to tell me what I get to think or feel about that. Ever."

He grinned then, totally disarming her. "I'm not the only one who needed to get away from Diablo Lake for a few years. There's nothing wrong with diplomacy, you know."

She nodded and they continued on their way. "I asked because you were good at it. It was a real compliment."

"Oh. Thanks. So maybe we got off on a weird footing today and we can have a do-over?" he asked.

"Welcome back to Diablo Lake, Mac."

He laughed. "Thanks. You too. I've waited a while before talking to Jace. I wanted to let him get used to me being around. Would you please let him know I'll be giving him a call this coming week? Believe it or not, Katie Faith, I don't want any contention between packs. It's a waste of power and energy." He shrugged.

That she believed with all her heart. And hoped he was as sincere as she thought he was. "I will. And I'll tell my dad you were asking after him."

They parted ways at the end of the block when she crossed one way and he headed the other.

Jace was outside the mercantile, loading big bags of animal feed into the back of a customer's truck as she approached.

She paused to take in the glory of the way he moved. So strong and confident in himself. Wearing his typical serious face, he was intent on his work until he stopped, sniffed the breeze and turned to lock his gaze on her.

"Sweet Baby Jesus," she whispered. He was so damned gorgeous she didn't know what to do with herself. She knew she was blushing like mad, but he looked at her, and then began to stalk over, like she was something he wanted to eat up in one bite.

"Hey there, Katie Faith," he murmured.

"Hey there, Officer. Whatcha up to?"

"Proving you right about bringing more people in off the street because the front of the place looked better. We've sold more pumpkins over the last week than we did all season long."

It made her so happy to hear that. To know she'd done something positive for him and his family.

"I love being proven right."

"I'd never have guessed. Now tell me why you smell like a Pembry."

She told him about her conversation with Mac as he frowned.

"You're going to have such a big wrinkle between your eyes from all that frowning by the time you're sixty. Jeez," she told him at the end of the tale.

"Why did he come to you? I don't like it." He crossed his arms over his chest and got all bulgy. She may have lost consciousness a second or two and she really wanted to jump on him.

"Maybe he came to me so you could get all your frowning and flexing done in advance. Or just maybe he thought I'd be a good person to approach you."

"Must be it." He snorted at her. *Snorted.*

"Suddenly I'm really thinking I'd rather not ride you like a stallion and leave you sweating and unable to move. I'm thinking I'm going to bed tonight *alone,*" she said as she began to walk away.

Panic washed over his face as he followed in her wake, trying to look casual so no one knew he'd pissed her off and was running after her.

"What are you mad for?"

She jogged up the back stairs and then to her door. "You know what I'm mad for. You snorted at me."

"I snort at you all the time. You say ridiculous stuff on a regular basis."

She couldn't really argue with that. But that didn't mean she was going to let him blow her off or underestimate her.

"Wolves aren't the only power in this town and don't you forget it."

"I haven't. I'm suspicious of his motives in coming to you, is all. I don't do anything without a reason and I figure he's much the same. Always was smarter than the others. He makes you part of this and it puts you at risk. I don't like it."

His pouty frown was even cuter than his alpha frown. "For what it's worth, I think he was sincere about trying to ease the tension between Dooleys and Pembrys," she said, wanting to reassure him. "You can talk to me about stuff, you know. I'm not dumb. I won't betray a confidence and I might have something to offer."

He heaved a sigh but didn't say anything else and she finally lost her composure. He'd been holding back about the fight and she knew whatever had happened was eating him up. If he thought to protect her while he managed something terrible on his own she'd kick his butt.

"When are you going to tell me what the hell happened at the fight between you and Darrell?"

He jerked as if she'd hit him. "What do you mean? I told you what happened."

"No. You gave me a basic overview. He was insulting and goaded you into a fight. You kicked his ass.

His daddy had to come save him. Blah blah. I know that stuff. I'd gotten phone calls about it before you got home that night. This was different. Things between you and Darrell are personal but not about me. *Tell me* what's going on."

He stood so still, muscles appearing to lock into place as he fought some sort of internal battle.

She moved to her kitchen and got a kettle on for a cup of tea. "There's leftover spaghetti in my fridge if you want to stay for dinner," she called out. "I'm going to change."

Jace had been shoving aside talking with her about what had happened ten nights past between him and Darrell.

She hadn't pushed, which he'd appreciated. But he'd also used it to hide behind as an excuse to just let it lie.

He got the leftovers out and set about heating them up while making a batch of garlic bread and some cucumber and onion salad.

By the time she came out, her hair down, face scrubbed clean of makeup, wearing soft pants and a T-shirt, he'd managed to get her tea steeping and found the words he needed.

She saw his progress on dinner and smiled. "Thank you."

He nodded, pushing the tea at her.

"I bought beer, it's in the fridge," she told him.

"I saw. Thanks for thinking of me." He sat. "Do you know much about my father? About what happened to him?"

"Not much. I mean, there are rumors. I'm sure you know that."

"Rumors of what? I want you to be honest and tell me. You don't need to soften it for me."

"That he was executed for violating pack law and that it'd been about a woman. I always figured it had to be pretty bad, much more than just an affair. I mean, that code of silence thing is pretty hard core and only for the worst of crimes, right? But you and your brothers weren't outcast and you're Prime, so I gather whatever it was didn't blow back on you."

"That's pretty much it. I don't know the whole story myself. The sentence was handed down in secret. He was executed and his name was struck from our records so all I had was rumors really. The same ones you heard I bet. Before I beat the hell out of Darrell, he brought it up. And so did Scarlett to you." Jace licked his lips. "I hate that they can talk about it, hell, that Darrell and his momma probably know the details and I don't. Because my family obeyed the law and theirs isn't. And they want to use it to hurt me and hurt you and my pack and it's not something I'm prepared to let continue."

The outrage coursed through him at the utter unfairness in that.

"I imagine that's got to suck. The not knowing. And then Darrell maybe knowing instead? I'd punch him too. How can he get away with that?" She was so angry on his behalf and it mattered so much.

She made things better.

He got the feeling the Pembrys would use anything they could to hurt Katie Faith because she was his only real weakness. Though she made their pack stronger, she was someone he'd die for, which was a way to get to him.

"I made an official complaint about it. Of course

making that complaint to the father of the offending wolf and the husband of another doesn't do much for my confidence anything will be done."

"And in the meantime, they could end your career as a cop." She frowned. "I know Dwayne declined to file a complaint, but I don't like threats like that hanging over you."

That she'd be so angry on his behalf was just another reason he loved her. "Thing is, I've been realizing I didn't really have much of a future in law enforcement anyway. Not as a cop. I'll be Patron soon enough, which means my loyalties would be divided and I'll have to resign. I think the people in this town deserve more than that. Until then though, I'll work as long as I can because my salary allows me to stash money away for our future."

"You're saving for our future?" She blinked back tears as her mood softened.

"Hell yes. You think a mug like me can keep a prize like you without a nice house and money in the bank in case we need a new roof? I can't afford a mansion, but I can keep you well. Our kids will go to college so we'll need to save up for that. Braces maybe. It's my responsibility."

"I don't need a mansion. I just need you. And I need you to not focus so much on braces for children we don't even have because it's making you stressed and grumpy. We've got time."

"Wolves are planners. It's what we do. I guess I assumed you knew that. Why I didn't figure Darrell was lazy with you too, I don't know." He put his palms over her hands. "You're my woman. My mate. Of course it pleases me to take care of you. Thinking about our future doesn't stress me out. Witches like numbers and wolves like plans."

She laughed a moment. "Fair point. You're a lot like engineers at times. Which involves numbers too. But in a way you guys seem to take to from the cradle." She licked her lips. "I love that you want to protect me. Even if I push you when you go too far, you make me feel safe."

It was exactly what he'd needed to hear.

"Your wolf needs to listen to me and trust me." She took his face in her hands and he loved her so much it hurt. "No one wants more for you than I do. We're together in this. So I need you to lighten your load with me sometimes as much as you need to unburden yourself. I'm not fragile. I won't fall to pieces if you share with me. Okay? I don't want you dealing with this crap on your own."

Leaning in, he touched his forehead to hers. So grateful he had her. Letting that knowledge soothe his agitation.

"I want a life with you. Forever. Wolf and man trust you utterly."

"Then what's bothering you? Are you worried about my ability? Or that I'd leave like I did after Darrell dumped me?"

He shook his head, kissing her slow as he backed her into the bedroom. "I'm not worried about either of those things." Hell, he was proud of what a powerful witch she was and he knew to his toes they were together for the long term.

He pulled her shirt off, followed by her bra. All her pretty skin aroused him. Bared just for his touch. For his mouth and gaze.

He drew his fingertips up her ribs, sucking in her gasp as he kissed her once more. Restless and needy, she writhed to get closer. "You're my witch and I'm your wolf. There's special magic in that bond. Can you feel it between us?" He spoke, his lips against hers.

"From the first moment you kissed me I wanted you. Even when I shouldn't have. I never imagined feeling as if I belonged with someone. Not like this. Belonging *to* someone."

Her breath hitched as he cupped her breasts and flicked his thumb back and forth across her nipples.

That was all the last bit of proof he'd needed. Darrell had never even halfway loved Katie Faith. A wolf took mating very seriously. It was more than marriage. It was a true partnership even as he'd continue to protect her however he had to.

"Planning our future will never be a source of stress for me. It's what I'm supposed to do for us. You're my mate. Taking care of you, building a life that makes you happy and keeps you safe is what I was born to do. Nothing pleases me more than our connection."

After a rather hectic few moments of kicking clothing off, they fell into bed, tangled, heated, sliding skin to skin.

He ached with how much he needed her. His pulse a drumbeat in his cock. Her smell aroused him beyond bearing as he licked a trail from one nipple to the other.

She reared slightly, groaning as her nails dug into his ass.

It set him on fire that she demanded her pleasure. So sexy and fierce. He slid kisses down her belly and over to each hip. Her taste beckoned and once he took that first long lick he hummed.

"Delicious."

She shivered as he petted her with covetous hands, kissing her, tasting her as she warmed, heated under his touch.

All his. Every beautiful, tasty inch of her. The strength in her muscles as she strained to get more from him.

He gave it to her, reveling in all that soft, sweet honey between her thighs. Here she was vulnerable and open to him utterly.

The sounds she made drove him, battered at his control as he feasted on her, wanting her orgasm, craving that rush of magic she threw off as she came.

Her fingers tunneled through his hair, pulling him close as pleasure seemed to rush over her skin like a shiver.

Even as she came she wanted more of him. Knew she'd never get enough even if she spent the whole of the rest of her life at his side.

And she planned to do just that.

She tugged his hair. "Inside," she managed around a desire-thick tongue.

"Yes," he growled as he went to his knees at the foot of her bed and brought her to the floor with him, settling her on his thighs as he thrust up into her pussy in one movement that stole her breath.

It drove her wild when he used his strength like that. He could pick her up like she weighed nothing.

So. Hot.

He ran his hands over her skin, sending ripples of sensation through her. In contrast, he fucked her hard and fast.

All she could do was hold on as he sent her careening

over cliffs and into the sea. He was a rollercoaster of a force in her life and she'd never been happier.

"I tell myself over and over that I want you slow but once we get started I can't stop myself from gorging on you," he murmured against her collarbone before kissing the hollow of her throat.

She wrapped her arms around his shoulders, holding him close so she could nibble on his earlobe to make him snarly growl that way he did when she licked him in one of his favorite spots.

"Gorge away," she said as he slid impossibly deeper, resulting in an unladylike grunt.

He gripped her hips, pulling her forward on his cock, sliding her clit against the line of his cock as he ground up and into her.

Just when she was sure she wasn't able to come again so soon, it hit her, sucking her under as she held on, her teeth finding that spot on his neck where he loved to bite her too.

He shuddered hard with a groan and held her in place as he climaxed.

For long moments they panted to get their breath back, still in a tangle.

"I do apologize for doing this on the floor but I seem to have lost control of my lower extremities," he muttered, making her laugh.

"Just don't look under my bed because there're dust bunnies. Oh!" She wriggled free, grabbing a lost sandal. "There it was. Now it's not even sandal season, of course."

"There's such a thing as sandal season?" he asked her from his spot on her bedroom floor.

"Duh. Do you wear sandals in February? No. You wear them in July. Sandal season."

"Well there you go. Learn something new every day, I guess." He rolled to his feet and she had to pause at her closet door to take him in.

"Damn, look what I got in my bedroom. It's a wonder I ever leave."

He grinned at her. "Darlin', if it were up to me, you never would. We'd just lock ourselves in, fuck, sleep and eat. That's all we need."

The way he saw her—his gaze roved slowly from her toes up to her face—left her a little faint.

"Never in my life did I imagine someone who looks as good as you would look at me the way you do," she told him.

"Never in my life did I imagine being able to look at someone like you and know you were all mine."

He didn't tease. His voice was serious, which moved her to seek him out, burrow into his embrace.

Chapter Twenty

Katie Faith knocked on Patty's door as she called out a hello. She didn't want to just barge in and her hands were full anyway.

"Katie Faith?" Patty came into the front room from her kitchen with a smile. "Come on in!" When she got a few steps closer she noted the things in her visitor's arms and hurried to open the door for her.

"Hey there. I got a little crazy with pumpkin and ended up baking all morning long. Want a share of my loot?" She desperately wanted the matriarch of the family to like her and if it took pumpkin nut bread and spice cake, she'd darned well bake her heart out.

"I just made a pot of coffee. Come on in and have a cup with me," Patty told her as she led the way through the kitchen.

She'd been in Patty's kitchen a few times before. Always with Jace. Katie Faith had to find her own way with each member of Jace's family, most especially the woman who had been the only mother he'd had for most of his life.

"I'm glad you came by. I know you've been busy with your daddy and the Counter but you made time to redecorate the front of the mercantile so nice." Patty indicated she sit at the table.

A cuckoo clock on the wall above the fridge chirped once. "I love that clock. I don't think I noticed it before."

Patty carried coffee and plates over for the treats Katie Faith had brought. "I have to disable the bird when JJ is home. We had to come to an understanding about that about thirty years ago or so." The grin she turned Katie Faith's way reminded her of Damon. "Some battles you lose to win the war."

"An excellent relationship tip."

Patty chuckled as she stirred two heaping teaspoonfuls of sugar into her coffee. Jace was the same way. Most werewolves had a wicked sweet tooth. "How are things?"

"In general or anything specific?"

"Let's start with in general and see where that takes us." Patty tipped a fat slice of the pumpkin bread onto a plate for herself.

"I'm doing pretty darned good all things considered. I just finished my dress for the dance. Aimee took pity on me and helped with some of it. I'm the worst with buttonholes. She always has been a whiz at that sort of thing. Business is up. Everyone is so excited about Collins/Hill Days so they're out more. May as well have a hot fudge sundae before heading to get a pumpkin down your way."

"Avery okay?"

"Yes, thanks. As long as he keeps calm, he's okay. He's back in his garden, which means he's not under my mom's feet and there's no incidents with frying pans. He's also back at the Counter three days a week. Says he likes it when he doesn't have to be the one in charge.

I think it's more that he likes that I clean up the mess after he makes it."

"I like that you came over here without Jace. Shows you want to be part of this family more than just his main squeeze."

"I better be his only squeeze."

Patty laughed. "I can see why he fell for you. Some sweet, soft thing would get run right over by him and this family. You know you're going to have to shove him when he muscles into your business. Male alpha wolves are a big pain in the butt. JJ still feels it's necessary to tell me how to make peanut butter cookies after six decades of marriage."

"I love Jace very much even when he's constantly in my business. Trying to protect me like I'm a toddler with a fork near a light socket."

Patty smiled. "Even when he was just a preschooler he would herd his brothers. Make sure they never got hurt. Oh, they beat the snot out of one another plenty of times, but heaven help anyone who came at one because they got all three for their trouble. His mother was like that." She folded a napkin, pressing the fold over and over until it made a sharp pleat.

Katie Faith knew Patty wanted to say more, so she remained quiet. Waiting.

"All his life he's worked to prove he wasn't Josiah." Patty spoke at last. "Sealing what happened only makes it more mysterious when really it was ugly and tawdry and unnecessary. And now they want to use that to hurt him."

"Scarlett and Darrell, you mean?"

Patty nodded. "Twenty-five years have passed and

it's still an open wound. Out of sight is never out of mind. It's always there."

"Someone needs to tell Jace the whole story. I know there are rules about it. Secrecy and all that. But it's going to come out somehow and when it does, don't let it sucker punch him. Please, Patty."

"I took an oath. Like the one you'll take one day when you rule this pack at Jace's side. I gave my word I wouldn't reveal the key details from what happened. I'm bound by that."

"Shouldn't Darrell and Scarlett be bound by that too, then? How is it they get to know and he doesn't? Don't you all know how it eats away at him?"

"They're skirting the terms. It's still a violation, but it's not within my power to make them tell Jace or I'd have made it happen a long time ago."

Katie Faith vowed to find out herself then. She hadn't taken any oath to keep the truth from Jace. He deserved to know what happened. Another wolf might get into trouble for it, but she wasn't a wolf or a Dooley by marriage yet, so she'd damn well do whatever she could to keep him from getting blindsided.

They finished their coffee and sweet treat before Katie Faith said her goodbyes and headed out. She wanted to stop by to check on her mom and TeeFay, who were supposedly spending the day canning but more than likely they were drinking margaritas and watching romantic comedies together instead.

She found them both on the sofa in the TV room watching a movie about male strippers. "I can't turn my back on you two for a second," Katie Faith told them as she came in.

"Canning is done. Why not share some eye candy?" TeeFay held her glass aloft. "Come on in and sit a spell. Tell us why you have that look."

"I brought pumpkin chocolate chip muffins and two bottles of wine."

Her mom grabbed the remote and turned the television off. Aimee came in the back door a breath later, calling out her hello as she stumbled into the room and saw the three of them.

"Well you're just in time, Aimee. Katie Faith brought chocolate and booze so she's got *something* big to say," TeeFay told her daughter as she dropped a kiss on her cheek.

"I don't have a glass yet," she told Aimee, who came back with a jelly jar.

"Bigger than a wine glass. You look like you need it."

She opened the bottle and poured herself and Aimee a glass. Her mom and TeeFay topped off their margaritas.

"If you're pregnant maybe not drink that wine," her mother told her in an undertone.

Katie Faith laughed and gave her mom a one-armed side hug, careful not to spill any liquor.

"I'm not pregnant. He…well he sniffs me and knows when I'm fertile. Pretty cool if you ask me. Anyway. It's about Jace. I need to know what happened with his dad," she said finally. "The wolves have pack law. And that says they're supposed to not speak of whatever the hell his dad did. But Scarlett and Darrell have hinted around it. Used it to hurt Jace and I'm not going to stand for it."

He'd said to her that it was unfair they got to know

and he didn't and that was doubly true when they used that to hurt him.

"They have rules for a reason, Katie Faith," her mother warned pretty halfheartedly.

"I'm not a goldarned werewolf and I'm not married to one either. I don't have to obey their rules about this."

"All we know are rumors because it involved another wolf and you know how close they keep their business to the vest when it's about this sort of thing. Whatever he did got him killed. Not just killed, but struck from their records. JJ and Patty had to officially adopt the boys under pack law or they'd have suffered the same fate."

"For goodness' sake, why? That's awful. Damon and Major were babies. Jace couldn't have been much more than three or so. How could they have been punished for whatever their daddy did?"

"Like I said, this is all mainly secondhand because of all the rules they have."

"Well, that's dumb." Katie Faith fumed on Jace and his brothers' behalf.

Aimee nodded. "Totally dumb. I bet a man made that rule up."

"The same one who invented stiletto-heeled sandals so your toes start to hang off or hurt after about an hour."

"Katie Faith, I know we've talked about your tendency to wander around a point. This is one of those times," Aimee told her.

"Am I wrong about the shoes and your toes?"

"About them having anything to do with the topic at hand? Bless your heart. It's nice you're so pretty."

Aimee patted her knee as they snickered. "And damn I hate those shoes."

"I think they're more sarcastic than we ever were," TeeFay told Nadine.

"Probably."

"So what happened?" Katie Faith repeated.

"There was a girl. There always seemed to be at least one. Boy, I always did feel bad for Jace's momma. He used her beauty right up. And then her hope. That light in her she had all through school had been drained away. He wasn't just a tomcat. He was sort of predatory about it. He'd hound and hound a girl until he finally got bored or she had someone threaten him away."

TeeFay took up then. "Always shifter girls. He never was one for witches, thank heavens. That's part of the reason this has remained such a well-kept secret. Whatever he did back then, he did it to another werewolf and they aren't talking. I just know he was here one day and then the wolves—down to a one—left town. Didn't see any of 'em for several days. Then we woke up and everyone was back except Josiah and none of them were talking. Their elders sent someone to talk to Miz Rose's daddy and later it just sort of made its way through town that no one spoke his name. Time passed and it fell from our minds, I guess, as things like that do."

"It took years for the Dooleys to get themselves back together after that. Pembrys solidified their power then and they've held it pretty tightly ever since. Whatever it was, he did it to a woman or because of a woman, and he caused so much damage he got executed and then erased for it. I just know it was bad or they wouldn't have done what they did. Whether you like it or not," her mother added. "You go marrying into their world, you best realize they're not humans and they have their own rules."

"Why is everyone talking marriage today? We're dating. Seriously yes. I'm in love with him and I don't doubt we'll be together—married and all—for the long haul. But it's early days."

"Is not."

"You're not helping, Aimee." She glared at her best friend.

Naturally, Aimee ignored the look. "Early days my butt. You two are inseparable. You live across the hall from him. You're with him every day even if it's just, um," she darted her gaze over to her mom, "a few minutes before you go to sleep."

Katie Faith rolled her eyes as she struggled not to blush that her mom had been right there when Aimee pretty much said they slept together every night. "Nice save there."

"Oh for heaven's sake! You don't think TeeFay and I know you and Jace are having sex?" Nadine flicked her wrist. "There'd be something wrong with a gal who didn't avail herself of a man who looked as good as Jace Dooley."

Katie Faith dropped her face into her hands, laughing and horrified all at once.

She'd missed this side of her mom when she'd been so very concerned about her father. But that sense of humor, the steadfast strength of Nadine Grady had settled in her once again.

Still didn't mean she wanted to really get into sex talk with her mom. "Okay, moving along."

Aimee spoke. "That's right. Back to the subject. The front of the mercantile? Pumpkins and hay bales and flower boxes? *Come on.* You've known him for a very long time. There's no early days for you two. Not anymore. You're long past that. You're over here finding out what you can so you can skirt around rules everyone else has to obey except those who're trying to hurt Jace. Anyway, your momma's point was that if you go into his world, you have to deal with their rules and customs. Just like he'll have to deal with ours. That's how this works." Aimee sat back and gulped her wine.

Katie Faith sobered a little. "I do accept the rules of his culture and his pack. If I actually was married to him, I couldn't be doing this." Not until he was Patron. Maybe then they could drag the Dooley wolves into some more modern rules. "But I'm not. He said something to me. That I was his witch and he was my wolf and we had a special bond because of it."

Nadine and TeeFay shared a quick look.

"What was that all about?" she asked them.

"He said those words exactly?" TeeFay asked.

"Exactly? I don't know word for word. It was the feeling it gave me. Like we were making a promise. And part of that is me protecting him like he'd protect me," she said.

"Did he say you were his witch and he was your wolf?" her mom asked.

"Yes. Those words. And then he said we had a special bond because of it. He did say bond specifically. Why?"

"There is a special kind of magic between some witches and shifters. Sometimes it's not romantic or sexual at all. Just a union of two people that creates an old magic. Protective magic. That bond, that promise between you, is impenetrable. It's strong, ancient energy these woods don't generally favor folks with on the regular."

"Since all this stupid political marriage crap started to get more witches into the packs, it's happening less and less, wouldn't you say?" TeeFay asked.

Katie Faith's mom nodded after she thought a few seconds. "Yes, I would. But it'll be something to ask Miz Rose because she's the best source for that sort of thing. But it goes to her point that this kingmaking the wolves have been up to with our people has changed the balance here. If you and Jace have this connection I'm glad of it. As your mom because it means you'll be safer and stronger. That this thing you have with the man you love is genuine and special. I couldn't wish for more for you. At the same time, you're going to be involved in so much nonsense. I don't like that they'll hurt Jace through you. And I don't like that they came at you through your daddy. I have some things to say when Scarlett returns my calls."

"You called her?"

"After she did what she did to you in the market? You bet I did. She's lucky you didn't send that buggy straight up her ass."

"God, Momma you have no idea how much I wanted to." Katie Faith giggled. "That wine is kicking in. Here I am, day drinking with my mom. Good times. Hey, do they even make that peanut butter with the jelly swirled into it anymore?"

"Don't let her lead you off topic. She gets worse when she's tipsy," Aimee warned them.

"See if I let you have the last piece of pizza next time," Katie Faith muttered. "So, you called Scarlett.

Did you give her Severely Disappointed Mom or Mom-deusa?"

Nadine laughed. "Momdeusa?"

"Yeah. Like you get so mad snakes pop out of your head and you turn everything you see to stone. Usually accompanied by all three names a child is born with."

"That's a good one. I can recall you making me go momdeusa a time or two. I went more quietly threatening. I'm not disappointed in her. She better run if she sees me coming. But I will have my say to her face before this is over."

"So, in the pro column I have this special old magic connection thing with Jace. It makes me stronger, which also goes in the pro column." She glanced up at Aimee. "In this town the more power you have, the more independence you have. The more choices you have. I'm a big fan of that. Jace is strong. I make him stronger. I'm also a fan of that."

"I saw JJ last week," Aimee said. "He's better. Spending more time with his brother out at the lake. Fishing. Staying out of things."

"Jace has been Prime long enough to prove several times over he's capable of being Patron. I don't think anyone will challenge him. But right now, he, Major and Damon are running the pack in a time of heightened tension and doing a fantastic job. And I think JJ is a crafty old wolf who knows exactly what he's doing to stay away and let Jace lead right now."

Nadine gave Katie Faith a raised brow. "You're going to be good at this Patron thing. That's what you're taking on along with marrying that man."

"I know that's what I'm taking on. And I think it'll be sooner rather than later. I'm not so sure they'll be as excited to have my power because it comes with my brain and my mouth." She laughed. "Well that's not entirely fair. I think there are a lot of shifters in this generation who really do want to make some changes and do what's best for the future of all the wolves in the pack. Just like most Pembrys are more like Mac than Darrell."

She thought about it a bit.

"Really, I'm window dressing. I don't know how I'm supposed to do this any other way. I'm not a werewolf. I can't know all their issues the way one of their own could."

Contrary to popular werewolf folklore a bite from a werewolf didn't "turn" anyone. It could easily do damage, maybe even death without a whole lot of meaning to. Which was why they kept to themselves out there in the middle of nowhere Tennessee.

She'd never be a werewolf like Jace. She was already shaky on the idea of being a wife, she really couldn't make sense of telling Dooley wolves what to do. So she'd lend her strength to Jace and keep on learning all she could about their world—both from inside and outside it—and hopefully she'd be able to be his sounding board as well.

"Does he want to know about us?" TeeFay asked.

"He's curious about magic and the witches here in Diablo Lake. I'm still working on understanding. But he's respectful. And though I have no doubt he'll offer up his opinion on all sorts of things—Lord, that man—I do think he'll continue to be respectful as he learns."

Two hours later, she headed out, grateful she'd decided to walk. The crisp air would do her some good, as would all the decorations on lawns, in front windows and at businesses.

But what did her the best was the feeling that she was home and that Diablo Lake had taken her back with open arms.

Chapter Twenty-One

Jace tapped on her door, waiting for the sound of her footfalls. She'd come, open up, chide him for not letting himself in with his key. Then she'd remind him he was the one who wanted her to lock her door in the first place.

He just liked to see her face as she opened up for him. Liked being invited into her space. Not that he didn't mark it all with his presence once he was there. But he liked that little ritual. It felt like being met at the door. And he loved when she did that too.

But he didn't hear her after a minute and another knock. She was usually home by seven and they often shared a late dinner once he got off his shift.

"Hey!" she called out as she came up the stairs at his back. "I meant to be here by now but I was a dumbass and forgot what the grocery store was like this close to Halloween and Samhain. It was a full-blown crazy-pants mess in there."

He took the bags as she passed. "You should have texted me. I could have met you and helped carry these up."

She smiled, holding the door open. "Well there are a few more down there now, please and thank you."

"Okay. Well. Good." He put the bags down and then headed to her car to get the rest, finding her in the kitchen, unloading items into her fridge.

"Let me drop in the biscuits to cover the chicken I put into the slow cooker earlier."

He pulled her close. "Evening, darlin'."

She snuggled in, hugging him tight. "Did you have fun fighting evil today?" she asked as he put her away from himself and kissed the top of her head.

"The usual Collins/Hill Days stuff. Vandalism of the toilet paper and egg variety. Maisie Ephram made me hot chocolate that she served with a huge slice of apple pie when I found her ratty ass dog once again. So that happened, which puts me in the win column for the day anyway. And now I'm here with you, which means I'm definitely winning."

She paused in her food prep, laying her things down. Making her way back to him, she tiptoed up to kiss his lips. "You're being very sweet. Thank you."

"Sweet? Ha. I sit here and watch you whip up scratch biscuits you'll make to go on a dinner you've been planning all day. For me. I'd be a monster not to be sweet for that."

"Still. I think Maisie is gunning for a win in the apple pie category at the contest on Founder's Day. How's she doing? I just had a slice of my mom's—with a lattice top and crystallized sugar."

"Too much nutmeg for me. But it's a slice of pie and hot chocolate on a day I got yelled at by a bunch of grumpy old guys upset over the usual shit I can't do anything about like leaves blowing off trees when it's windy."

She pulled a beer out, cracking it open and handing it over. "You're home now. Eat something warm. Hang out with your super hot girlfriend. Forget about grumpy old men for the night."

As she dropped dollops of the dough on top of the chicken she looked up a moment with a teasing light in her eyes. "I only want to think about one young grumpy guy."

"I'm not grumpy. I'm efficient."

"You sure are." She gave him a cheerful smile.

"It's two months today since I kissed you the first time. Well the first time since you'd moved back home. It's been sort of crazy, but you, you're everything good."

Katie Faith tossed herself at him. Laughing, full of love, he caught her, holding her against him as she dropped kisses all over his face.

"I love you. Grump and all. I see through all that curmudgeonly attitude anyway. You have a soft chewy center."

"You say the weirdest shit, Katie Faith."

"I'm unique. You're efficient. We're perfect for each other."

Sweet Jesus, they were.

"Something like that. I've never done a Samhain celebration before. I mean of course we did them in school and I've seen the basics. But I want to do this right. What do I do?"

"You want to? Oh. Wow. Well, yes, I'd like that. You there with me. We do different rituals and events over the four days before Samhain but you don't have to do them all. Friday night after work I was going to make an ancestor's altar. Just a way to celebrate those who came before. If you want, you can add your mom."

Jace liked the idea of that. He looked over to where he thought her altar already was. "That's an altar there, right?"

He didn't know as much as he should have about her magic. He wanted more of her.

"Yes, that's an altar. It keeps me centered. Helps me remember to be mindful of what I am. To use my magic wisely and with respect to those who came before. When I was like six or seven, I had trouble focusing enough to use my magic. It felt like a sneeze that didn't quite happen. But all the time. My magic was right there, I just didn't have the ability to shape and own my intent enough to use it."

He bet she hated not being good at something. Witches were very competitive and six or seven was late not to have control.

"My Grandma Opal came over after church one Sunday and she took me outside to find the materials for what turned out to be my first altar." She picked up a river rock, smooth and dark with flecks of gray. "This rock." She put it back on a pretty scarf she'd draped over a table in her living room. With a flick of her wrist, she indicated a smooth disk of wood, some small candles, a silver figurine and some acorns. "And that piece of wood is what's left. I've built it, changed it, added or removed things over time as I need to. But what she taught me then, and what I do today, is that focus and intent take mindfulness. Control and respect for the power Diablo Lake gives to her witches. I didn't get it at first. But after about two months I figured it out."

So fascinating. He took her hand and kissed her wrist, pleased at the way her pulse jumped against his lips. "I bet you did it that first time 'cause you got mad the others were better than you at it."

Her grin told him he'd been right.

"It wasn't that I needed to be the best. There are witches here in Diablo Lake who are far, far stronger than I am. But I just couldn't tolerate Missy Shacklee being able to do something I hadn't managed."

Wisely, he kept his smile mild instead of the laugh threatening his belly.

"Anyway, I write in my journal here. Do my working and spellcasting here as well. The ancestor's altar I planned to put over in that corner. It'll be part of my Samhain altar. I'll put pictures of people who've passed. My Grandma Opal, for instance." A sad smile touched her lips a moment. "My cousin Lorie. You remember her? She got killed in a rollover accident three years ago now."

"I do remember her." He pressed a kiss to Katie Faith's forehead. "So the key is to find something that I could put here that would be a way to think about my mom?"

"Yes. Or some forebear who paved the way. You can have more than one. There's power in ritual. I'm as Protestant as you are, right? But when we sing together in church, or when we pray we engage in ritual. Ritual is a form of memorization. Intense focus." She blushed.

"Are you embarrassed?"

"I guess I've never really described it to anyone else before. It sounds weird to an outsider, probably."

"To the guy who transforms into a giant wolf at will? Really?"

She smiled again.

"I think what you just described sounds beautiful. It makes sense. I never thought of it that way, but yeah, it makes sense. Thank you for sharing your world with me."

"Samhain is a very contemplative time. A lot of people I know do their own rituals and remembrances as well as the ones all the witches in town do together. We do stuff with everyone else in town on Halloween. But the night before that, we do a walk to the graveyard. On the way back we gather up a bunch of leaves, berries and the like to make the decorations for the big feast on Samhain night."

"You do a bonfire too, right?"

"I should have known you'd notice fire. Boys."

He set the table, ignoring her tease. Mainly because she was right. He loved to watch a Samhain bonfire but he'd done so from afar, never really having the reason to be part of the celebration itself.

"Yes, there's a bonfire. Then after that, a huge community dinner Miz Rose hosts at her house every year."

"I'd heard...well, you use game when you can. Right?"

She nodded as she spooned up dinner on plates he then carted to the table.

"Not everyone does I wager, but yes. Being out here it's easy enough to have the stew be venison. Or to have wild turkey instead of store-bought. Samhain feast food is comfort, stick to your ribs stuff."

"I'd like to contribute. To hunt and bring you the deer and turkey."

"You...you would?" Tears sprang to her eyes and he struggled to figure out if it was good or bad.

"I'm a werewolf. I never use *store-bought* turkey."

He snorted at the very idea. "Did Darrell bring you store-bought turkey?"

She curled her lip as she peppered her dinner. "Darrell never came to any of our Samhain rituals. Said it made him uncomfortable. I wasn't going to force him. That's entirely not the point."

"He never did? Even when you were going to get married?" Darrell was so relentlessly a shitass.

"Scarlett thinks it's of the devil. Pastor Tomkins disagrees with her on that point, but whatever. Scarlett's perspective on God is none of my business. I wish she'd keep it that way instead of screaming it in everyone's face."

Jace withheld a growl. "Well, *I'll* be with you and I'll be bringing you the meat already dressed and cleaned for the feast. And maybe a picture of my mom for the altar."

"I'd like that. Thank you. It means a lot that you want to know this part of me. To share it. It's a time of reflection for us. Contemplation is a major factor for me. And the more I think about my life, the more grateful for you I am."

"Now who's being sweet? Damn." He pointed his fork at the chicken and biscuits on his plate. "This is so good. I needed something like this after the last few weeks."

"I like taking care of you, goofball."

"I like being taken care of." He breathed out carefully. "I'm having coffee with Mac tomorrow."

"It's about time."

"It's been best to let it lie a bit. Now that things have calmed back from boiling over, we can see what's what."

"Weren't you guys friends? Back in the day I mean," she said.

"He was two years ahead of me in school but we ran in the same circle at times. I played football, but I wasn't a star like he was. Or like Darrell had been. Still, he was a good guy. I hope he still is. I've never had any trouble with him and I'd like to keep it that way. I imagine he's got enough of his own problems to keep him busy enough from borrowing mine."

"From your lips to God's ears. By the way, your grandmother said something about a Halloween dinner? I'm to bring macaroni and cheese. Which I took as a compliment because of its relative importance on every southern table."

"She mentioned the pumpkin bread you made. You impressed her. Not that I'm surprised because you're very impressive." He didn't tell her the dinner was for all the wolves in town, as well as the cats and they had it at the grange. There'd be at least five different macaroni and cheeses there, but if his grandma told her to do it, she had a reason. She always did.

"The kids go out to trick or treat and when they get back, we have the dinner, which takes a few hours and will be many courses. After that you can head out. There's a big run so you're not going to want to stick around for that part."

"Okay. I'll make plans to meet up with my friends after dinner while you're four legged, eating bugs and stuff."

"I don't eat bugs. I eat rabbit and small game mostly, though this time of year I might take down a deer. Since I need something for Samhain, I might hunt for you that night."

"I'm all for skipping the part where you bring down a full-size deer with your teeth if it's all the same. Of course I'm sure it's quite impressive, but ew."

He laughed. "All right then."

Chapter Twenty-Two

The next week went by in a blur of activity. Samhain preparations and celebrations as well as the same for Halloween and Collins/Hill Days had overtaken the town.

Katie Faith was glad of it. The more time she spent planning, decorating, working and being with her family and Jace, the less time she had to be nervous about Halloween dinner with the Dooleys.

She'd made four different types of macaroni and cheese that week, scoring each. She made the winner late that afternoon once she'd closed up over at the Counter so she hoped it was as good as it looked.

Out front of the mercantile, Damon and Major had turned the lawn into a spooky maze to the candy bowl where Patty and JJ handed out caramel and candy apples, along with popcorn balls to all the kids in town.

Trick or treating was usually over by seven or so, which was when people began to pour over to the grange. Cats and wolves carrying platters, bowls and all types of food and drink headed inside.

She watched from his window as she waited for Jace to hurry his butt up.

"Calm down, darlin'. We won't be considered late

for another hour. We have plenty of time," he said as he came in from the bedroom.

"This is my first big thing with your family. And I seem to notice a lot of shifters going in that building. If I didn't already know from Patty that this was an all-shifter event I might be annoyed with you for not telling me."

"I didn't want you to be nervous." He took the box with the food inside, picking it up easily as they headed out. "You're going to be fine. Everyone already knows you."

"Some of them even like me."

She linked her arm with his as they got to the street.

"Most of them I bet. And the ones who don't, we don't care about."

He really was the best thing ever.

Inside was a swirl of feral magic. Cats and wolves, sleek and fierce as they broke bread, their kids running all over the place as adults kept an eye on them, keeping them out of harm's way.

"It's impressive to see how many shifters there truly are in this town when they're all in one place," she told him as they made their way over to the cluster of tables the Dooleys had taken over.

Plenty of folks called out their hellos as she and Jace passed. It made her feel welcome, which took the edge off. She'd known these people all her life. She had no call to feel like a stranger, but she had when she'd walked in and everyone had stared for several long uncomfortable moments.

But she'd survived their little test and it was time for some serious eating. "Man, it smells so good in here."

"The elders from each pack or family show up at

dawn to start preparing the meat for cooking. They have special recipes they guard with threats of violence," Damon told her as they sat down. "You'll know why when you try that boar Joey Cuthbert has been cooking all day."

Shifters didn't mess around with burgers and steaks for their feasts. No. They had to have boar like showoffs. Still, it smelled pretty freaking fantastic when the first platters of it made their way through the crowd and to the tables followed by trout, turkey and what seemed like an endless parade of sausage.

Each dish had its own flair. Salty sweet, tangy, spicy hot, and each came with a wave of sides. Not everything was a winner or to her taste though.

Her mac and cheese got served up with some jacked up mess of squirrel someone had made. But then, because people were avoiding squirrel with prunes and pineapple, the contrast with her macaroni and cheese meant everyone loved it and couldn't get enough. Mainly because they were hungry, but whatever, Katie Faith would take the impression she left.

She'd definitely need to thank Patty, who had maneuvered this moment for Katie Faith to shine. It was simple. Nothing about it ruffled feathers but it definitely was a positive thing.

It had been sort of easy to assume Patty was good at running a household but it was JJ who handled all the politics of running a pack. But the longer Katie Faith knew Jace's grandmother, the more she realized Patty was a clever tactician in her own right.

Boy, that was embarrassing. But she knew better now than to underestimate someone at first glance.

Though the hall was full to bursting with shifters,

there were a fair number of witches in attendance too, including several of the children running around. One of her second cousins was married to a Pembry and had two kids, one witch and one wolf. It was a nice symmetry. One she'd not given a lot of thought to, really. She did want kids and she'd happily take what she got because she and Jace were going to make some cute children no matter if they turned furry at will or could wield magic.

But seeing all that love, all that life across many generations made her feel, well, so very satisfied with her life. She'd made some dumb choices, had taken a few lumps and now she was part of this wonderful community.

Damon tossed a roll past her face to Jace, who caught it in a quick movement. She and Patty gave them a look they both ignored.

The Pembry section was across the large room, but right in their line of sight. Aside from a few dark looks, it was all smiles and laughter.

At one point though, she realized that whatever Josiah had done, he'd done it to this community. What must it be like for the wolves who loved whoever he'd hurt? To not be able to speak of their own tragedy would be its own kind of punishment, wouldn't it?

Feeling the need, she leaned her head on Jace's shoulder. He put an arm around the back of her chair, holding her close as he continued to listen to some story Damon told.

Major smiled at her from his place across the table. It was so very nice to belong here. She'd protect them, she realized. At Jace's side, she would protect what they had here. The community and connection.

The men cleaned up because it had been the women who'd served and done most of the cooking. Jace walked her over to Aimee's house, just the two of them under what was a very full moon.

"I had a really good time tonight. Thank you for including me," she told him as they paused at Aimee's front gate.

"Thank you for including yourself. For jumping in the way you have. They're your family too, now." He kissed her long and slow as the moon's magic lit against his skin.

"I'll head over when we're finished with our run. All right?" he asked, his lips against hers.

"You can text first if you like. Save yourself a trip over if I've already gone home."

"I don't take my phone with me when I'm wolf. I'll see you in a few hours."

He was going to do whatever he wanted to so she just let it go. "Have fun. I hope you find a nice fat deer for me to cook with tomorrow. Oh, and I love you. Don't look at any of the pretty wolves out there with you."

He growled, swooping her up in his arms to kiss her again. "Tell me again."

"Not to look at butts?" she teased, knowing what he wanted to hear.

He nipped her bottom lip hard enough to sting.

"I love you."

He put her down carefully, kissed her once more and stepped back. "I'll see you later tonight. I love you too."

He watched until Aimee opened the door and let her inside, jogging away into the night.

"Looks as good going as he does coming," she murmured to herself.

"No lie detected there," Aimee said. "Now shut the door and get on in here. We're drinking disgusting marshmallow vodka and eating caramel apples."

"Good lord above," she said, laughing as she went to join her friends.

Three days later, Jace approached his grandpa and great uncle as they sat on the dock, their fishing poles in the lake, hats on, beers at the ready.

"You here as Prime or as my grandson?" JJ asked holding a beer out.

Jace took it. "Both, I guess." He glanced to his great uncle and waved him to keep sitting.

"Grab yourself a chair then. Let's hear it."

He did, settling in, glad he had a beer and the sun because the breeze coming off the water was chilly, even for him.

"I'm going to ask Katie Faith to marry me," he said after a few minutes.

"I expect so." JJ cackled. "She's a catch. Your grandma sure does think you did good. I 'spose I do as well."

"I was going to wait until Valentine's Day or something like that. But I don't want to."

JJ cackled again. "Even when you was barely out of diapers you hated to be told no. Katie Faith isn't a pushover. I wasn't too sure at first. Girl's flighty as hell. But she's steadfast. After I saw her at Halloween dinner I knew she'd be good for this pack. Hell, I find it hard not to run when I see Scarlett Pembry out and about and your little scrap of a girl held her own. Marry the girl so you can take over as Patron. It's time."

Jace heard the exhaustion in JJ's tone. He should

have stepped down a decade before, but he'd stayed, even while he was sick, to give Jace the time to grow and be ready.

"She's got a few hot buttons around marriage. Stupid Darrell. It may take a while. I'm going to let her take the lead on the date. I have to ask her first."

"Did you talk to her daddy yet?"

"That was my next stop. I had dinner with them all last night for Samhain so I talked a bit about it with both her parents then." They'd been good to him. Even after the way Darrell had treated her, they welcomed him to their feast and to their community.

"It went okay?"

"Nadine Grady has no tolerance for shenanigans with her daughter when it comes to wolves."

"She's a scary one. Avery, he's got some power, but she's the one with the real ferocity of the two. I like that the girl came back here for family. And I like that she comes from good people. You two are a good match. She's already brought more to the pack."

Having powerful witches in a pack meant the shifters were able to change much faster and with far less pain. After the Halloween dinner it had been the Dooleys who'd made the change the quickest and plenty of people noticed and commented on it.

"Be aware that once you announce your engagement, them Pembrys is gonna throw a shit fit," JJ said.

Jace didn't much care at that moment. This was about him and the woman he was born to love. Werewolf stuff would always be part of his life, but how Scarlett might feel about him marrying Katie Faith meant absolutely nothing.

"Mac and I had a reasonable talk about reasonable

things." Mac Pembry was up against a mountain of shit because of his moron of a brother and seriously out of control mother.

He didn't seem particularly interested in making a power play, but Jace expected it all the same. It was how things were with wolves. A hierarchy had to be set and right then it was in flux.

Eventually, he and Mac would have to come head on at one another. But for the next several months as they hunkered down through winter, Jace wanted to strengthen his own position so when he became Patron there'd be little change for their people to have to deal with.

First he needed marriage as part of that new hierarchy for his pack. They needed to know they could trust Katie Faith. Count on her like he already did.

It was a careful line for her to walk and he understood divided loyalties. The more he learned about witches and their real, integral connection to Diablo Lake being such a safe haven for shifters, the more he'd developed a deep sense of loyalty to them.

But he was still going to lead his pack. And that part of him knew that the proposal would bolster his standing against anyone contemplating taking a run at him for Patron.

"Hot button or not, the girl can't drag her feet too long or it'll make you look bad."

Jace knew that too. But he wouldn't push her. That wasn't to say he couldn't woo the hell out of her, though, to speed things up.

"I have some moves, Grandpa. I got this."

"Go talk to your grandma. She's got something you might want before you propose."

And with that, the Patron gave his blessing to the marriage and to Jace taking over the pack.

He stayed a while longer to listen to a story he'd heard a dozen times before but it got better each telling. Jace figured by the time his grandpa hit a hundred or so, there'd be dragons in it.

He'd walked out to the lake from town, so by the time he got back he'd more than burned off his beer. His grandma strolled up, a basket full of books in her arms.

"Hey, darlin'." She thrust the basket his way. "I've just been picking up some things to take out on visits. Tommy Moore has a chest cold. Donnagene is playing nursemaid to him, her mother and two of her kids all down with the same thing as Tommy. Books never go amiss when you're stuck inside."

Being isolated meant they were responsible for taking care of their own. Patty had been making visits to all the members of the pack for decades now. It occurred to him he needed to talk with Katie Faith about this side of running a pack.

"If you wait about an hour, I can drive you. I just have an errand to run first. I'm going to talk to Nadine and Avery to tell them I'm going to propose to Katie Faith. I just got back from talking to Grandpa and he said to come see you. I would have done that anyway."

She directed him on where to load up what in various baskets and plastic tubs and containers with the things she'd take to the people she dropped in on. Food to those who might be struggling in some way. A friendly face with some pretty flowers when someone has been ill. Clothes, diapers, whatever people might need.

And then she led him into the house and bade him to sit while she ran to get something from her room.

Not a difficult task when he noted the heaping plate of cookies there. "Okay," she told him as she returned to sit next to him. She passed a black velvet ring box his way. "My mother left me these rings and though several of my sons have gotten married, I've never felt like these would be right for any of their wives. Katie Faith, though. Well, you take a look and tell me what you think."

He opened the box to find two rings. A gold band with diamonds set in it and an engagement ring with a solitaire diamond stone. Old-fashioned and very feminine but made for a woman who worked with her hands. The rings seemed to hum with energy.

"My Pop made the band himself and my mom wore them every day until she passed. They had a good, strong love. The kind of connection you and Katie Faith have. That connection will serve Dooley well. I'm so pleased for you. She's a good girl. I surely do like her."

"This is beautiful. She's going to love that it came from my great grandmother. Thank you." He looked up to catch her gaze. "I don't know what I'd do without you."

"You and your brothers are my boys. I love you all so much. You're doing such a wonderful job, all of you. I can't wait to see what the next decade has in store for you."

Chapter Twenty-Three

"I need to borrow your black pumps." Aimee came in to Katie Faith's bedroom barefoot, heading for her closet.

"Did you even give them back after you borrowed them the last time?"

"I can't believe the things you accuse me of, Katie Faith." Aimee slid the black pumps on. "So cute. Now you. Damn, girl."

Katie Faith turned in front of the mirror, making her skirt fly out and then fall gracefully. Deep dark green, the dress hugged her best assets like her boobs, and gave plenty of camouflage to her thighs and butt.

"I hope Jace likes it."

"He's a guy. It shows off your tits, makes your butt look good. You're a hot momma right now. All fecund and gorgeous."

"Fecund? Ooh, fancy pants. But I like it. Full of life. Yeah. But not ready to start popping out babies just yet, thank you very much."

"You gonna tell Jace about those jerks you had to kick out of the Counter today?" Aimee asked as she looked through the lipsticks in her makeup bag.

"Not unless I have no other choice. It's Founder's Day. I'm going out with my gorgeous boyfriend to a dinner and a dance in a beautiful dress. Like I want to ruin that with some recounting of a bunch of teen boys pushing and shoving over ice cream. It's dumb. They knew it. I handled it."

"I'm just sayin'. He's only going to pout like a big, dumb baby—no lie, he'll look good doing it—if he finds out from someone else."

"I'm a business owner. I sell food products to the public. Do you know how many stupid and unpleasant people I have to deal with on a weekly basis?"

The young adult werewolves had a lot more testosterone going on of late. After a quiet, albeit tense, period with no open hostilities between Dooley and Pembry, it had slowly inched its way back. Once they'd had their run after the Halloween dinner without incident it was like they were done being nice and the scuffles and snarls had begun to show up again.

"Can I tell you a secret?" Katie Faith turned on some music and got closer to Aimee. "I'm afraid the dance tonight will blow up into a full-on battle if I bring it up."

"It's only going to get worse until it explodes. My mom says about every twenty-five years or so they have some sort of kerfuffle."

They kept their voices low, standing near with the music still playing. Shifters had amazing hearing but they'd be all right if they stayed quiet.

"I don't want to be in the middle of some stupid turf war between werewolf packs. I didn't come back here for that. I didn't fall in love with Jace for that. I'm trying to get used to it."

"For crying out loud, Katie Faith! Stop it. You're in or you're out. Suck it up. You love him and his family. You already chose a side. You're not in the middle unless you keep resisting where you already are. Which is with Jace."

She shot Aimee an aggrieved look before putting on her earrings and then her lipstick.

"What if it goes wrong again? You know? What if my judgment is so messed up and I make the same mistake? And here I am having to choose sides? I'm in over my head."

Aimee hugged her quickly. "Are you so perfect you really see getting dumped at the altar by a guy who never loved you at all as some sort of character flaw *you* possess? Darrell was just a punk ass loser. You went away. You grew up in Chattanooga. You did it on your own. And then you came back different and better. Smart enough to know Jace isn't a damned thing like Darrell. They're barely even the same species. This is forever and I've never seen you so utterly certain of anything as you are Jace. You made the decision to love him way back when you first moved in here."

"I don't know how to be an alpha! I don't know how to be a wife like Patty. She seems like all she does is bake and clean but damn, Aimee, she's a powerhouse. How can I compete with that?"

"Don't compete with that. She's his nana. Everyone fucking loves their nana," Aimee said. "She helped make him who he is, but he chose you. For real, your man has faith in you and your ability."

"No pressure there," Katie Faith mumbled.

"Oh boohoo. Too late to be worrying about that stuff. Has it ever occurred to you he's letting you take your time with this even though you both know what's what? What do you think it costs a guy like him to give you the space you need? Even though if you did marry him he would be stronger and he could take over as Patron with you at his side. The weight would firmly be with Dooley and we could move on to some balance with them in charge a while. No, not *them* anymore. *You.* If Jace trusts you, and I trust you, how about you trust yourself?"

Katie Faith had to look up at the ceiling to keep from crying as they hugged. "Thanks for the pep talk. I really needed it," she said. He wanted them to move in together. Wanted to sleep not in his bed every night, or hers, but theirs.

And she did too, but living together with his grandparents just an acre away and her parents less than two miles in the other direction made her a little nervous. It wasn't that she didn't know they figured out she and Jace had sex. It was her hang-up she was sure.

"I want tonight to be fun. I want it to be romantic and wonderful. You'll dance and I'll dance and we'll have a nice dinner and it'll be great if we can avoid talk about stupid twenty-year-olds measuring their peckers in some sort of dominance display at the Counter. I'll tell him tomorrow. You're right, he should know. But let me have tonight as something akin to normal. Please."

Aimee gave her a hard look before she sighed. "Fine. I'm glad we can agree I'm always right. Let's eat and have cocktails and look pretty, shall we?"

Jace waited downstairs with his brothers so he didn't see her right away. It gave her the chance to watch him without his knowing it. His hair needed a trim, but she didn't really mind. He looked like a pirate. A werewolf pirate. That book so totally needed to be written.

He wore his serious face. He had dozens of versions.

This one said he was patiently amused with his brothers but would still kick their asses if they pissed him off.

It made her smile and that's when he looked up as if she'd said his name out loud.

He broke from the group he'd been with, making his way to her, pulling her close and swaying just a little. "You look gorgeous, little witch."

She grinned against him. "Says the hot werewolf in a suit."

"You ready to get going?" he asked as he set her away from him and took a long leisurely tour of her outfit. "Can't wait to show you off. Damn, darlin'."

"I'm so hungry," she muttered as they got there a few minutes later. He'd wanted to walk but she had heels on and nixed that idea right quick.

"Works out nice then, that inside this building will be a lot of food." He handed over their tickets at the door and then with a hand at the small of her back, guided her to a table already half filled with friends and family.

"I didn't realize half these people were couples," she said to Aimee once they'd gotten settled.

"Me either. I'm a little bummed, I can't lie, to see Mason Braithwaite with a date. I was hoping to snag his attention a while," Aimee replied as she passed around the bread basket.

Katie Faith buttered a piece of cornbread and tried not to inhale it. It had made sense earlier to save room for all the food at this dinner. But now she was bordering on hangry so she needed to get something in her belly.

Plus, the cornbread was really good. Good enough she had no remorse for choosing it over the rolls in the basket.

The energy in the hall was excited. Humming with holiday cheer, crackling with the tensions between packs.

Sharon, sitting next to Darrell across the way, sent Katie Faith a dirty look, which ruffled her feathers.

"I never did a thing to her. It's all been at me from her and Darrell. She's got some nerve to give me dirty looks."

"I feel bad for her." Aimee turned over her ordering card to the server who'd come to collect them. "I'd hate to think of an ex who was as pretty and talented as you are. It would seriously mess with my head. Plus, he's a dingus so you know he probably hasn't said much to reassure her."

"Aw, I feel so bad." Her tone was sarcastic, but there was some truth to it. "Having now, you know, found the person I'm meant to be with, I can't hate her that she found it with the guy I thought was mine. I didn't have this." She motioned with a hand over at Jace, who blithely ignored her. "So I couldn't know the difference. But I do now. If she hadn't come along, I'd be a different person and not one I'm sure I could have really respected."

"And you don't have to worry about him running off with someone else." Aimee tipped a chin at Jace.

"I'm not a fool, that's why," he said. "Stop getting her all worked up." He frowned at Aimee, who made a rude sound.

Katie Faith grinned. He was so sweet beneath all that grump. Even Aimee saw it to tease him like a big brother.

"She's going to be worried the whole of her life that he'll do her the way he did you." Aimee happily dug into her salad as it arrived. "There's a very high bacon to salad ratio here. I approve."

Even though Sharon had been giving her the stink eye, Katie Faith was hit with a bolt of sympathy. Being loved with total surety wasn't anything she could have understood before Jace. But now, well, she didn't know if she could claim she wouldn't do whatever it took to be with Jace.

And if she didn't have that, she had a man she couldn't trust. Which was a fate she truly wouldn't wish on anyone.

Years later, mainly all she had for Sharon was pity. Darrell she had no respect for. He was in the DTM file. Dead to me.

Ignoring him had been a good strategy over the last several weeks since his dumb ass nearly taunted her father back into the hospital. But if she saw him in town she looked right through him. She wasn't going to give him the satisfaction.

She'd chosen a fantastic onion soup with a cheesy piece of bread broiled on top. But once she'd finished, Jace stood, holding a hand out.

"Come dance with me, little witch."

She waved her napkin at her face a few times before standing and letting him lead her to the dance floor where Otis Redding's "Long Time Coming" started playing.

"You noticed, huh?"

He swayed with her, holding her close enough to envelop her in his heat and the scent of him beneath that.

"You like to play it when we fuck," he murmured as he bent to her ear, sending shivers through her.

"You're naughty," she told him as he stood again.

"I can only make you feel as hot for me as I am for you right now. Truly, you're a sight. That dress is the prettiest wrapping on the best present I've ever been given."

"Wow. You're really working it tonight. I like it." She smiled up at him as he twirled her at the song's end and led her back to their table.

"You're making everyone look bad," Damon said as the appetizers came out.

"On account of me being so awesome?" Katie Faith asked as she grabbed some stuffed mushrooms for her plate before passing it to Aimee.

Damon looked over to Jace, who just shrugged.

"Oh so you know she's a weirdo?" Damon demanded of his brother.

"Like I have a say in it?" Jace asked.

"I'm such a cross to bear," she tossed in, before turning to Aimee.

"Are you mad at me now, Katie Faith?" Damon asked. "I don't think she's mad," he said to Jace.

"If she was mad, you'd know it. She's not one of those silent suffering martyrs. She'll shove her grievances up your ass until you pay attention."

Major thought that was hilarious. Jace had to admit it was pretty funny. And sexy. She wasn't just going to sit around and mope or hope things happened. Everything she did, she did for a reason.

Just another thing he adored about her.

"I can't help if you all have no game and feel outdone by mine," he told his brothers.

"You had a song arranged for her. Everyone here knows it now." Damon shook his head. "I can't recall a time you did something sentimental like that."

"I can't recall ever wanting to before she barreled into the apartment across the hall. Seems like decades since that moment."

Funny to think about that. They'd just fit, closely and well from the start. He reached out for her and she was there, warm and giving. She was smart and fierce and was, as his brother said, a weirdo. But in just under three months his entire world had changed and it felt like it'd always been just waiting there, patiently holding until that time when they came together as they were supposed to.

He didn't normally go in for all that stuff, but in this case, it felt like it was meant to be. Not back when she was in high school. Not when she'd left town. He wasn't right for her until this precise moment in time and for that, he had no choice but to believe it was part of some bigger, wiser plan.

More food came as the entrees appeared. A few couples' spats had broken out and he'd been keeping his eye on a few wolves who'd been drinking pretty steadily for the last hour. He just wanted the evening to go well if for no other reason than Katie Faith wanted to have a nice night out and what she wanted, he'd bend over backwards to give to her.

He didn't much like the renewed outbreaks of trouble between Dooley and Pembry around town. Darrell appeared to have sprung himself free of his time out and was talking dirt all over town. Striking tempers and getting everyone all wound up once more.

If Dwayne didn't hurry up and control his wolves, he'd lose a lot more ground than Jace first figured. On one hand that was good for Dooley wolves. But on the other, it wasn't good for the town as a whole.

"Stop thinking about work, honey," Katie Faith said in his ear as she put her fork down with a happy sigh.

Aimee had gone out to dance, along with a lot of other folks, leaving their table deserted at their end.

"I could say the same for you."

"Me? Dude, I just ate a slice of cake as big as a side of beef. I wasn't thinking about anything but cream cheese frosting and your abs. At the same time."

Their little game had been escalating all evening, starting with that dress of hers, though he did his part with playing Otis and making that comment about sex music. She had a penchant for Otis Redding and so every time he heard it now, he thought about the way she looked, rising above him, candlelight on her bare skin, gleaming against a sheen of sweat.

"You were just thinking about sex right then," she accused, leaning in close.

"How do you propose to know that?"

"Well, a non denial is a pretty big indicator." She sent him a raised brow that made him hard. "When you think about sex you get this faraway look—pretty similar to when the pizza is on the way from the kitchen at the pub to our table."

He couldn't stop the laugh at that. She knew him really well.

"Remember that time we ate pizza while we fucked?"

She blushed right down to the pretty cleavage on display at the front of her dress. "I remember."

She'd not only showed up at his door wearing nothing under her robe, carrying a pizza, a six-pack and a really giving heart. She'd even turned on the game in the bedroom, not that he watched anything but her making all his wishes come true. He might have absently kept track of the score, but he'd deny it if asked.

She probably knew anyway.

"You know me pretty well."

"When it comes to you thinking about sexytimes, yes, I think I do."

"And yet, you're right there, looking up at me and trusting me to my core. How'd that happen so fast? How'd you become everything so fucking fast?"

Her cheeks darkened a little as she blushed. "I'm so strange for getting turned on at how mad you sound at the very idea of loving me like that. Grrr, feelings, I'm so mad at you!"

He took her cheeks in his hands, kissing her. "You should marry me."

It was out of his mouth before he'd thought about it a little more. He'd planned to ask her, yes, but he had a plan to ask her once they got back home. He had champagne chilling already back at the apartment.

She pulled back, looking at him carefully.

"I know I sort of tossed it out there." He pulled the ring box out. "But I actually had plans to ask you in a more romantic way than a blurted thought."

And then he dropped to one knee in front of her.

Though there wasn't an actual scratch across a record album sound, the whole room was suddenly looking at them as the music went down about half as everyone blatantly gawped and eavesdropped.

"Takes some stones to do this right now with the whole town watching," she said, one corner of her mouth hitched up.

"I think we've established the state of my stones, Katie Faith. What do you say then? Marry me."

Her gaze went down to the rings.

"Those belonged to my great grandmother. My grandma passed them on to you."

A few tears dropped over her cheeks as she tore her gaze from the rings to his face. "Wow. Wow. They're beautiful and," she ran a fingertip over them, "they still have a trace of the magic she made with your great grandfather when she married him. Patty passed these on to us, so there's a kind of magic from that too."

"Answer the man, for goodness' sake!" someone called out.

"Oh! Shit. Sorry. Yes. Yes, I'll definitely marry you."

He lunged to his feet, bringing her with him as he kissed her soundly. "Thank god that worked out. I was starting to worry that you'd say no."

"No you didn't. What kind of fool would I be to say no? I'm not any type of fool."

"I talked to your parents already. And my family. But look, I know you want to go slow. So we'll take it at whatever pace you need to," he said, his forehead to hers. "If you want to wait until this whole mess quiets down, I understand."

Everyone began to get back to their tables, or over to the bar to get something else to drink. Friends and family rushed over to congratulate them in a pretty solid stream for the next hour or so.

By the time that had settled down, Katie Faith should have known it was too good to be true that they could get through an event without nonsense.

Scarlett lumbered over, giving them both a look. Nadine got between them, surprising Scarlett into stepping back.

"You keep away from my daughter. You hear me?"

Nadine crossed her arms over her chest and dared Scarlett to say anything else.

"All I was going to do was wish them well and tell her I hope things turn out better for her than they did his momma. The Dooley men have a spotty track record."

Katie Faith didn't even have the time to jump on Scarlett and beat her dumb face in because it was Nadine who did it first. Nadine who was at least three inches shorter and fifty pounds lighter than Scarlett.

Nadine who had a lot more magic than people gave her credit for and a whole lot of anger about what had just been said to her daughter.

There was a scuffle as Nadine got the first few blows in, mainly due to surprise. Chairs flew to the side as they went at one another. She kept her magic to a minimum, which was good as it was for self-defense as Katie Faith had done and Scarlett hadn't shifted form.

"Y'all are trash," Scarlett yelled out.

Dwayne waded in, trying to get her talked down.

Katie Faith got between the two women. "Momma, please. It's over. You made your point and Daddy is going to get worked up if you don't chill out."

"You're the one acting like you're on a reality television show. No one asked your opinion of this engagement. You got no call to say that mean-spirited stuff about my daughter. No call at all," Nadine said to Scarlett, still pissed off. "What is *wrong* with you? You got grown children and grandchildren and you just did that? You should be ashamed of yourself!"

Katie Faith turned her mother in her arms, aiming her away, using her body to propel them both from the scene as the yelling continued at her back.

"Mom, I need you to focus. Calm down." She managed to get them both outside where TeeFay and Aimee waited.

"I will not abide that woman one more moment." Her mom tried to get past but they managed to get her held back.

"Nadine!" TeeFay grabbed Katie Faith's mom's shoulders and gave her a good hard shake to get her attention. "Get yourself under control. Avery needs you right now. We got Katie Faith's back so you can handle him. Get him home."

"She wished my daughter to die in childbirth. She wished my child to a loveless relationship with an abusive piece of garbage. How dare the likes of Scarlett Pembry even think that much less say it aloud? I can take her."

"Mom!" Katie Faith hugged her mother tight as she yelled. "Stop. Please. You're totally freaking me out now."

Shaken, she let go when her mom slumped in her arms and scrubbed her hands over her face.

"It's not all right," she whispered.

"I know. But I'm not going to die in childbirth and I have a really wonderful boyfriend, well, soon-to-be husband now, who loves me. I trust him. Nothing she can say is going to hurt what I have with Jace. She just showed her ass to the whole town in there. *Think about that.*"

It was all Katie Faith could think about once she'd managed to get her parents in a car and on their way home.

"You guys should go home now too. It's okay. I'm going back in there to be with Jace." Katie Faith turned to TeeFay. "I don't know what I'd have done without you tonight. Thank you. And for having my back with that whole mess."

TeeFay hugged her tight. "Girl, you're like my own. I've always got your back. As for your mom, I haven't seen her that angry in a really long time. Maybe only three times her whole life."

"What Scarlett says doesn't matter. I don't care about her."

"Katie Faith, some things once they get said gather a sort of power. Some superstitions are based on real things. Some words can't be taken back. You know? Your mother doesn't want that bitch putting any sort of negative energy out there waiting to hurt you. And it's outrageous to say what she did. She's lucky your mother didn't snatch her baldheaded."

Aimee hugged her too. "We're here until it's time to go." They linked arms and headed back inside where things appeared to have calmed down enough to sharp discomfort.

"Oh and congratulations again," Aimee said in a whisper.

She grinned. "Yeah, despite all this chaos, it's a nice night."

"Do you have a wedding date?"

"He said I could take my time. Wait until things calmed down. Until I was sure."

Aimee cocked her head. "He's nearly perfect except for that control freak streak. Giving you more space even though you know he's champing at the bit to move forward. Once a wolf makes up his mind, they don't seem to let up."

They all watched Jace and Dwayne have a very tense conversation in one corner for a moment.

"I notice something." Aimee turned back to Katie Faith. "The witches are here at your back. The Dooleys are here at your back. Outraged on your behalf one and all. Know who isn't over here? Who didn't stand up for you during that fight and right after? Pembry."

"I've been trying not to make any overt declaration that might affect wolf business. But no matter what I do I'm making a declaration. I just need to think about what I want to say."

She caught Sharon's eye, the two looking across the room for long moments. That attack hadn't come from her, it had come from Scarlett. Katie Faith wasn't going to blame Sharon for that and she was done blaming her for breaking up with Darrell which was for the best anyway.

Carl stepped between the two wolves and Katie Faith hurried over.

"That's enough for one night. This should be a celebration. We had an engagement this evening. Love is a good thing. We'd been peaceful and you're damned well going to hear me tell you peaceful is a good thing."

Katie Faith moved up to take Jace's left hand, careful to leave his dominant hand free. "I have a lot of ideas for the wedding I'm excited to talk to you about. So let's shine this mess on. If Pembry can't get itself together, that's ultimately their problem."

Dwayne's eyes widened. He hadn't been expecting her to take such a public stand. Even after his wife had said all that!

Jace stood taller at her side, glowering back at Dwayne.

"You're not Patron yet, boy, know your place," Dwayne snarled.

"As soon as they get married, he'll take over. What's it to you anyway, Pembry?" JJ said.

"Talk to me then," Dwayne said.

"Shut up, Dwayne." Katie Faith took a cue from Jace and stood taller.

"You got no call to speak for wolves," he said.

"And *you* got no call to decide who speaks for Dooley. In any case, I'm speaking for the witches in this town."

The leaders of the consort, except her parents, fanned out at her back.

When she saw his shock she sneered at him. "Yeah, that's right. We're not invisible after all, huh? You come at one, you come at all."

"I thought you were going to stay out of wolf business," Dwayne challenged.

"I did until you all made it town business." She shrugged before turning her attention to Jace. "If you'll take over as Patron once we get married, I think we can pull off a wedding pretty quickly."

"I meant what I said. Take the time you need," Jace murmured.

"'Course you did, which is why I love you. Anyway, you and I both know this town is never going to calm down so if we waited for that, we'd get old and gray."

"You best watch the steps you're taking." Dwayne reminded them he was still there, being a giant asshat.

"I'm entirely sick and tired of you and your family threatening me. I know which steps I'm taking. You need to be sure to do the same. I'm done with all y'all." She held up a hand toward Dwayne and spoke to Jace. "I'm going to go home now. I need to check on my parents after this mess and there are plenty parts of this wolf crap I want no real part of."

Jace smiled down at her, bending to kiss her. "Big, bad, tough witch. I like it. I'm done here too and I want to go with you to see Avery and Nadine."

"Tell your daddy I'll stop by soon," Dwayne said and Katie Faith turned back from where she'd been walking away.

"You won't be doing that. You're not welcome. You've done enough so back off."

"I've known your—"

Katie Faith interrupted him. "I don't care about anything you're going to say right now. I told you what was what. Keep your ass off my parents' property or I'll handle you myself."

He stepped back as if she'd slapped him and she wished she had. When she was assured he wasn't going to say anything else, she and Jace left with all the witches and Dooley wolves. The cat shifters had already been edging away, but once Katie Faith had reached the door, the cats had made their way out too.

Chapter Twenty-Four

Jace's jaw hurt from keeping his control so tight. With Katie Faith upset, her parents upset and his pack worked up, they all needed him to keep it together.

They'd gone to her folks' place, where her mother had convinced Avery to go to bed but Nadine was still worked up. Which got his little witch upset all over again.

They'd stayed long enough to get Nadine talked down off the ledge before heading home.

"I'm sorry," he managed to say once they were alone.

"For what?" She kicked off her shoes as she climbed the steps leading up to their apartments.

"Tonight was supposed to be our night. A good time. A wonderful memory."

She sighed. "There are parts that are most definitely wonderful memories. It's not every day a gal gets proposed to. The rest? Like the part where my mom got into a brawl? Well, sometimes things don't go the way we planned. Oh shit." She came to a halt and he nearly ran her over.

The hallway outside the apartment doors was lined with Dooley wolves.

"What's going on?" he asked Major.

"They need some reassurance," his brother said quietly.

"I'll make some warm apple cider while you talk to them," Katie Faith said, unlocking her door and disappearing inside. "You may want to run and get some cups so everyone can keep warm while they wait," she called out to Damon.

Major looked his way and Jace nodded. "Let her be. It'll keep her busy and I could use some warm cider anyway." He clapped his hands. "What can I do for y'all?"

It had been as if a switch had been thrown. The scene at the dinner dance had catapulted him into the leadership position in such a definite way and the wolves who'd shown up out of nervousness or anger, whatever their reasons, had done so without hesitation.

Jace figured he'd done something right, at least, for them to have shown up. To have waited patiently and calmly as Katie Faith brought them out cups of warm cider to enjoy while they waited.

Major showed Imogene Hadry in.

"Mrs. Hadry, it sure is nice to see you. What can I do for you?" Jace asked as he helped her into a chair before he sat.

"I surely don't like all this upset. My granddaughter is having a baby in a month and all this fighting makes her anxious. That's not good for the pregnancy."

Jace leaned close enough to take her hands in his. "She's lucky to have a grandma who cares so much about her."

"She's young. Young enough not to remember what it was like when we were truly at war with the Pembrys.

Her mother and father look to me for reassurance and I'm here looking to you."

"That's what I'm here for. I'm doing all I can to set this all straight. But I won't stop until I feel like my wolves are safe and taken care of. Plenty of Pembrys are fine, upstanding citizens of this town. Our friends and family. There's no reason to think we can't get through this rough patch like we have before. So your great-grandbaby can have as wonderful a future as possible."

He knew her granddaughter so they talked about that for a while. About growing up and having the next generation of wolves to fill their pack.

She just needed to be heard. To feel like she could tell her family things were going to be all right and the world that baby was going to be born into would be protected and safe.

And after she left, and several more wolves came in with the same sort of need, Jace lost his hesitance and embraced his role. The role he'd been trained for his whole life.

Still, it was after one in the morning by the time everyone had cleared out. Katie Faith came over, having changed into soft pants and a long-sleeved shirt, tucked herself onto his couch at his side and listened as he talked with his brothers about the whole situation.

"I think you managed to calm them all down," Major said. "Grandpa wanted to come deal with them, but Grandma made him go home and told us to call you if you didn't return within the hour."

"We stopped off at the Gradys first. Just wanted to make sure they were all right."

Major looked to Katie Faith. "I have to say, I've been scared of your mom my whole life but I never really knew why. She's tough, but she's always been sweet to me. After that scene at the grange I now understand it was my subconscious telling me she was a predator." He patted her knee. "Your daddy okay?"

"They're both okay. Or they were when I left. Tomorrow, or I guess later today, will be a challenge because I feel like she's not done," Katie Faith said. "I've never seen her so outraged. Not even after I was left at the altar."

Jace put an arm around her shoulders to hold her close. He *hated* her being unhappy. It sent his wolf to pacing.

"Thank you guys for defending me tonight when Scarlett said all that about your mom. I know it hurt you too."

"It's no secret that she died in childbirth. I just can't imagine what Scarlett thinks to gain by reminding people of that. This town may not like our dad, but they all seem to have liked our mom." Damon frowned.

"They *pitied* our mom," Major corrected. "Not the same as liking her. But I think Scarlett is past thinking about what the outcome of her actions might be. Which makes her a bigger threat than I first imagined. She's truly out of control and Darrell isn't helping."

Katie Faith exhaled sharply. "I don't care. I mean, I do care that she's affecting her wolves, but she needs to be removed. And if Pembry won't do it, they deserve what they get."

All three males looked at her with some surprise.

"What? You don't think I can't be vicious when I need it?"

"Darlin', I think you're plenty vicious." Jace kissed

the top of her head, not allowing himself a smile at how adorable she was to protest that she was mean.

"You were pretty fantastic tonight, all things considered," Damon told her. "Here and at the dinner."

She'd treated his wolves like her own. Already tending to them, seeking to soothe and comfort. He wondered if she'd even noticed that.

They visited a while longer until finally his brothers headed off to bed and he was alone with her once more.

"So, I think tonight will go down as one of the most memorable Founder's Days in history."

Tucked into his side like a kitten, she managed a laugh.

"Did you really mean it when you said we could get married soon?" he asked. "I know it was the heat of the moment."

She shifted to sit astride his lap, facing him. "Do you think I don't know what it costs you to give me space and time?"

Surprised into momentary silence, he thought about her question and realized maybe he'd just done it without thinking because she needed it to be that way. And he told her so.

"You're an alpha wolf. The Prime of your pack. It's an indelible part of your nature to want to take care of those you feel responsible for. I took that for granted a little."

Before he could argue, she put two fingers over his lips a moment.

"No. Let me finish. I love the way you love me. I'm spoiled. Used to the way you put me first. I don't need any more time. I've thought about this a lot and had long conversations with Aimee about it.

"I know I want to be married to you. It isn't *early days* when you've known someone pretty much your whole life. When you make me feel like I belong to something bigger than myself. I guess I have to ask you if you still want to marry me after that brawl earlier."

He shook his head, stretching up to kiss her quickly, his hands then settling at her hips.

"If anything I want to marry you even more. Nadine will be an awesome mother-in-law. Damn, she didn't waste her time with any bullshit, did she?"

She giggled. "Oh my god, Jace. She flew at Scarlett. If she hadn't gotten the upper hand through surprise…"

"Your mother can handle herself. She went straight for a punch to the face. Made Scarlett's eyes water. Blood went everywhere, freaked people out. Nadine made her point. Don't think she didn't. Scarlett won't come at you without a second thought again."

"But she will come at me again. Let's be real here."

Jace was pretty sure that was going to be true. "Yep."

"When she does, I need to be ready. I'll use magic to defend myself."

"Don't say it like you're warning me. I *want* you to use your magic to toss her off like a flea. Remember, you're my woman. You'll be Patron when I take over for my grandparents. I'd assumed your strength would be your brain. And I still think that. But how could another wolf take you seriously enough to let you lead them? And then I saw you tonight and I understood. You're a force to be reckoned with because you're brilliant and powerful with your magic. Nadine didn't need to be a shifter to blacken Scarlett's eye. And you don't need that either."

Once he'd spoken the words aloud he realized what a huge thing it was that he'd just accepted.

She smiled at him with a little cunning at the edges and his cock throbbed at the sight. "You know what it does to me when you get vicious, right?" he asked her.

"I know enough to let her come at me first so I'll have the ability to use my magic to defend myself."

He growled as he yanked her down to kiss her.

"I have to confess something though. Before we go any further." She pulled back, her lips kiss swollen and her hair a sexy tumble around her face.

"Am I going to like this?"

She grinned again, swiping her thumb over the line between his eyes. "That frown line is so sexy. I don't know what to do with myself sometimes."

"I have some suggestions. If you face that conundrum again, I mean."

"I told myself I'd be circumspect once we married. Let you make all the decisions." She shot him a look. "About the pack I mean. I told myself that even after we marry I can do my witch thing and you do your wolf thing. But I'm not sure now."

"What do you mean?"

"I have opinions about things, Jace."

"Good Lord, Katie Faith, did you think that was a secret? You have opinions on lots of things. Hell, most things."

Snickering, she gave him a quick kiss. "Har har. I don't think I can be married to you, be Patron at your side, without truly being involved."

Relief flooded him. And then so much joy that she wanted to be a real partner in the running of the pack.

"Like tonight?"

"They stood up for me." Her bottom lip wobbled a little, but she sucked in a breath and kept going. "Dooley wolves defended me tonight. They cared about me and I don't know. It feels like a special sort of magic happened tonight between me and you and your wolves."

He agreed.

"I'm going to remember who defended me tonight. And who didn't. When we marry, my magic will make you all stronger. The power balance will change. I know it and to be truthful, I want that. Because unless new leadership takes over Pembry, they'll just get worse and worse."

"I didn't expect you. Not to be this. Hell." He rubbed a hand over his face. "I didn't expect to love someone so much it hurt a little sometimes. The way it feels to watch you switch gears from sexy lady about to have hot sex with her man to concerned alpha when we got to the top of the stairs and saw everyone waiting. I don't know that I'll ever forget this night for as long as I live.

"Not for the fighting, but for the myriad things I learned about us both. You're not just my witch, though you most assuredly are. You're Dooley's witch. I really do think that. When are you going to marry me then?"

"No way. You can't say all that sweet stuff and not let me coo over you a bit." She tried to look stern, but the kisses she laid all over his face belied that. "The Dooley wolves *are* mine. I feel that too. Strange. Wondrous. I'll have to figure out how to work with both parts of my life, but I figure that's a situation by situation thing. I'll learn as I go along how to be a witch who loves the wolves she's responsible for even though she's not a werewolf."

"When are we getting married?" he repeated.

"I need a few things. A dress being one of them. Carl can perform legal marriages. You'll have to handle the wolf side of things. I don't know enough and I don't want to leave anything important out."

"Well we eat raw deer liver under the full moon."

She reared back, her lip curled and he burst out laughing.

"Hey!" She punched his arm. "Not funny, mister."

As he was still laughing, he disagreed.

"You've planned a wedding to a werewolf before. I'm more handsome and my family is less crazy than that one. You're good. We could go to city hall and have Carl do our vows. All I need is you. The ceremony around it doesn't change the commitment." And he didn't want to have to wear a suit if he could avoid it.

"Darrell didn't count. On pretty much every level. This is the first time I've done this. I didn't feel for his wolves the way I do ours. I never felt for him not even the tiniest bit what I do you. So the wedding was a silly, fluffy, fun thing for me, but it wasn't necessarily a commentary on who or what I was. Most assuredly not about my relationship with Darrell. Which I suppose explains why we didn't get married.

"This is our forever."

He drew her close, resting his chin on the top of her head.

"So, in a month? A week? Tomorrow?"

"I have to set up a few things. We don't need a big church wedding, but my parents will want to have a party or reception of some kind. I expect Patty and your aunts will too."

He growled again, annoyed. He wanted her right

then. But would he deny her this? Not a chance. If it pleased her, he'd make it happen.

"Give me two weeks. Okay? That's not even very much time, especially with Thanksgiving coming up and you know we'll hear about that."

Two weeks was doable. He could live with that.

"I imagine my grandma has some help she'd love to give."

"Of course. The rings, they're special. She gave them to you for me?"

"She told me she'd had them and was waiting for the right woman to pass them on to."

"That's a really nice thing," she said sleepily, her body a warm, comfortable weight in his lap. "I'm sure my parents will want to do the food. How many do you think will be there? Is this a whole entire pack feed four hundred thing or what?"

"Dooley will feed our guests. The wedding will be open to the entire pack. So about six hundred or so, but most likely not all at once."

"Darrell didn't do that. That's a lot of wolves to feed. Will they all come?"

"The Prime is marrying, of course they will. As for what your last fiancé did or didn't do, he's a poor excuse for a wolf."

"You have such low self-esteem."

He smiled at the slowing of her voice as she got sleepier and sleepier.

"If you talk to my dad, he can coordinate with you on the food. It's going to be a big job."

"It's my job to provide for my mate and my wolves. It's who I am, Katie Faith. We'll hunt, all of us in the Dooley family, then we'll feed our people."

"Oh. Well that's nice. Given where the mercantile is, how about we do something there? We can use the lawn, get some tents up for the reception." It took her a while to get the whole thing out and he knew she teetered on the edge of sleep.

"Darlin'? It's late. What time do you have to be up?"

"On a normal Sunday I'd get up at nine or so to be at the Counter to open by 10:30. But we both know it's not going to be a normal Sunday. I have until about seven. I need to stop by my parents' place, go see Miz Rose and then go in to prep for what's going to be a big day once church lets out."

"Gawkers." He curled his lip.

"Whatever. I will make sure not a one of them gets away without having spent at least five dollars. I'll make it a contest for myself."

He smiled. "You're a pain in the ass on purpose?"

"I have a business to run. If the people in this town want to come into my shop to stare and gather stuff to gossip about, they will most assuredly do it with a soda or a milkshake or whatever in their hand or they can get out. I have bills to pay. A wedding dress to find and purchase. They damned well better spend money in the Counter."

Jace certainly had no plans to tangle with her. He'd throw his money down happily to watch her make him a chocolate malted any old day.

"I've been putting money aside for us for a few months. I'll get you added to the account so you can pay for that dress."

She snorted and he heard the tired in it. "No you won't. It's very sweet of you to be saving for us." She sniffled. "But the dress is something I want to do myself. And just stop that growl you're about to give me. I know you can't handle being told no. But if you want me in your life, you're going to have to get used to it."

He swallowed it back but tightened his hold a little. She wriggled, but it was more to get closer than anything sexual.

"You're a pain in the ass."

"I know. How on earth do you put up with me?" she asked sleepily.

He smiled, let her hear it in his voice. "It's a trial at times."

Her harrumph didn't have much behind it. Then, she got a little heavier as she sighed, dropping into sleep right there in his arms.

After a few minutes more, he carried her into the bedroom and settled at her side, curled around her. A last touch, his fingertip slid across the ring she wore that marked her as his. That metal she said carried the magic of the women who'd come before her.

She fit into that line well, he thought as sleep began to sink hooks into his consciousness.

Chapter Twenty-Five

Mac Pembry strolled into Salt & Pepper as Katie Faith shared some dinner with her friends the next day.

He headed right to their table as several Dooley wolves in the place kept a very close watch on him.

"If you're here to start some mess, Mac Pembry, I'm happy to give you some," she warned.

"I'm here to talk to you about what happened last night."

"This is something between you and Jace. I'm not going to let you put me between you."

He smiled, tipping his head to indicate the empty chair. "Can I sit? Have a few minutes of your time? You worried Jace might get jealous?"

"Oh, you think you can say that and not piss me off?"

Two wolves at a nearby table shot to their feet, catching her attention. She nodded her thanks, but waved them back to their seat.

"Don't you try to get to me through Jace, you understand? I don't take kindly to such talk."

"You're right. I apologize for that. May I have a few minutes? Here in public. If you don't like what I have to say, I'll go."

"What?" She indicated the chair. "Say it and be done."

"You're still mad about last night," he said.

"Is that what you have to say?"

He gave her one of those earnest handsome guy faces. "You're being hard right now, Katie Faith," he added a charming smile.

She just stared at him until he sighed.

"She didn't mean it the way you think she did."

She goggled at him a moment. "Really? Are you referring to the ugly stuff your mother said last night that set off a fight in the middle of a Founder's Day dance? The comment wishing me better than the mother of three sons standing right there with me? God, no wonder y'all are so messed up with that as a mother." She shook her head, really mad now.

"She's still my mom." His voice took on an edge and that made her even angrier.

Aimee put her hand on Katie Faith's arm, just a touch to let her know she wasn't alone. "What is your problem?" Aimee asked Mac, defensive of her friend.

"This is more complicated than you're making it out to be." He glared at Katie Faith and she glared right back. "Yes, it was a bitchy thing to say, but she didn't mean it to say she hoped you died."

She snorted. "Oh well then it's *totally* okay for Scarlett to have said such a thing in front of three men who lost a mother. Or maybe Annie's sisters, who were there too. I'm sure all those folks who lost someone they loved mean nothing in the never-ending quest your mother has to be the ugliest, pettiest citizen of Diablo Lake."

His eyes widened then as he reared back, offended. Good.

Katie Faith waved a hand at him. Dismissing him.

"Get out of my face, Mac. I'm not joking around now.

Your mother or not, she's broken rules. You know it. How can anyone take Pembry serious when you don't handle that? She'll tear y'all apart. And good luck with it, because it has nothing to do with me. What she said was meant to hurt Jace and his brothers. Scarlett is a mess and I won't play pretend that she *didn't mean* what she said. And I sure won't take any responsibility for what she said. We're done here."

"You're just going to let this keep going until it ends up in open war?" he asked her.

"I'm going to what now? You're truly sitting there after what your mother and brother have done and saying this is about what I have or haven't done? Is that what you learned in your fancy school in London then?"

He growled, but it wasn't cute like when Jace did it. She didn't like it one bit so she crowded closer, fighting the urge to get away from him. If she meant to do what she told Jace and truly lead at his side, she had to think and act like a wolf at times like this.

"I'm doing what I can. But you make it harder when you act this way. Everyone starts feeling like they're losing power and position and they make bad choices."

"It's not my job to make your life easy, Mac. The scene at the grocery store? Your mother started it. Continued it even as I literally ran away from her. Darrell getting his ass tossed into the street when he threatened me? He started it. He came into the Counter and got my daddy all riled up. Your mother deliberately ruined my engagement and said cruel things. Getting *my* momma upset, sending my father to bed early. Your brother started a fight with Jace, got his ass kicked, called for his daddy and your daddy hasn't done a damned thing to shut him up. So. As I said, we're done here. This is a Pembry problem. Not a Katie Faith problem. But if you make it a Katie Faith problem you're not going to like my response." She looked at her phone. "I have to be somewhere just now so I'll even make it easy and leave first." She stood, leaving money on the table for her food.

Aimee looked across the table at Mac for long moments as if trying to puzzle him out before she joined Katie Faith at the front door.

"I'll talk to you later on." She needed to stop by her parents and then head home to meet up with Jace.

"Yes. I want to hear on the dress situation." She gave Katie Faith a hug. "Don't let him get you all upset, you hear?"

"This whole mess makes me upset."

"I know. But try not to let it anyway."

Sighing, Katie Faith headed to her car and over to check on her mom and dad, who'd taken the day off and stayed home to rest after Katie Faith harassed them and even resorted to tears.

It was bald-faced manipulation of her dad, but she'd have done it again in a heartbeat if that's what would be necessary to keep him safe and healthy.

He was still pouting when she arrived. But Miz Rose was there, sitting at the dining room table with her mom, when Katie Faith came in.

"Hey," she said, giving her grumpy dad a smooch before heading over to the table to do the same with her mom and Miz Rose.

"Hey, darlin'. Miz Rose and I were just talking about the dress. She brought hers, I have mine and we've got your Grandma Abel's dress too. But we also want you to know if you don't want any of the dresses we won't be upset. This is your day."

"Let's go try them on and see what's what first? Then we can decide if I need an entirely new dress or if we can do some alterations."

Two of Miz Rose's daughters had worn the dress and Katie Faith knew why. It was a beautiful, simple silk sheath. It was what she'd always considered elegant. But perhaps more suited to a long, lean body instead of Katie Faith's, she thought as she checked herself out in the mirror.

"Even with alterations I think this wouldn't flatter you," Miz Rose said as she frowned.

Her mom nodded. "Try this one." Grandma Abel had been Rose's second cousin and Nadine's great grand-mother.

A white satin undersheath went on first, followed by a lace overdress with two tiers. There was a sharp nip at the waist, but it was a higher waistline. It should have been too much. Or not enough. But it was…perfect.

"My great grandpa Mike went off to the city and came back with the dress. It sat in the back of a closet at your grandma's house for years and years. I found it in a garment bag. It's in perfect shape for a dress that's at least a hundred years old."

"It's very old fashioned." She cocked her head and looked at herself.

"Edwardian, I believe, is the style and time period." Miz Rose gathered up Katie Faith's hair, twisting it back at the base of her neck. "It suits you."

"Feminine without being overly fussy. I wouldn't have thought the tiers would suit you so well. You look beautiful. What do you think?" her mom asked her.

It was totally different than her dress the first time around. That one had been a poofy, floofy confection with seed pearls and the like.

This dress was sort of like Jace and their wedding itself. Improbable, but it worked.

"I think it's the most perfect wedding dress I could have imagined."

Her mother stood behind her on one side and Miz Rose on the other as they stared at the dress and Katie Faith in it.

"If you cry, I'm going to cry and it'll be a mess," she warned her mother.

Her mom sucked in a breath and stood up straight. "I think you're perfect in it. There's a veil."

She pulled out a length of tulle and Katie Faith gasped at the pretty embroidery at the edges. Delicate whirls and swirls of tiny flowers and leaves.

In her hands, the magic of it seemed to flare to life.

"This wasn't bought in the city, though. Someone who loved the bride very much did this over painstaking hours of work."

She held it at the back of her neck. "Here. We can pin it into the bun. Give it a little bit of modern to go with the traditional dress that way."

They did a little measuring and pinning to adjust the fit better. Her mom would do the alterations and Miz Rose volunteered to handle the flowers as her son-in-law ran a floral delivery service out of his landscaping business.

"His greenhouses are absolutely bursting with roses right now. What about something with fall colors?"

Witches were badasses when it came to growing roses. All winter long the roses climbed up the trellis at the side of her parents' house because her dad had such a gift with them.

"Corals and yellows with some orangey reds. Yes. Nothing else. Long stemmed. We can tie them with ribbon or the like. Jace's boutonnière should be one of those colors. He's going through the mercantile to order a tux. He pretty much just let me choose it."

"You're not giving us very long to plan. Are you sure you're not pregnant? Because if you're not, if you gave me six weeks, that's only a month longer than you already had chosen. If you give me six weeks we can do up such a pretty wedding at the church."

She ignored the pregnancy comment. "I'm so relieved it was booked." She set the veil aside carefully before taking her mom's hands and squeezing. "Honestly. I want to have Carl do the honors on the front porch of the mercantile. Then we can put a big tent up on the lawn for food and dancing after. I want to marry Jace. I want to do it with my family and friends there. I'm really happy with all the plans."

Her mom kissed her cheek. "Your aunts and I will be baking the cake. No arguing."

When she was going to marry Darrell, his mother had insisted they buy a cake from some bakery all the way in Tompkins Creek. She'd sneered at the very idea of making a wedding cake like common people.

"I'm not arguing at all. I can't wait." She was as common as they came and thank goodness for it. Especially if it meant she'd take a cake baked by people who loved her over a store-bought one any day.

"Jace told me earlier that the pack would provide the meal. I don't remember that at all from Darrell and said so. But then he got that face of his and explained that

Darrell was a lame wolf anyway. Cake is ours though, I'll let him know that." Once she told him why, he'd be all for it.

"Where on earth are we going to get all the chairs we'll need for the ceremony? Six hundred plus, he said?" Her mother looked heavenward.

"What I think would work best is if we can work with city hall to get the permit to shut this part of the street down. Make it into a block party type of thing. But I'm thinking the ceremony party will be less crowded than the rest. You give people cake, food and drinks and they'll come out. We can rent chairs." Normally she'd get them through Pembry freight but she didn't want to have anything to do with them at the moment. "Aimee says she knows someone who knows someone. It'll happen."

"An operation this size will be bound to go wrong here and there. Long as we've got enough chairs for the elderly and enough food, we'll be fine," Miz Rose said as Katie Faith got dressed in her street clothes once more.

"The only thing I can't deal with going wrong is the actual wedding part. Everything else we can handle as it comes up."

Jace had been chopping wood when one of his cousins came over to tell him about what Mac Pembry had done to Katie Faith earlier that day at Salt & Pepper.

Katie Faith came into the yard five minutes later, when he was still working through his mad as he put things away in the moonlight.

"Whatcha doin' out here?" she called out.

"It would be nice," he said, trying hard to keep the

anger from his tone, "if I found out things from you instead of other people."

Her smile fell away. "What are you talking about?"

"Mac Pembry getting up in your face in public and me hearing from my cousin instead of my fiancée."

"You listen here, buddy. I've been with my mom and Miz Rose fitting *my wedding dress* and planning the reception. Do you think I was going to toss that—actually important thing—aside to run to you to tell you Mac Pembry acted like an alpha wolf in the middle of a restaurant? Is that what you think I should have done? Because I don't. Would you like to hear what happened from someone it happened to instead of some tattletale cousin?"

Then she poked him in the chest and he was so stunned he started to laugh, pulling her into a hug. "Can we start over?"

"I think that's a good idea. I just got back from my mom's house. I have a dress. The alterations will be made. I chose flowers and we even got the ball rolling on gathering all the things we'll need to try to accommodate a thousand people or so. I wanted a small wedding. Remember that? You're the one who was like oh well hey we need to invite all six hundred of my friends."

She then laid out all the different details from the dance floor to tents to be set up. "I'm leaving the food to you, because that's your thing. But the cake is my thing. My mom and my aunts will make it. That's what they do when one of their own gets married."

"I admit all that is more important than rushing over here to tattle on Mac Pembry. But how about a text instead if something like that happens in the future? And it most likely will since you'll be leading them with me and you'll come to see what a pain in the ass it can be to sit in the leader's chair. Tell me?"

"If I'd have texted you, you'd have rushed over to my mom and dad's place and demanded to know exactly what happened. Don't pretend otherwise. Now if you cool your jets a little, I can tell you what happened."

She told him about the weird interaction she'd had with Mac earlier. He didn't like it. Not one bit. He should have approached Jace rather than going around him to Katie Faith.

When she'd finished, she looked him over carefully, wagging a finger. "That face of yours. Stop. I'm here. He didn't scare me. Like, at all. He was doing the bidding of his family, but he's not Darrell. And I did insult his mother."

"That's because she's out of control. Still, there—"

"Are rules. I get it. He should have talked to you. Which is what I told him repeatedly. All he did in there was look like a jackwagon and I underlined for him that I wasn't going to be put in the middle and that he needed to speak to you."

She kissed him even as he kept frowning.

"I don't like that he came at you."

"I know. But it wasn't threatening. I would have said so if that was the case."

He wanted to storm over to Mac's place a little less than he did just a few minutes prior.

"I really do hate being told no. It'd be much easier if everyone just obeyed me," he muttered as they went up to her place.

"Yeah, well. I told you the other day that if you mean to have me in your life you'd better get used to hearing it. Also, there are four wolves in the hallway outside your apartment. You might need to have office hours or something so they don't all have to wait around."

He walked a careful line, especially until his grandfather stepped down. He didn't want to shove JJ out. So as they slowly transitioned, he let his grandfather set the pace. It had been his seat for decades and Jace could learn from him for the rest of his life and still not know everything.

"Let me handle this. Will you let the wolves know I'll be up shortly? I'll be over at your place after that," he told her, kissing her quickly before she hustled off toward the mercantile building.

Chapter Twenty-Six

On the Monday before the wedding, Jace came home from work to find a note taped to his door. An invitation to dinner for him and Katie Faith from his grandmother. She advised them to show up with a big appetite at no later than five thirty.

Which was about half an hour from that moment.

He turned on his heel and knocked on Katie Faith's door.

She opened up with a smile. "Hey."

"We've been asked to dinner in half an hour over at my grandparents' place." He kissed her quickly.

"Tonight?"

"Yes. I'm going to clean up a little while you gussy up a little. Come over to my place when you're ready and we'll head over."

She might have muttered that he was bossy, but he couldn't argue so he didn't.

Once they arrived, he wasn't surprised to see his brothers and uncles at the table already. This had the hallmarks of some sort of official pack business.

There was hugging and kissing all around. It pleased Jace to see how easily Katie Faith had adapted to their more touchy-feely ways, giving and receiving caresses and reassuring touches.

"Just in time." His grandmother motioned them to the table. "Tab, honey, bring in that big platter with the pork chops. Jace, bring in the potatoes."

JJ gave the blessing and within a few minutes, all chatter had quieted down to get serious about eating.

They weren't really used to girlfriends at the table, but Katie Faith wasn't really that. She was more. Someone they'd all known since childhood and she fit with them. Mainly because that's how she was, but he wasn't unaware of how hard she worked to learn about pack law and custom.

After some small talk and wedding detail stuff that had him daydreaming about fishing and maybe some tent sex, he noted his grandfather had taken over and Jace paid better attention.

"Patty and me, well, we're going to move out. This is the Patron house. Jace will be Patron soon enough. He and Katie Faith should move in after the wedding."

Everyone nodded like it was normal to just up and give your house away. He'd grown up in this house. It had always felt like home. Once he allowed the idea to root, he couldn't shake the vision of Katie Faith hollering at their kids not to slam the screen door when they went out back to play.

Katie Faith looked to him, waiting for his expression. Waiting, he knew, for him to show how he felt before she did the same.

Love swamped him then, shoving away all those broken edges that scraped him raw sometimes. He gave her a small tip of his chin and she smiled, reaching out to take his hand.

Lauren Dane 321

"This is a very fine gift. Thank you." To refuse would have been the worst sort of insult. "But we don't want to put you out of your home."

"You know we have a cabin at the lake. I've been spending time out there over the last months, making it a place your grandmomma will be happy. I got my dock. I got my poles and my privacy. My life has been noisy a long time. I like the idea of some quiet."

Jace heard the weariness in his grandfather's tone. He'd been in charge for pretty much his entire adult life. Had lived through tragedy and brought his pack back from utter chaos. It took a toll and he wouldn't begrudge his grandfather wanting to retire.

"We've been moving things over there since before your engagement. The kitchen and bathroom are finished. Hell, nicer than what you've got here." His grandmother winked at him. Telling him it would be all right. "It's how things work. I moved in here with JJ after he took over, just like you will."

"There's very good magic in this house," Katie Faith said, making Jace love her even more. "The house was built with love. It's lived here and given magic to these walls and this ground for a very long time. Babies and grandbabies only brought it more light. It's a safe place."

His grandmother blinked away tears. Major handed her a tissue and she laughed, holding him to her for a moment.

"The Patron lives here. This is where you and Katie Faith belong. I was thinking we could have the Patron ceremony either on your wedding day or close to it," JJ said.

They were skipping the honeymoon. He knew she'd be too nervous to leave town with her father still recovering and this situation still raw between Nadine and Scarlett.

A honeymoon would keep until next year, he'd told her. But what she'd said was that she'd rather spend their money and effort on a house.

Ever practical. He liked that about her.

Now they had that house. One he'd have to update because, like his grandpa, he wanted his wife to be happy. Wanted her to feel as if it was *hers* and not someplace she was a tenant.

Still'd be less costly than building from the ground up or buying something if they were lucky enough to find what they needed on the market.

"I'm sure we can work the Patron ceremony into our wedding day. I mean, the whole pack will be there anyway," Katie Faith said.

"Let's you and me talk over some details and then we can work it out with my grandparents," he told her. Jace got the feeling she might think it was something akin to wedding vows but there was a lot more to it than that. And it wasn't something the whole town could be part of.

He leaned over to kiss her and murmur his thanks before catching the second pass of the mashed potatoes and loading up another helping.

Katie Faith watched a bunch of gorgeous shifters hefting tables, chairs, tent poles and all other manner of items they'd need for the reception in two days' time. Out beyond the mercantile they'd erected a massive kitchen. They'd been preparing the wedding feast for the last two weeks as freezers, fridges and root cellars began to fill up with all the supplies.

She sat on the roof outside her apartment, Aimee at her side.

"I can't believe how well this whole thing is coming together. In two weeks. You're a beast." Aimee clinked her root beer to hers.

"I haven't done much. Not really. All those cute Dooleys are the ones who've handled the setup. You and Lara are the ones who found all these chairs. Miz Rose handled the flowers. My mom did the alterations on my dress. The wolves have been hunting and fishing for the last two weeks. They've even got smokers set up and will start cooking some of the meat tomorrow. All I've really had to do is stand around and thank folks who've done things for me. It's pretty rad."

Aimee laughed. "People love you."

"I hope I don't suck too terribly at being a wife and a werewolf Patron who's really a witch." Katie Faith said it so fast she was pretty certain that if it had been anyone other than Aimee they wouldn't have been able to understand her.

"You're going to be amazing at all that."

"I don't know." She shook her head. "Patty is one of them. She knows what it's like to be a werewolf. She understands them in a way I can't. Ever. And she's so steady. I'm weird. Wolves don't know what to make of weird."

"You need to slow down there, sister. You're heading off that ledge and there's no reason," Aimee said. "Patty is amazing. I totally agree. But it's not like they expect you to be her. And she'll still be in Diablo Lake if you need advice or help."

Probably. Werewolves were all so damned nosy and

in one another's business she had no real doubt Patty would continue to be an active part of pack life.

"I'm going to be the first non-shifter Patron in Diablo Lake history. How's that for pressure?"

"But not the first mixed marriage by a long shot. Right this moment I can name at least ten couples who live here now. You count their friends and family, their children and grandchildren and you're not alone. And even if you were, you're going to handle this because you're capable that way. You just are. Organized and energetic. Except for mornings but we won't speak of that though I take it he's tolerant of your flaw in that way."

Katie Faith groaned. "He's *so* fucking cheerful in the morning. And he likes morning sex. I have to be up anyway so I may as well go on ahead and get on board with that."

"Well, sure. You show him your tits! Of course he's tolerant of what a shrew you are until you have coffee and or some sort of baked good."

"He does seem to enjoy them. And he lets me brush my teeth and pee first. I can't get on board with all that sex until then."

"With the door open? No way! He must be a wizard in bed."

They dissolved into laughter as Katie Faith blushed furiously.

"Well, I'm just sayin', he vanquished the balrog and he's like a level 15 sex paladin. Or whatever, I don't actually know what a paladin does. So that's not going to work as a wise crack."

Aimee patted her shoulder. "Such a pretty face."

Which started off a fresh gale of laughter.

"He's awesome in the ways of sexing. Enough said.

However, no one is awesome enough to make me down with the door open during peeing. Or god forbid, just walking in to get something when I'm peeing. Were-wolves have boundary issues, I'm telling you." She winced as she realized how much emotion she'd put in that last sentence.

"We're on the bullet train to tangent-land, aren't we?"

So much had changed in such a short period of time, Katie Faith had a bit of whiplash. His family though, they just sort of barreled into every room as well as her life. They were total busybodies and now that Jace had been taking over, at least five of them seemed to constantly be underfoot.

"You mock, but you know you want to hear it. Am I right?" Katie Faith taunted.

Aimee made a *get on with it* motion.

"They just like to hug and lay on you so no complaints there. And he sleeps nice and warm. But they come to him now. His pack members I mean. Every night they wait for him to talk to him and I have less time with him to just hang out than I did before. And I know that's part of the deal. So I'm trying to learn from him. Trying to learn from Patty and JJ. His brothers have been great with history lessons and the like.

"They're all good to me. The Dooley wolves have welcomed me. The Pembrys didn't welcome me. Not like that. I mean, they didn't shun me or make me feel bad or anything. But I never felt like each individual wolf was part of my family." She swallowed hard. "Hell, they just built a dance floor that they'll then use to make the deck on the back of the Patron house."

Which was the capper on all this panic.

"JJ and Patty will like that. The view over the backyard and the forest just beyond sure is a pretty one. They could have a barbecue out there too."

"Monday night we went to dinner over at JJ and Patty's. Right after I got my second roll buttered, they up and announce they're moving out of the Patron house and giving it to us. They've had a place out on the southern end of the lake for years now. JJ needs the quiet and she needs him to be healthy so they're headed there. They started a while ago, apparently, and just told no one. But for real they've begun loading up furniture and moving it. Like today."

"Wow! That's unexpected and sort of fast. I mean, great. It's a beautiful house and all. How do you feel about this?"

Katie Faith said, "I guess it just made it a whole lot of realness at once. Getting married. Taking on a new family including six hundred or so folks who are as good as family. Moving out of my apartment to move in with Jace after moving out of my apartment in Chattanooga to come back here. I've lived on my own for my entire adult life and now we're not only going to be married, but living in the same house, a house that he grew up in. Jesus on a pony."

She blew out a breath.

"He's so sweet about the whole thing. I can't hide it from him that I'm a little freaked. But I'm trying to keep it to a minimum."

"Do you have second thoughts?"

Katie Faith shook her head immediately. "No. I'm utterly certain I love him and I want to marry him. We already live together pretty much so that probably won't be such a big deal though he's a mess. I hope that bathroom has double sinks because he leaves so much water everywhere when he shaves."

"Okay we're headed toward tangent-ception at this point. Stick to one side topic at a time or I get too confused." Aimee was so great at keeping her reined in.

Katie Faith grinned a moment. "Anyway. So I think I've dealt with anxiety over the living together part. And the marriage part too. But wow, this Patron thing. It's like his whole life. The heart of who he is. And he's so good at it. I'm seriously impressed with how much they trust him. They come to him and wait in the hall outside our apartments. And they do that to ask his advice on stuff. Should they try this new business, or should they ask their sweetheart to get married. They come to him when there's been some sort of dispute because they trust him to solve it in a fair and just manner. The grumpier he is, the more they love it. I don't even get it but it makes me love them all even more in return. The aunties, oh God, they swarm all over him, asking for his help, wanting his reassurance. It's adorable."

Aimee said, "You got yourself some kind of life. I'm not jealous, because that's a negative thing. I'd like to have that someday. To have someone look at me the way he looks at you. And you have such a blazing, bright path into your future. I love that for you because only someone as perfect for you as Jace is good enough."

"He's so good at being Patron. And his grandparents were too, even during a time of crisis, you know? And I'm not a werewolf, as we've already established. I'm such a newbie I squeak when I walk. Moving into that house, which he's of course remodeling any way I want, just makes it all so *immediate*. It's just…a lot to take in and I know I'm going to screw stuff up."

Aimee hugged her, laughing.

Katie Faith knew Aimee would say all the right things, which was why she finally confided all her anxieties and obsessions from over the last two weeks.

The Dooley wolves *did* seem to like her. They trusted her. Sought her out in town. Made a point to come by and say hello if she was working at the Counter. They'd opened their arms up to admit her to their community.

She really liked that.

"My best advice is to be yourself because that's who we all love. Weird or not. You said yourself you're certain you love him and you want to marry him. So, those are the two biggest deals. Then you said you already pretty much live together and that wouldn't be such a big deal to adjust to. You're nearly all the way to okay by this point. The rest is you learning how to lead with Jace and I don't imagine you'll be anything but great at it, because you're too competitive not to be." Aimee's cockeyed grin eased the last of her anxiety. For the moment anyway.

"I'm so glad to have you back in my life every day. I do feel better. Thanks for the pep talk."

"I admire you so much, Katie Faith. Which means I have every possible confidence you will be great at all this. You'll mess up, yes. Everyone does. But you have Jace at your side. You got this."

Katie Faith hugged her oldest, dearest friend before catching sight of Damon.

"I need to talk to Damon about something. I'll be back." Katie Faith darted off.

He smiled when he caught sight of her as he put tools back into the shed. "Hey, sweetheart. Do our preparations meet with your approval?"

She hugged him. "It looks fantastic. You're making this day so much more special. Thank you."

They'd gotten permission to close off the street surrounding the mercantile. The tables and tents would be scattered on the huge lawn that fronted it and the Patron's house next door, spilling out into the road where a dance floor would go. A live band would play.

Though not the small wedding she'd originally wanted, it'd be a damned fun party so she'd just up and invited the whole town. She'd told Jace they might as well make it an event to unite instead of divide. If Pembrys wanted to come—as she counted many among her friends and family, she hoped they did—they would be welcomed. If they didn't, she couldn't help that. The other event, the one that had booked the church was for a christening and a party after. So Katie Faith had told them to stop on by after that if they wanted cake.

Things were going to be all right.

She and Jace could do this.

She blew out a shaky breath, holding on to that. "Do you have a minute? I need to talk to you about something."

His expression sobered. "Always."

"I know that once I marry Jace I'll be subject to pack law. Specifically when it comes to discussing anyone who's cast out."

The answering expression on his face told her he knew exactly what she was going to talk about.

"Until then, I'm in a gray area and I hate the idea of things being used as a way to hurt him. Or you. So I can tell you I know *some* of the details about what happened with your father, but nothing really specific. I've been going back and forth as to whether I should tell

Jace what I do know. You and Major understand him better than anyone. What do you think?"

He sighed. "It's hard to see past my own bias. Maybe you might tell him what you told me and let him decide if he wants to know more. I do hope once you take over, you'll re-think some of our laws. Silence hurts a lot of people."

She nodded. "It's on my radar, for whatever that's worth. I love you all."

Damon hugged her. "Thank you."

"You planning to try to steal my woman, Damon?"

She turned to catch sight of Jace approaching, along with several others who'd been setting things up. Damn, he looked good enough to lick.

"Cute as your brother is, I seem to only like one flavor of werewolf these days."

He hugged her and she sniffed him. Clean sweat always smelled so good on his skin. She managed a lick at the end of a kiss she pressed to the side of his neck.

"We're headed out for a run. Is everything all right?" He tipped her chin up to look into her eyes.

"Yes. Go. Have fun. I'll see you later. Come by if it's not too late. Even if it is."

He flashed her a grin and within moments, they'd all swept off, heading toward the edge of the forest behind the Patron house.

Jace caught up with Damon just before they took the shift. "Everything okay with her?"

Damon nodded. "Yes. She wants to talk to you about something. But it's not dire. There's nothing for you to worry about or I'd have told you up front."

"Then why'd you overexplain just now?" He gave his brother a careful look.

"Because you'd have asked me all those questions so I just went on and answered them first." Damon quirked a brow.

"Okay. Yeah. Okay." He breathed out carefully as they reached the little outbuilding they left their clothes and other belongings in before they took on the wolf.

She was fine. Not in danger. Very happy. When he'd just had her in his arms she'd been in love with him.

He stood on the dirt, pine needles, leaves, loam gone a little wet from condensation. The moon hung overhead, three quarters full. The magic of the earth seemed to suck him under and he let go of his human self.

Wolf took over.

Paws hit the earth this time, gaining purchase and tearing into the deeper forest ahead.

The entire world around him might have been black and white, but it was the scent and taste that rendered everything in full color to his senses.

Strength roared through his veins like a river. Power drove him as they hunted. Hunted to feed this mate and their pack. Their family.

He led them through, using keen senses and his connection with them to flank and bring down prey the wolf knew men would remove to be presented to her.

He chuffed out a breath, pride driving him to continue. Wanting to please her, the other part of his heart, no matter her form.

After he'd cleaned up from the run and made sure the dressing of the game they'd hunted was nearly done, he came home wearing human skin to find her tucked up on the couch, waiting for him at his place.

She looked up from her laptop where she was most

likely doing work of some sort. "Did you have a good run?"

He settled in next to her, wanting to touch her. "We did. We've got more than enough meat for the wedding now. I was thinking we might go on more regular hunts like this to be sure freezers are full through the winter. If we did it as a pack, we could share and no one would feel like it was charity."

Pride was important to a wolf but not at the expense of your family being hungry. It was his turn to lead. His place to be sure they were fed, clothed and safe. He couldn't do everything, but what he could do, he would.

"That's a great idea. Patty already has a list of families she likes to make sure get a little extra here and there when she goes on her visits."

"She also has a list of people she calls whenever someone in town has excess meat or fish, vegetables from the garden, all that."

"She's the heart of your family. I don't think I can fill her shoes."

He turned her, pulling her into his lap and settling back, arms wrapped around her body.

"She's got sixty years of experience. She created all sorts of processes you'll be able to plug right into, which is a huge help. But they don't expect you to be her. You'll be your own kind of Patron."

"Aimee said pretty much the same thing. I have to tell you something," she blurted out.

"This have anything to do with whatever you and Damon were talking about earlier?"

"Yes." She told him about the discussion she'd had with her mom and Nadine and that she'd asked Damon for his advice on whether or not to come to Jace and what he'd said.

"When I was a boy I used to imagine he was some hero who'd been wronged. A victim of a terrible injustice. But that didn't last very long. You can say someone should be erased from pack records, but he didn't do whatever he did in a vacuum. My assumption, given what I've been told and what I could figure out, is that he did something horribly violent and most likely to a woman. A Pembry woman. I'm a cop. I can figure it out if I really wanted to." He let that hang a little, chewing it over.

But it had felt invasive, and whether or not he agreed with the way the pack handled that sort of erasure, he was still bound to pack law.

She nodded, understanding. "Okay. But I think pack law is wrong. I think the wolves who loved whoever your father hurt not being able to grieve openly is a terrible idea. I think it must have led to festering resentment, how can it not? What about you and your brothers? Innocent in all this. You have a right to know your own history. I'm not a wolf and I can't understand your ways the way you all do. But it's cruel and it doesn't serve any goal. There's enough secrecy in our lives as it is."

"You've done some thinking about this, I see."

"I'm trying to prepare to do this job. This life commitment not only to you, but to your pack. I have opinions. Remember? I warned you when you asked me to marry you that I planned to be fully involved as your wife and the female Patron."

He hugged her to him a little tighter. She had, and it pleased him deeply.

"I won't argue with you. I need you with me. We'll get through this together."

She kissed his neck before scrambling to her feet. "Come on."

He grabbed her hand as he rushed past, rushing to the bed, falling to it with breathless laughter and a tangle of limbs as clothes came flying off.

He rushed to get more, loosing his need as he roved over all her bared skin, with teeth, lips and tongue until she writhed, breathless beneath him. He loved driving her to this state of impatience.

Her scent had ripened. Nearing her most fertile time of month. He licked a trail up her inner thigh to her pussy, tasting all that sweetness for himself.

She arched into his mouth on a gasp before he flipped her over and slid inside as deep as he could go.

Her nails dug into the sheets as she sought purchase to thrust back. He pulled her up to her knees before curling around her as he continued to fuck himself into her body.

Her skin shimmered with sweat. The scent they made together began to rise between them. When he reached around her hip to get to her clit with the pad of his middle finger she made a sound as her body squeezed him so tight he grunted.

His.

She was his as he was hers. He wanted everything. Wanted it right then as he wrenched an orgasm from her that dragged him down in her wake.

He fell to the mattress, still inside her as they lay there stunned.

Chapter Twenty-Seven

The day of the wedding broke with a few clouds that threatened rain, but held off as everything began to come together.

Katie Faith had gone to the Patron house—her house as of that day—met by her mother, TeeFay, Aimee, Miz Rose and Lara. Patty brought in champagne and they all visited and helped Katie Faith not be nervous.

In truth, she was too busy to be nervous as wolves and witches alike stopped over to fill her in and update her on the progress of all the last-minute preparations.

Finally, once she was done, her hair pinned with an antique comb her mother brought over, the veil reaching her fingertips but mainly out of the way at her back, she took a deep breath.

"You ready for this?" her mother asked.

"That day with Darrell seems like it happened a decade ago. Knowing all I do now, it seems pretty obvious he and I wouldn't have worked. This is different in every way."

Her wedding. Planned for them by friends and family with what she wanted in mind. The place was one she chose, not a fussy church she'd never belonged to anyway.

Aimee arranged the veil just so. "It feels different too."
It did.

Miz Rose took her hands, joined by her mother on
one side and TeeFay on the other. "Oh, you've made
your engagement ring the talisman where you store your
excess magic." She smiled over at Patty briefly. "This
was a good gift. All right, Katie Faith, my girl, we've
got a spell for you. A blessing, you could say."

Katie Faith made sure the handkerchief was at hand,
tucked at her waist where no one would see but would
be quick to retrieve for tears.

"It's been my pleasure to watch your magic coaxed
to life again," Miz Rose said. "Since you've been back,
you've dug your hands into the dirt and done the work.
It's been hard, I know it has. But you've done it and I'm
so proud of you."

Being a witch wasn't riding on brooms or curses. It
was being in tune with the ground at your feet, the sky
overhead and the trees all around. It was shaping energy as she willed it.

Not to hurt. But to defend.

And to grow flowers, but that was part and parcel of
being a witch, especially one with such a green witch
as a daddy.

They surrounded her, linking hands with Katie Faith
at the center of their circle. As they chanted, the air all
around her began to tingle against her skin. The spell
seemed to knit around her from her toes upward.

Love and strength seemed to flow into her as these
women she trusted so deeply gave her the gift of this
spell they'd made just for her.

Protection.

Wisdom.

Patience.

Compassion.

Curiosity.

As each one of these things jointed the daisy chain they draped around her, heart and soul, Katie Faith gave up trying not to cry and dabbed her eyes as tears came forth.

They loved her.

They believed in her.

She was part of something so much bigger than she'd ever thought. And that would guide her through even the darkest of times.

Her magic, already threaded through theirs, tightened, strengthened.

And when they finished, the spell seemed to *pop* and she could hear the outside world once more.

What a gift they'd given her. A piece of them lodged within her heart and the soul of her magic forever. Made her better.

"Thank you," she said around tears as she hugged each one.

Patty, who'd been crying too, added her hugs. "Thank you for letting me share in that. It was beautiful." She took Katie Faith's hands. "Welcome to the family."

"Before all the rest of my makeup gets cried off, we need to get moving." Katie Faith tried to sound gruff.

They walked out, circling to the back of the mercantile to meet up with her father. He smiled at her as she approached.

"You look so beautiful. When you were born, I had no idea what having a daughter would be like." He kissed her cheek. "It's been wonderful. *You're* wonderful and today you're going to be married to the guy you've been waiting for all along. I'm so proud of you and the woman you've become."

She slid her hand through his crooked elbow and her mother took up at her other side. They were both going to present her to Jace and his family for joining.

When they came around the front it nearly made her gasp. Flowers seemed to overflow everywhere. The boxes along the front porch railings had exploded in a riot of color.

"Miz Rose and I thought we could add a bit of our own floral magic," her father whispered.

"Oh, Daddy. Thank you. It's the most beautiful wedding ever."

Hundreds and hundreds of people stood, watching. The combined power from a crowd of shifters that big, spiced with pretty much every witch in town made her a little dizzy.

And at the top step he waited for her. Solemn with a little tiny curve at the corner of his mouth just for her.

His black tuxedo looked smashing on him as it spanned his wide, muscular shoulders, tapering down to his waist. His hair was tamed. Sort of. The edges played at his collar, but it worked on him.

"Happy anniversary," he said, holding his hand out to her.

"Katie Faith Grady is our only daughter," her father said to him. "A most precious gift. Don't squander it."

They took her hands and placed them in Jace's before stepping back.

"Hey there, Jace," she said.

"Hey there, Katie Faith. You ready to marry me?"

"Yeah. I am. Let's do this because I'm super hungry already and we have the Patron ceremony later."

He kissed her, much to the crowd's delight, as they headed to the spot Carl stood waiting for them.

The ceremony was a mix of old and new, of witch and wolf. Her parents offered their new marriage a spell of blessing and the pack laid pelts and horn aside for them. The elders had made them a wedding ring quilt she'd put on their bed, which they'd moved into the house earlier that day.

Never in her life had she felt like she was doing exactly what she was supposed to be. Not until that moment as Jace slid the band on her finger, snug up against the engagement ring as she said her I do.

JJ threw back his head and howled, long and loud, followed by pretty much everyone in the crowd—Pembrys in attendance as well—as the witches looked on.

And it was done.

She was married to Jace and her whole life beckoned, wide open and full of possibility.

Later, as she moved between one group to the next, a glass in her hand and a smile on her face, she nearly ran right into Scarlett.

Katie Faith groaned because there was no way her appearance meant anything good.

"You weren't invited," Patty said, stepping between them. "Get along home now."

"So you're not even acting like wolves anymore? Your Prime doesn't even have a real wife. He's got an imitation wife."

"And your pack has no Prime. Now I'm not saying this again, get the hell off my property." Patty's voice ended on a snarl. Katie Faith had never seen this side of her grandmother-in-law before.

But Scarlett must have. Enough to know Patty meant business.

"I'm not a real wife?" Katie Faith pinched her own arm. "Huh. I sure feel real."

"You got no call to talk about my kids," Scarlett yelled.

Jace hustled over with Damon at his side.

Mac also rushed over, putting an arm around his mother's shoulders as he threw them an apologetic look. He'd promised to be sure everyone behaved and looked pretty pissed off that wasn't the case.

"Y'all are garbage! Look at this mess." Scarlett kept talking as she went. "If you're so dedicated to your pack, where's the ceremony? How can you not do the full ceremony to take over as Patron? My daughter-in-law Sharon will be there and not acting like some human."

"Shut up, Momma!" Mac managed to get her moving down the block and around the corner.

"This isn't over, Jace Dooley! You got some answering to do for your daddy's sins!" was the last they heard.

"No you don't," she told him.

"If she'd only read the invitation she'd have seen you're doing the Patron ceremony after the reception," Aimee said. "But I guess it's garbage to read maybe."

Things weren't over.

Scarlett had lost her marbles and was going to continue to be a problem. And it was clear, given her last comment, that she was going to use Jace's father as a cudgel.

Katie Faith took Jace's hand in hers. She'd do whatever she had to, to protect him and their pack. Scarlett still hadn't figured out the humiliated young woman who'd run off years ago had come back grown up and ready to draw blood to protect those she loved.

"You ready to take a run on a wolf's back?" he asked.

If anyone ever asked her what it was like to be carried on the back of a pony-sized wolf as it tore through the forest, surrounded by hundreds of other wolves, Katie Faith could tell them to take pain reliever.

Her bones still felt a little jangly from all the bumping around as her feet finally touched the ground at the copse of giant trees about three miles from the mercantile in the deep forest.

When her sneakers made contact with the earth, the magic there rushed up to meet her. To greet her enthusiastically enough to bring a gasp.

All her life she'd been told her magic worked differently outside Diablo Lake's sprawling town borders. She knew it to be true after living away for several years. Her magic was still there, of course, when she'd lived in Chattanooga, but it had been a lazy stream.

Jace, still in wolf form, fought a ceremonial battle with his grandfather, who surrendered after the metallic scent of blood hit the air. And in that moment, that lazy stream, which had become a busy river, was a massive, never-ending, wave. A wall of power and energy so strong, so eternal and natural in her body.

In that very moment her potential unlocked and she was the witch she was born to be. At her wolf's side.

And as he transformed so quickly and powerfully, she knew it was her magic that made it possible.

"I'm not just your witch, Jace. I'm the pack's witch. You're all my wolves. My magic is part of yours now and always."

That hadn't been part of the script, but it needed to be said for the magic of that moment to be right. To shimmer and settle into place. A covenant between wolf and pack, and witch and wolf.

She knew her wolves lived in her, their joys and sadnesses.

Jace kissed her, getting blood on her chin.

"Dude. Ew."

He laughed, hugging her tight.

"I love you, Katie Faith. Let's go home now."

He took wolf form again and she clambered back on board before he tore off into the trees.

* * * * *

Acknowledgments

Thank you to the entire Carina Press team who are, as always, totally wonderful.

Thanks so much, Angela James for putting up with me and always knowing what to say and how to say it so my author brain hears it. And to Kerri Buckley who has stepped into that place with remarkable ease.

My beta readers: Mary, Fatin and Renee – thank you for your advice and your time and all the love you give my books (Lillie, I add you to this list!)

The spouse who is my best friend, a great sounding board and the inspiration for all my alpha heroes in some way or other – I love you.

About the Author

Lauren Dane is the *USA Today* and *NYT Bestselling* author of over seventy-five novels and novellas in the romance and urban fantasy genre. She lives in the Pacific Northwest among the trees with her spouse and children.

You can check out her latest releases, backlist and upcoming books at her website: www.LaurenDane.com or you can write her at LaurenDane@LaurenDane.com or via her PO Box: Po Box 45175, Seattle, WA 98145

And don't miss the next book in *New York Times* bestselling author Lauren Dane's Diablo Lake series: *Diablo Lake: Protected.*

The powerful witches of Diablo Lake are taking back control. No longer will they be pawns in the town's misguided power plays. Chosen to lead the charge, Aimee Benton can't possibly fall for a werewolf—especially a Pack Alpha.

Problem is, Mac Pembry is as irresistible as he is infuriating…

Chapter One

Aimee pulled her car into a spot at the rear of the mercantile. She'd walk over to Katie Faith's house from there because her driveway was currently housing construction stuff they were using on some remodeling going on.

The breeze on the back of her neck was unfamiliar, but she sort of liked it. She loved the soft fuzz at the base of her skull.

She headed across the lawns, pausing to breathe in the life her best friend had brought with her when she'd moved in. Roses burst forth over every planter box. They climbed up trellises and spilled across the edges of all the walks.

In December, this sight would be totally unreal in any other place but Diablo Lake. In Diablo Lake, roses in December meant a witch lived there and gave the earth her power.

A bunch of gorgeous men stood outside her best friend's place, all sweaty from building things. She paused to take it in, because life presented you blessings and it was disrespectful not to enjoy and appreciate them.

Hot werewolves with tools. It should be a calendar. Aimee made a mental note because, come to think of it, what a fantastic fundraiser idea for the organization she worked for.

She hummed her delight at the thought, and being werewolves with super hearing, the group of 'em all looked in her direction. They hadn't been alarmed, which meant they'd recognized her scent and most likely her magic.

"Hey, y'all," she called out, pretending she'd been thinking about cobbler instead of pecs and abs glistening in the sun.

Jace, Katie Faith's husband and most assuredly a gorgeous werewolf, paused, his eyes widening and his smile of welcome dropping into surprise. "You cut your hair."

Suddenly she went very shy and sort of embarrassed before reminding herself that hair grew back.

"I like it." Damon, one of Jace's brothers, stepped a little closer. "It's got blue in it. I didn't see it at first because your hair is already dark. Saucy. Diablo Lake definitely needs more saucy."

Saucy she could do.

Moment of panic passed, she said, "Thanks. I just thought a change would be nice and since the wedding is over and I don't have to worry about pictures, I figured why not do something big?"

Katie Faith came out onto the porch. "Did I hear Aimee out here?" Then she gasped, rushing over to get up in Aimee's space to get a look at her new haircut.

"It's fantastic. Flirty. So sexy. Mysterious even. My

God, why do you have such perfect features for short hair?"

Aimee, used to the way her best friend talked, understood it was all compliments and let herself be drawn into the house as she said her goodbyes to the others over her shoulder.

Once they were out of immediate earshot—though if they'd wanted to, the wolves could easily overhear though it was considered good manners to attempt not to eavesdrop—Aimee grabbed Katie Faith's hand.

"Spill this story." Katie Faith pointed at Aimee's head with her free hand. "This is a reaction haircut. With some get-me-over-something colored tips."

"This calls for liquor."

Katie Faith nodded and led the way. In the large and old-school kitchen, her friend poured them each a shot of tequila and then she clinked her glass to Aimee's. "All right. Let's hear it."

"So, Bob called me yesterday. Totally out of the blue."

Three years before she'd met Bob through her job as a rural social worker. He worked for one of the agencies the grant that funded her job came from.

They'd been on and off over those years. Meeting when she went to Knoxville to check in with some of her clients and at the main office of the social service agency she worked for.

Katie Faith's "bullshit" eyebrow rose. "Did he, now? In a booty-call way?"

Aimee got up to paw around through the cabinets until she found some chips and came back over.

"Well, it was weird. You know, he and I finally and

truly broke things off more than six months back now. I haven't seen him or spoken to him since. And, well, I know this sounds mean, but I really don't miss him. It was fun while it lasted, but it was never going anywhere permanent."

Even if they had both wanted to get more serious, there was still the problem of him not being from Diablo Lake. Bringing a human into town was a big deal. Marrying them into the community took dedication and a real match.

That was never what it had been with Bob.

"So," Aimee continued, "he told me he wanted to meet up because he'd been thinking about me and I was like, 'Dude, no, really it's okay. I've moved on, I'm not mad but I'm done.' So then he's like, 'Please can you just meet me? Just a few minutes.'"

She tore open the bag and stuffed her face in between the next two shots.

Katie Faith leaned back in her chair and gave her an appraising look before shaking her head slowly. "Oh, Aimee-girl, you're going to kill me with this story, aren't you? Last time you took this many shots of liquor in a short period of time it was the night I got left at the altar."

Aimee snorted, remembering that gawdawful scene when Darrell Pembry left her best friend waiting at the church to run off with another woman. "Well, this isn't as horrible as that, at least. However, you don't even know half. Just wait for it." She waved a hand. "So it was Friday and that's when I go down to Knoxville anyway. I agreed to meet him for coffee. Because, girl, no one gets between me and lunch and if it was going to go badly, I didn't want to mess up a meal."

They bumped fists. "So say we all," Katie Faith intoned, which made her laugh.

"I get there and he's sitting at a table already. I go over and he gives me the gracious-ex cheek kiss and hug and I'm like, he was a pretty good guy, I hope this can be cordial but I'm not feeling any tinglies at all. Not a one."

And at one time, they'd really had them.

"And then." She took a bracing breath because even remembering, it filled her with so much emotion. "Sweet, sweet baby Jesus. The man tells me several things. First, he's married. Has been for *fifteen* years." Nausea rose again at the feeling of betrayal that'd washed over her.

"Get out!" Katie Faith yelled it so loud Jace pounded into the room, looking alarmed. She winced at the sight and gave him a sheepish smile. "Sorry, honey. Aimee just told me something totally awful."

Jace turned his gaze Aimee's way, staring carefully. "Do you need us to teach someone a lesson for you?"

Aww, he'd just offered to beat a boy up for getting fresh like a real big brother would.

"As much pleasure as that would give me, I'm good. Thanks though," Aimee told him.

He nodded once before walking from the room, telling everyone to get back to work.

"But wait, there's more." Aimee thanked Katie Faith for the shot she poured. "Hoo, I'm going to be so drunk. I'm going to say something unwise and probably be hungover tomorrow. I'm making bad choices. Ugh. Bob also told me he has five children. Five." That still made her want to run him over with her car.

"I'm going to Knoxville right now to punch him right in the butthole!" Katie Faith snarled.

Thank God for friends. "That's a really good one. I'll tuck that aside for future use," Aimee told her.

"Honey, I'm so sorry. What a maggot-eating shitlord. What did you say when he told you this?"

"You're on fire tonight. I need to write that one down and you know how much I love *shitlord* as an insult. Bob is a *total* maggot-eating shitlord. So when he busted out that he had kids and a wife I said, 'What the fuck did you just say?' And I may have said it loud enough to get a look from a woman nearby. Then I said to her, 'He just told me he's married and has five kids. After dating me for nearly three years.'"

Katie Faith hooted with laughter. "Did you really? I am so bummed I missed that part."

"She said, 'You go 'head on, honey, that deserves all the bad words.' Then she told him she hoped his pecker fell off. It was a pretty righteous moment. Anyway I was like, 'Why did you tell me this now? We broke up six months ago, I haven't thought of you in about five and a half months. How could you involve me in something so shady?' And *then* he says he's also got a porn-addiction problem so he has to come to me as one of his steps to make amends. I tossed my still very warm drink at him and stormed out. Then I spent too much money on some boots and cut all my hair off and got blue tips because I'm a cliché."

Katie Faith shook her head. "You're not a cliché at all. That blue looks so cute. I'm surprised you didn't call me for bail money. I might need it after that. What are you going to do? We can borrow Jace's truck, load it with our friends and hunt him down. I have extra baseball bats."

This was why she'd come to see her friend. Aimee laughed, wiping away an embarrassed tear. "I was already done with him, you know? I would *never* have been with him if I'd known he was married. So I don't feel guilty. Not that way. But he *used* me. Made me into the other woman. I really hate that. And I hate that he told me all that to make himself feel better. It only made *me* feel worse! I'm probably going to take a five-hour shower now. I feel so bad for his wife and kids. How could I not have seen?"

She'd asked herself that very question over and over. But the place he'd met her was an apartment. One she thought was his and there was no way a family of seven lived there. It was a one-bedroom condo a single man lived in. Ugh.

"He had a single guy apartment. I wonder if it's his or if he borrowed it when I came to see him?"

"Like one of those fuck pads the guys in the movies get." Katie Faith nodded and Aimee settled in. When her friend got liquored up she said the best, weirdest stuff. "Remember that one we saw? The guy from *The Lord of the Rings* movies was in it. He was a Cheaty McCheaterson and he and his douche-canoe friends all shared this condo where they took their side action back."

Aimee nodded. "That guy's hot. But that one had murder in it. Ew. No. I hope I wasn't using the murder-my-mistress sheets."

"That would be a cliché for sure." Katie Faith gave a

dramatic sigh. "He's a pig. Good riddance. Thank God you used condoms. Your hair looks totally adorable and lastly, you didn't see because he's a cheater who crafted a life on the side meant to fool everyone in what was most definitely not a murder fuck pad."

With one last sigh, Aimee said, "So, that was my day. How was yours?"

Katie Faith, still frowning, hugged her tight before getting up. "We need to eat something. My dad brought soup to the Counter at closing time tonight. Since my mom has been keeping him at home to avoid all the drama in town, he's been cooking like crazy. Not that I'm complaining, mind you."

She puttered around the kitchen—one of the rooms they'd remodel come spring—getting the soup heated as Aimee let out some more of her guilt and anxiety.

But now the situation in town—heightened tensions between the shifters—came into focus once more.

A different sort of anxiety.

Katie Faith's father had suffered a stroke that'd nearly taken his life just four months before. Her family had needed her for support and to run the soda fountain and it had brought Aimee's best friend home, had given Katie Faith real true love and had come at a time to be a match to dry grass.

The wolves' constant back-and-forth had dragged the witches into the fray. Which had involved Katie Faith and, in turn, had only made her father's health more precarious, and her normally really easygoing mother actually got into a public brawl just the month before.

The town was a magical place. Literally. But the more drama and anger that was dredged up, the harder the land had to work to connect with the magic of all the witches. Everyone was at odds and it was exhausting.

"Dude, this is bananas. Like every last bit of today has been absolutely ridiculous and all this town stuff is bonkers. I stopped by to see your dad yesterday on my way home. He's looking better, but his energy is a little frantic."

All her life, Aimee's magic had been the nurturing type. She wanted to make things better for people and animals. And plants too.

She was a green witch. Happy to bring life wherever she went. It meant she was able to use those gifts in dealing with clients because she was empathic. Avery, Katie Faith's dad, was anxious for his family. Resentful that he'd been weakened and guilty because he felt he didn't do his job.

Aimee helped relieve some of his stress, talked him into a better place where he could more easily see he was doing so much more than he'd thought to protect his family.

"My mom told me you hung out with him for an hour having tea and listening to his country music. Thanks for that." Katie Faith had her own frantic energy, as she'd been at the center of a lot of the mess in town. Though here, in this big solid house, it was calmer. More steady.

"Your dad is great and he made hummingbird cake, so naturally I had to stay for tea." He'd started to loosen up, let go of the negative energy he'd been clinging to. "I encouraged your mom to get him away from town more often. I talked to Wade and he told me he's going to be traveling for work and he needs a house sitter to hang with the animals, deal with the gardens, all that stuff. I suggested he call your mom so that'll happen soon too."

Wade was Aimee's brother. He'd left Diablo Lake to settle in Asheville after college. He did employee training seminars on tech support so he traveled several times a year. His place was near enough, but far enough away that Katie Faith's parents could go and not feel guilty but be out of the drama.

"What a big old Softie Softerson you are." Katie Faith put a bowl of mushroom soup in front of her.

"Am not. I'm heartless and cruel. Oh, and I'm a strumpet."

Katie Faith snickered. "A strumpet? I was thinking more a floozie with loose morals."

Aimee nodded as she thought that over while she ate her soup. "I'll have to consider that."

"I couldn't talk them out of the Consort meeting though," Katie Faith said of the group of witches in Diablo Lake and their regular meeting. "I tried but my mom said she wasn't going anywhere until she got her say. So."

Jace wandered in, grabbed beers and left once more, pretending he hadn't been checking on them.

"He's so cute to pretend we don't know he's listening to all this," Katie Faith told her with an eye roll.

A while back her friend had told her of how nosy and bossy and in-your-business wolves were, and the more Aimee hung around them, the better she understood what she'd meant.

But at the heart of it with Jace was his wanting to

protect Katie Faith's well-being. And as Aimee cared about that too, she gave him some leeway.

If only the same could be said of *all* the wolves in town. The constant tussling over power had always been part of life. But lately it had been much more personal and hateful as some old grievances had resurfaced.

The witches had been pulled into the whole mess and they'd all had it. All that negative energy would degrade the heart of power all those who lived in Diablo Lake were protected by.

That heart of power the witches had taken an oath to protect, back in the very beginning of their peculiar little town in the middle-of-nowhere Tennessee, also happened to feed their magical power. The earth fed their magic so they were being impacted on multiple levels.

The Consort, run by the elder witches in town, had called a meeting to discuss the situation the following week.

"At least it's not before eight in the morning." Aimee didn't much mind getting up early. But on a Saturday when she'd had the week she had?

Katie Faith curled her lip at the very idea of getting up that early, though she'd do it if she had to. As her friend was a nightmare of a human being before she had coffee, Aimee was relieved on that front as well.

"Why don't you stay over? You can sleep in the spare room. We can watch something scary, even." Katie Faith's hopeful expression made her feel so much better.

"Thank you. But I'm feeling better now. I mean, I wasn't bummed we weren't together and now it makes me even more glad. I just feel dirty, and not the good way. I'll walk home."

"No, you won't. There are a jillion wolves here, and one of them hasn't been doing tequila shots so they can drive you home. But you don't have to go just yet, right? I feel like I haven't seen you in forever."

"You got married a week ago. I've seen you three days this week so far. I think we're okay." Aimee rolled her eyes, glad to have a friend like Katie Faith.

"Being married has been pretty cool."

"So you two still bang and stuff? Now that the thrill is gone?" Aimee teased.

"It's a chore, but we make it work. I mean, someone has to do Jace, it may as well be me."

"Glad you make the sacrifice."

Don't miss Diablo Lake: Protected *by Lauren Dane*
available now wherever ebooks are sold.
www.carinapress.com